Enthusiastic reviews for Lior Samson's novels —

Distant Sons

"[A] book that will stay with me, probably for the rest of my life, and that I know I'll read again. ... It enlarged my experience of being human."
— *M. Thornberg, author*

The Rosen Singularity

"The plotting is ingenious and the characters come through strongly."
— *Rebecca Goldstein, MacArthur Fellow, author*

The Millicent Factor

"A solid page turner. The author keeps the pace just right with action and chases ... and backroom dealings."
— *RJ Beam, author*

The Intaglio Imprint

"Super-realism and compelling rationale, ... an intricate and incisive creation,"
— *George Church, geneticist*

Bashert (The Homeland Connection)

"Samson writes with a crisp elegance, like John Le Carré, and weaves his plot magically,"
— *James A. Anderson, author*

The Dome (The Homeland Connection)

"An excellent read, and very highly recommended."
— *Midwest Book Review*

Web Games (The Homeland Connection)

"This extraordinary author has the ability to anticipate events. ... You will not put it down."
— *Alan Caruba, critic, BookViews*

Chipset (The Homeland Connection)

"[A] multi-dimensional thriller ... populated by flesh-and-blood characters."
— *Avraham Azrieli, author*

Gasline (The Homeland Connection)

" [A] great novel . . . high concept, flesh-and-blood protagonist, and realistic action. ... [It] will raise your blood pressure and make you think."   —*Columbia Review of Books and Film*

Flight Track (The Homeland Connection)

" Stunning, compelling, thought-provoking. To the book's broad scope and expert pacing, add three-dimensional, engaging characters."   —*M. Thornburg, author*

The Four-Color Puzzle

" [A]n authentic thinking person's ideal mystery; an eloquent feast of words and an excellent story."   —*Jeanie B. Clemmons, author*

THE DRUCKER PROXY

THE DRUCKER PROXY

by Lior Samson

GESHER PRESS

Gesher Press
Rowley, Massachusetts

5 4 3 2 1

ISBN 978-1-7326091-1-2

Cover and book design: Larry Constantine
Cover background photo: "There's light at the end of the tunnel"
© 2015, Thomas Whelton, used by permission
Set in Aila, titles in Agency FB

In memory of
Edward Yourdon (1944-2016), friend and collaborator,
whose legacy lives on

In this matter of immortality, people's beliefs appear to go along with their wishes. – Ambrose Bierce

Prologue

Night. Black. Darker than night, like the inside of a cave after the spelunkers have all turned off the lights on their hardhats and the last afterimages have faded: the black of the void, utter and absolute, without even the distraction of phosphenes. Nothing seemed to work for him, no feeling, no sensation. Slowly, in the distance, sparks of colorless light flared and coalesced into a shape, a bright grid, like a barred gate at the far exit of a long tunnel.

Thoughts intruded, unbidden, only to vanish before they could be comprehended, lost in emptiness like random cellphone flashes in the stands at a stadium concert, winking signals gone even before they could be fully experienced. A buzz, like erratic tinnitus, faded in and out, shifting in pitch but trending always lower until it was a slow and steady putt-putt-putt quietly mixing with an overlay of voices speaking a language that defied parsing.

"Coleman. Can you hear me, Coleman?"

"I don't think he's conscious. He can't hear us."

"Look. The numbers say he's there. Coleman? Coleman Todd Drucker! Can you hear me?"

One last confusing voice. "Well, enough for now. This is just a trial run."

Part 1

Each life makes its own imitation of immortality.
                                              – Stephen King

– 1 –

He was, for the moment, an Olympic skier on a giant slalom course. There was no snow, no alternating red and blue flags, only the narrow asphalt snake that was Old Topanga Canyon Road zig-zagging down toward California's Pacific Coast Highway.

With precision and concentration, Coleman Drucker powered into the next hairpin turn without easing up on the accelerator. Taking the outside lane gave him a clear view ahead through the deep shadows of early sun. He flattened the curve and fishtailed briefly while straightening out.

Pounding the dashboard, he shouted into the wind. "Yes! I love it. Every damn minute of it." He had the black-and-yellow Tensora Model N in full-manual mode, and he reveled in the sense of mastery.

It was all an illusion, of course, and Cole knew it, but willful ignorance allowed him, despite his vaunted technical background, to live on the edge, to feel as if he were pushing the envelope. His entire life had become a tapestry of interwoven illusions embroidered around the edges by his transgressive tendencies, particularly in personal relations.

He drove one-handed, left hand over his mouth as if he were hiding his growing grin. He inhaled. Gwen. The scent of her still lingered on his fingers. She led trail rides for his daughter's summer camp in Topanga. She was an agglomeration of contradictions: a smart businesswoman who underplayed her intelligence, a lithe athlete who kept her shirt on during lovemaking, a woman of some means who mucked her own stables. He knew the affair was going nowhere, and he hoped she knew it as well, otherwise things could turn messy—and possibly expensive. She was the latest patch in the messy cloak in which he wrapped himself, nothing more.

"Why do you do it, man?" he asked himself, then shook his head. "Because I can," he told the wind, "because it feels good. Like this."

The downhill race was an end in itself. He had hours before the first of the meetings that were the punctuation marks at the end of nearly two years of nerve-wracking negotiation. He rushed for no reason, save for the seductive sense of speed in the low-slung electric roadster. With the top down, the rush of air over the windshield whipping his thinning hair and the muted buzz of tires on asphalt were the loudest sounds.

He skidded around the next switchback, but it would have been nearly impossible for him to lose control completely and wipe out. The car itself was his invisible backseat driver, its cloud-connected artificial intelligence monitoring his every move, tweaking and adapting its responses to the slightest twitch of the foot or tug on the wheel, cameras tracking the roadway, computers keeping the customized car always within its performance envelope, never exceeding the safe parameters for speed, torque, wheel-slip, and acceleration.

There was no comparable backup for the business risks he was facing at the office. He had bullied and bluffed his way through his second acquisition in four years, a buyout that absolutely had to work. He was acutely aware that if the building blocks he had stacked with such care were to topple, the tumble would take him down and Drucker Technologies with it.

Switching hands to reach the center-console touch screen, he scrolled through his classical database and called up a Tchaikovsky favorite, the "Little Russian" symphony. He cranked the volume through the close-focus headrest speakers.

He was running through a mental checklist—open merger issues, updating his life insurance, reviewing the proxy papers—when he rounded a blind curve to face an oncoming motorhome hogging the two-lane road. He deftly twisted the wheel. As his right tires touched off onto the narrow strip of dirt on the inside of the curve, he tromped on the accelerator and squeezed through the gap, leaving a spray of gravel flying behind.

A warning flashed on the heads-up windshield display, and the steering wheel locked up. He jammed on the brakes, but the car kept flying toward the outside shoulder just beyond the end of the guard rail. In desperation, he tugged on the parking brake, and the car reluctantly came to a silent stop angled across the road.

"What the fuck?" The center console and steering-wheel displays were both blank. Cole pressed the power-on button and watched as the word "WAIT" flashed in red on the dashboard.

Suddenly he was not alone. "This is your Tensora Roadside Services operator." The voice seemed to hang in space in front of him. "Are you all right, Mr. Drucker?"

"Yes, I'm all right, but my fucking car just died on me."

"I'm sorry to hear that, Mr. Drucker. My name is Erin. I'm here to help. Our remote diagnostics package is already being executed. I see that you are headed south on Old Topanga Canyon Road in Topanga, California. Are you in a safe place? Do you need roadside assistance?"

"I need my goddamn car to restart, and I need to get to my meeting. That's what I need."

"My display is showing that the Master Controller has rebooted correctly. You should see a status screen on the center console display."

"I see a black fucking screen is what I see."

"I am sorry to hear that. I am initiating a remote system restore. This should only take a few minutes."

"And what the fuck am I supposed to do in the meantime? I'm in the middle of the road, blocking both lanes. I . . . Oh shit!" A dirt-spattered vintage F-150 was rounding the curve. Cole raised himself in the seat and flailed his arms wildly.

The pickup skidded to a stop just feet short of the Tensora. The driver, shocks of white hair spraying out from beneath his Dodgers baseball cap, looked down from the open cab window. "You need help?"

"No, I think I can handle this."

"Well, then, do you think maybe you could pull over so others can get by? If it's not too much to ask."

"I will, I will. Just hang on." He looked down at the display that was now showing a swirling Tensora logo. "Just waiting for this thing to reboot."

The driver in the pickup laughed. "Maybe you should

get a real car, mister, instead of an overpriced laptop on wheels."

Cole ignored the taunt and kept his eyes on the screen. As soon as the display normalized, he spun the wheel and pulled over to the side. The pickup squeezed by with a throaty grumble. "Hello? Erin? You still there?"

"Yes, I'm still here, Mr. Drucker. My system is showing that all indicators are nominal on your vehicle. The remote diagnostics report that all sensors, actuators, and subsystems are working properly."

"Then what the hell happened? I thought these things had triple redundancy and backup systems up the wazoo."

"I'm sorry, but I don't recognize wazoo."

Cole shook his head in sudden realization. "Wait, you're an AI, right? I'm not talking to Erin with a ponytail; I'm talking to a fucking computer."

"I'm Erin, Tensora Motor's automated Emergency Roadside Intervention Network. Can I be of any further assistance?"

"Yeah, just don't let this sort of fuckup happen again. Okay?"

"I have scheduled special maintenance for your vehicle for later today. I note from your profile that you have the Concierge Service Plan. Your car will be collected at,"—there was a pause and a shift in the tone-of-voice—"Drucker Technologies Headquarters, Building 1 executive parking, between 10 and 11 a.m. and returned before 4 p.m., or a loaner vehicle of equivalent model level will be provided should your vehicle need to be retained for service. Have a nice day."

"Yeah, right." He pulled onto the pavement and resumed his descent toward the ocean. The pleasure was gone from the drive. Nerves on edge, the illusion of control now shattered, he drove as if his high-tech car might, at any moment, suddenly refuse again to do his bidding.

– 2 –

Cole, sleep-deprived from the dawn departure and long dalliance in Topanga but determined not to show it, paced at the end of the conference table in his last meeting of the day. With a lazy flick of the wrist in the direction of his tablet computer, he brought up the last of the nineteen PowerPoint slides in his presentation. A twitter of strained laughter spread around the table as the image of a vintage twentieth-century factory-built home— a bland sand-colored double-wide with a green cranked awning over the entry door—steadily morphed into a postmodern high-rise complex.

"And that, people, is the future of construction integration, from adaptive exteriors that adjust albedo and permeability to the seasons as readily as to the time of day, through to the totally connected intelligent appliances, utilities, HVAC, and communications, all factory-built under strictest quality and cost control with turnkey onsite assembly. This"—he jabbed with his index finger—"is what is achievable from the synergy of Unified ModulArch leadership in large-scale pre-manufactured construction with Drucker's newly acquired expertise in systems management and our long-proven state-of-the-art mastery of IoT technology. With sea-level rise contributing to the biggest urban construction boom in a half century, the Internet-of-Things and the future of smart-building and smart-city architecture are being merged into a bold new vision: our vision. We are Drucker Unified." The new logo painted on the screen.

He paused as if waiting for applause. His people, in the outer ring, nodded affirmation; the ModulArch management had the seats at the table. It was a multilayered metaphor, as if those seated were more important, the focus, yet at the same time they were surrounded, being watched. It was another of Coleman's well-managed stage illusions. Drucker Technologies was buying out the much larger ModulArch, and he and his handpicked team would be calling the shots on the new corporation.

Even the attire declared the disconnect in corporate cultures. In Drucker Technologies, Coleman set the tone with his favored black jeans and blazer and open-collar shirts worn untucked. Bradley Pomerantz, CTO of Drucker, sported a denim sports jacket over one of his signature tee shirts covered in Python program code. In stark contrast, those seated around the table in their gray pinstripes could have passed for bankers. At first glance, one might assume they held the upper hand.

Coleman took his seat at the head of the table. "I know I don't have to sell any of you on this. The acquisition has already been approved by both boards, so it's too late for second thoughts now. Sorry, Bert, but you were overruled and outmaneuvered. We're stuck with each other,"—more forced laughter around the table while Drucker CFO Bert Jamison squirmed at the back—"but I wanted to set the stage today for the envisioning exercises scheduled for next month." He poured two fingers of water from the Raw-Water bottle in front of him, took a sip, and continued. "For the new company of Drucker Unified, the sky is, quite literally, the limit." Another hand gesture triggered the high rise building on the wall-size screen to start growing upward into a brightening sky, followed by fade-to-white.

The applause rippled around the room for a few polite seconds, then stopped when Coleman held up a hand. "Okay, let's talk."

— —

Coleman made a show of checking his smartwatch. The questions and challenges that had taken over an hour had mostly been carefully calculated to appear improvised, with each of the assembled executives making their moves to stake out positions without exposing too much of their private agendas for the fluid times to follow. Coleman, a wizard at reading a group, had delivered his selective disclosures in a way that promised nothing but allowed everyone to believe they were uniquely on the inside track. Throughout, he had sustained his upbeat persona, alternating between that of a cheerleading peer touting new horizons and a sympathetic senior counselor reassuring them all that nothing would change. Nothing, he thought, except I am now a billionaire and you're not.

"And so, gentlemen . . . and ladies"—he pointedly glanced toward Tonika Warner seated to his left, the only woman and only person-of-color among the top management of ModulArch—"that does it for the day. Action items for everybody: one, enjoy your weekend; two, get some sleep. The real work starts Monday with the first sprint to flesh out and finalize the roadmap for post-merger integration. We'll kick it off with our first all-hands meeting of the combined companies—remotes to Atlanta, Tokyo, and Madrid—the details are in your packets. Now, take a break."

As the rest of the transition management team gathered their gear and drifted from the room, Tonika Warner dawdled and fussed with her cellphone. Once alone with Drucker, she looked over to him. "So?"

"What are you asking? What do you want to know?"

"Where am I in this picture?"

"I would guess pretty much right where you want to be." He smiled at the sudden image of her straddling him. Tonika was his kind of woman. Smart, a smart dresser, built like a ModulArch high-rise, and soon to be deeply beholden to him. "Everyone knows the key role you've been playing in pulling the companies together, building a joint vision and shepherding stragglers. Plus, who on your side of the merger is as tech savvy as you? I mean, among your people here"—he gestured around the now-empty table—"these guys all came up from construction, manufacturing, production management. Hell, Decatur started out with a nail gun in his hand. By comparison, with your degree from Cal Tech and your record at ModulArch, you're sitting pretty for a future in what is really, at the heart, a technology company."

She closed her portfolio and slipped it under her arm. "You've been upfront with me all along, CT. I appreciate that. I don't know whether you realize how much it takes for a woman, a black woman, to get this far in a glorified construction company. Don't let the suits and ties fool you. These guys still drive around with hard-hats stashed in their trunks and diesel fuel flowing in their veins. In that culture, women have no place on the job site, and blacks and Hispanics are lowest on the totem pole, one notch below the robots that are starting to show up onsite. So, you see it was not accidental where I sat today."

"I figured as much."

"I know your roster might already be a little deep on the tech side. Still, I couldn't help but note you have three women on your board and your management ranks do not all bring to mind a wall of fresh plaster, if you catch my drift."

"I do. And we try. It helps having the right people with the right agenda in HR." He gave her a skewed smile that almost shaded into a wink.

"I've met your wife, remember? At the Construction Tech Xpo in Las Vegas when you first started putting the moves on ModulArch. She is definitely one of the smart ones, someone who knows what she is after and goes for it."

"Like you?"

"I hope so. Look, I have new IT infrastructure proposals to go over, so I better get back to my office. There's lots to do before Monday morning."

"It can wait. Get some R-and-R over the weekend."

"Easy for you, maybe, but—"

"Monday is a new week and maybe a new org chart. Trust me on this. Take the weekend off. You'll be fine on Monday."

She cocked her head and gave him a what-you-talking-about look. "Do I thank you?"

"No, not yet anyway. But I hope you like your new boss."

She narrowed her eyes and nodded. "See you Monday, Mr. Drucker."

— 3 —

Drucker glanced at his smartwatch where an appointment flag was pulsing slowly. Damn. He should never have agreed to the interview. It was that woman—what the fuck was her name?—the one who was chasing some story for some article for some online magazine. Kelsey would know.

Kelsey Underwood was the guardian at the gate who stood between him and a hostile world and who kept everything on schedule and in place. He was usually good with details, but only if the subject matter interested him, which narrowed the topics to fewer than a handful, starting with making money and ending with making money. In between was sex, but wealth was job one, the means to every end, from the beach house to the wife who would meet him there in a few hours. With wealth came options, he always told his friends, and he had every intention to keep exercising those options as he saw fit.

He tapped the pulsing icon to acknowledge it and gave the screen a quick finger swipe. "Kelsey," he said into his wrist, "put my four o'clock in the small conference room and tell her I'm tied up on a call. I'll be there in ten. Oh, and have the new Existendia proxy papers on my desk to sign." He gave the twist of his wrist needed to end the message before retrieving his tablet from the podium. There were already several "urgents" and "importants" from ModulArch people. He scanned the sender and subject lines and dragged a couple toward Kelsey's inbox icon. She was good at reading his mind and knowing just how to handle the annoying day-to-day intrusions without explicit instructions from him. The message from Brad Pomerantz he flagged to handle himself. But not now. Get this woman in the conference room taken care of, then meet Barbra to celebrate.

It was all happening, for real. My first billion, he was thinking. I'm forty-seven and already made my first.

— —

The woman in the conference room was hunched over, squinting at an outsized smartphone as her fingers flew over a foldable Bluetooth keyboard. Her magenta-streaked hair was undercut on the left side, shoulder length on the right, and a diamond stud glinted high on her left cheek. She did not react when Coleman entered.

He cleared his throat. "I'm Coleman Drucker. You wanted to meet with me?"

"Yeah." She kept typing. "Just a minute."

Annoyed, he was about to snap that he was busy and that she should reschedule with his assistant, but she folded the keyboard and flipped the smartphone face down. "Sorry about that," she said, "but even freelance feature writers have deadlines." She stood and extended her hand. "I'm Dana Carmody."

"Ah, right. Oh yeah, I remember. Carmody Central. Funny stuff." He smiled, thinking of her geeky online comics, some of which had become internet memes.

"That was all a youthful brain fart. I string for the *LA Times* these days. And I'm working on a long piece for *Harper's*. That's why I'm here."

"And this piece for *Harper's*, it's about developments in the construction industry?"

"Not really. I understand you own a piece of Existendia."

"That's not . . ." He was about to say it wasn't true, but changed his mind. "That's not public knowledge. And not for disclosure. If you're here to discuss my personal investment strategies, I think we can probably cut the interview short. Very short."

"Well, I hope we can keep talking. And maybe you don't know that LATech Online reported on your investment over a year ago. I'd call that public knowledge."

"Okay, didn't know that." It wasn't true, of course, but he always preferred for others to think he knew less than he did. "So, right, I bought a piece of Existendia. I'm very future-oriented; my portfolio reflects that."

"You and a lot of other Silicon Valley entrepreneurs seem to have common interests."

"This is Santa Monica, not Santa Clara."

"Geography doesn't define culture, Mr. Drucker. The Valley, Seattle, Boston's Technology Archipelago atop the new harbor barrier crescent—it's all one big boy's club, the inroads of the last decade of female empowerment notwithstanding. There's still a glass ceiling, even if in high-tech it's Lexan. So, Mr. Drucker—"

"Cole. You can call me Cole, provided you get to the gist of this interview."

"The gist, Mr. Drucker, is that I'm interested in the quest for immortality and its associated illusions."

"Talk to your priest. Or your spiritual guru. Whatever. I'm just a glorified software engineer, despite the title on my office in the C-suite. I figure out better ways to connect and use internet-connected devices. And better ways to make money from those devices. Now I've got a company to run, a company that just tripled in size. Which you would know if you read LATech Online, since they've lately been all over us with their derisive drivel about . . ." He was interrupted by the tickle on his wrist. Kelsey was trying to reach him with something urgent. "Look, I have to go. I think that will have to do. I'll get one of the guys to show you out." At the door, he paused without turning. "Good luck with your piece."

— —

In his outer office, he smiled at Kelsey. "Thanks for rescuing me. What's up?"

"That's what. I figured you didn't really have the time for the charming Ms. Carmody."

He gently lifted her hand from the keyboard wrist rest in front of her and bent to kiss it. "You are so good, an absolute mind reader."

"I am. And that's why you'll be giving me a fat raise after the reorg."

"There you go again, reading my mind." He glanced at the time. "You better ping Barbra that I might be late."

"Already done. She's finishing up and will meet you at the beach house. Anything else?"

What Cole was thinking could get him in trouble. From where he was standing, he had a good view down her dress. He made a show of looking at the spreadsheet on her monitor, but figured she had probably noticed. "No, nothing now."

"Very well, then."

She had noticed, of course, and he knew it. He also knew that if he followed up with anything other than a nod and a grunt, he could be staring down allegations of sexual harassment from Kelsey—maybe worse from Barbra, who drew the line at workplace shenanigans. He struggled to keep a lid on his impulses, but the urges were always there nonetheless. Barbra might be the wet dream of half the men in the company—and maybe no small number of the women—but Cole was a sensation seeker at the core, always in pursuit of something new. Gwen, with her horse stables up in Topanga, was new. It would go nowhere, he was certain, but just the thought of her riding at his side, her ponytail bobbing in the wind, shortened his breath.

"Ah, I'll see you on Monday, Kelsey. Barbra and I are—"

"Off to the beach house for the weekend. I messaged the house earlier to crank the A/C up and to do inventory to make sure the fridge and bar have been restocked."

"You are amazing." He bowed, figuring that was an inoffensive gesture.

She grinned and turned back to her spreadsheet.

— —

In executive parking, a man in a blue service uniform was sitting in Cole's Tensora, talking into the air. "Hey, I know I was supposed to swap cars by four, but the freeway was a parking lot. I had to go surface streets. Then there was the stop at the shop. Der! Plus, the damn rent-a-cop at the gate here gave me a hard time." He looked up to see Coleman standing beside the car, hands on hips, eyes narrowed. "Shit, gotta go. The man's here." He thumbed the button on the steering wheel to cut off the call.

"Ola. Er, hello, sir. I'm Hernandez, uh,"—he looked down at the clipboard on the passenger seat— "Mr. Drucker. I'm here with the loaner for you for the weekend. We got, lotsa calls, you know, service requests, so we couldn't get to your car as fast as we could, you know." He nodded over his shoulder. "That's your loaner car there. It's the new NX. It's what they call a preproduction model. We thought you might like, you know, to see what you think of it."

Coleman shook his head in bemused impatience. The guy was acting like a parody of a dropout car jockey.

"Go ahead and get in. It's already keyed to your passcard. I just gotta finish some, like, paperwork here."

Coleman turned to check out the copper-and-silver Tensora blocking the exit. "So that's the new NX, eh? Okay. I'll give it a try."

He slipped in and tapped an icon on the screen. The top of the car split into four pieces to do a speedy and near-silent imitation of a Hollywood-style transformer as the roof segments disappeared into the body.

"Well, that's cool." He backed up, spun the wheel, and stepped on the accelerator. The car shot toward the rear gate of the campus.

Glancing at the rearview screen, he noted the man in the coveralls now had his head buried under the open hood of his Tensora. That struck him as strange, but the beach—and Barbra—were waiting. He waved his passcard in the air as if announcing his presence to a gathering crowd, and the back gate opened just in time for him to slip through without having to touch the brakes.

— 4 —

Traffic had been so bad that his own long driveway gave Cole the first opportunity to floor the NX. It plastered him to the seat. Then, just as he was about to grin with the pleasure, the autopilot cut in and applied the brakes to keep him from driving through the back wall of the garage. The momentary rush started him thinking about Gwen and the road up to Topanga, but he was already committed to a celebratory weekend with Barbra. That should be good. From the beginning, Barbra had been good in the sack, and she understood the art of expressing gratitude.

He hopped out of the car without opening the driver-side door. The house recognized him and opened the door from the garage for him. "Tandi," he said to the house. "I'll take a glass of the Willamette Valley viognier-gewürtz, please. Send it to the deck. Well chilled, of course."

"Right away."

— —

The doorbell surprised him. The house would have let Barbra in and would have sent away almost anyone else. He turned his phone right-side up to see who was at the door. Magenta hair. What the . . .? What did the woman want, and why had Tandi not sent her packing? He studied her face on his phone. The door cam was not flattering, but he had to admit she was cute. What was she, maybe mid to late twenties? Young, obviously a bit on the wild side, what with the hair and the hardware. That could be a good sign.

He glanced at the time-date banner on the top edge of

his phone. Knowing Barbra, she wouldn't get home for another couple of hours. He was all too keenly aware that she was becoming even more serious about the business than he was. Her stake dictated by the pre-nup was a lot smaller than his, which meant she had to work that much harder.

The door chime sounded again. Persistent little bitch. Okay, let her in and see if you can get her out of her pants in time for a quickie before Barbra arrives. It could be risky, but that would just make it all the more exciting.

"Tandi, let her in and have her wait in the foyer."

Drink in hand, Cole took his time getting from the deck to the front of the house.

"Ah, the charming and persistent Ms. Carmody. How did you persuade the house to pass your button-pushing through to actually ring the bell?"

"You ought to be able to guess that, Mr. Drucker. It's—"

"Cole, call me Cole. Please."

"The Internet-of-Things, Cole. Everything's connected and always listening. You just have to know how to talk to the stuff."

"You're kidding. Not my house. It's a Drucker Technologies fully integrated smart house. We have the best tiered security in the business."

"Fully integrated, that's the operant term. Everything in the whole place is on the network, Wi-Fi linked and internet connected. The more complicated the system, Mr. Drucker, the more holes there are to plug. No tiered security can protect everything against a determined hacker. Determined. That's me."

"Cute. That's cute. You are, too, I might add. But you gotta tell me how you did it? What did you breach."

She grinned. "I should make you work to get it out of

me, but it was really too easy."

"What if I ply you with one of the very best white wines from the Willamette Valley?"

"Ply away."

"Tandi, bring another glass of the viognier-gewürztraminer out to the deck. Now, Ms. Carmody, how did you do it?"

"The doorbell. I didn't have to hack the whole system, just bypass the intercept on the ring-through. It's a factory-set code that nobody thinks to change, since who would ever think of a ringing door chime as a security threat."

"Wow, now that's fuckin' clever. You just earned yourself a glass of wine and a private one-on-one with Santa Monica's latest billionaire. Follow me out to the deck."

"Really? Suddenly you're a billionaire? I would have pegged you as a few zeroes short of that club."

"Ouch. Don't tell me you don't know about the merger, the new Drucker Unified. It was in your own mag, LATech Online."

"Not my mag. Like I told you. I do read it, but I don't write for it."

"And here we are." He waved to make the slider open for her. "Isn't the view magnificent?"

"Nice. But it's the same damn rising ocean as your neighbors see, at least until you all get washed out into it by the rising seas."

"Yeah, but none of them have a Drucker Technologies home. And none of them are being interviewed by the amazingly clever and terminally attractive Dana Carmody, who is not above hacking into a supposedly secure system just to get an interview. So what is this really about?" He swiveled a deck chair so he could see her and watch the incoming tide at the same time.

"As I said before, I'm working on a piece about men—and a couple of women—who are desperate to outscore the actuarial tables—by big margins. Rumor has it that you have some opinions about some of these people and their investments in immortality. Take Craig Freiburg, for—"

"Freiburg is an idiot. He's old and scared. When he was younger, he was into wheatgrass and calorie restriction, oxygen therapy and cleansing fasts. Didn't buy him much. He still earned his quadruple bypass at fifty-four and two rounds of chemo at sixty. Have you seen the man? He's not even seventy and already looks like death on a beanpole. Now that he can hear the Grim Reaper scything toward him through the fields of his wheatgrass, he's all in to hedge his bets."

"You're saying?"

"Cryonics is a crock, the biggest sucker bet ever on offer."

"How is that?"

"None of these guys who have purchased perpetual preservation at three hundred below zero have thought through the end game—Freiburg included. Their fantasy is that science will someday be able to revive them and cure whatever disease or fix whatever trauma killed them. But why? Why would some future society want to go through what is almost certain to be an immensely complicated and surely risky and expensive process of trying to revive some old and ailing relic whose knowledge and abilities, even if they can be recovered, will be hopelessly out of date?"

He took a sip from his Riedel glass and savored the floral spice of the wine. "Mmm. An amazing and daring blend. Not one of my wineries. Not yet." He set the glass on the teak-top table beside his chair. "None of us is irreplaceable,

Ms. Carmody, or even ultimately all that important. Even genius is cheap. Something like 150 million geniuses are born every year. Why would we, in the future, squander scarce resources on bringing back some decrepit egotist from the technological dark ages when we have an endless supply of new recruits?" He noticed her hand in her pocket. "You taking notes?"

"Mind if I tape this?"

"Be my guest. I'll just rant on." He took another sip. "Since 1967, when Dr. James Bedford became the first man to be put into cryonic suspension, thousands of sad cases have had their bodies frozen. Even more pathetic are the hoards who can't afford the whole-body freeze and opt for the cheaper option of beheading before the iceman cometh. They're deluded. I'm sure you remember the mess with that Italian doc and his head transplant debacle."

She nodded. "But medical science keeps progressing. Someday we will almost certainly see a successful full-body transplant."

"Maybe, if civilization survives with enough resources to spare. But why would medical science risk trying to attach a perfectly good body to an old thawed-out head when they have some young Cal Tech science whiz whose torso was just yesterday crushed in a lab mishap. Think about it. Reviving the dead makes no sense when we have an overabundant supply of the living."

Her eyes narrowed. "In the case of Craig Freiburg, I understand his estate is charged with covering the cost. The longer it takes the science to catch up, the more his estate is worth."

"No matter how much his estate is worth, it probably won't matter in the end because dead is dead. They can't freeze you instantly. The moment your heart stops, brain cells start dying. The hippocampus, critical to forming memories, is dead within minutes. The chemical infusions they use to protect cells from damaging ice crystals are kept out of the brain by the so-called blood-brain barrier. The best evidence is that there isn't going to be much of anything left of the brain worth reanimating. It's all just reassuring stories, like myths of Valhalla or pretty promises of Heaven."

"So, you don't care if you die?"

"Don't be silly. Of course I care, but betting on medical science to bring you back someday is only marginally more stupid than betting on it to keep you alive. The young of the world—that's you, love—are already starting to balk at the drain on resources of an aging population, especially in keeping the oldest oldsters still going. Ninety percent of lifetime medical costs are incurred in the last few years of life. For the most part, even the most extraordinary efforts are yielding only a few extra years, often miserable ones at that."

"So I take it you are not into resveratrol and calorie cutting."

He patted his rounded cheeks. "Does it look like I'm starving myself in a desperate bid to buy a few extra months? Now as to resveratrol, that's different. I'm a big fan of red wines, big fan. I even own vineyards in Napa and the Columbia Valley. We're bringing in the zin crush next month up in Napa. You oughta come by to check it out."

"Not what I meant. But let's go back to your buying a stake in Existendia. Isn't that more of the same? Wildly expensive, largely unproven technology?"

"Not the same at all. Look, we really don't need to spend

our time on this. You can read the Existendia online prospectus. If you haven't already. The article in *New Scientist* from last year was also pretty good. I don't have any insider information to share. Besides, with their IPO on the horizon, I know better than to speak out of turn. I play hard, but I don't play with insider trading."

"I already read all that. I do my research. I didn't stalk you all the way out here for a technology rehash. I want to know about you. What are you looking for? Why are you in it? And are you an Existendia client?"

Cole worked his mouth for several seconds and shifted his eyes to the side for inspiration. He looked back at the determined Ms. Carmody and pointed with both hands. "Who are you, anyway? Are you this, this body in front of me? Nice body—don't get me wrong—even with its retro-renegade hairstyle and aggressively chewed fingernails. Are you your brain, the hundred billion neurons balled up inside that half-shaved head of yours? Or are you your personality, whatever it is that makes you stand out and be something special, something different from your friends and fellow workers?"

"How about all of the above."

"That's the lazy answer."

"Or the ambitious one."

"Whatever. In any case, what makes me *me* is my personality, all the quirks and traits and distinctive ways I deal with myself and others, plus everything I know and remember."

"Which is embodied in your brain,"—she pointed toward his head—"in your neurons and interconnections. And maybe even tied to the microbiome in your gut."

"Maybe. But you said the operant word: *embodied.* Who

says that who I am has to be embodied in wetware, in a biological substrate? I can still be me in silicon or in magnetic bubbles or in transient data in 'the cloud'. Take all the stuff that defines who I am, the sum total of the signals and wiring in my head, and upload it to a computer—"

"A supercomputer."

"Okay, a supercomputer, and . . ." He looked up. Barbra was standing in the doorway to the deck, shaking her head, turning her bobbed blonde hair into a gently waving flag. She had loosened the top buttons of her blouse, and the jacket of her power suit trailed from one hand. "Wow, honey," he said. "Here you are, earlier than I expected."

"And here you are, Todd, with . . . with who?"

Dana stood up and offered her hand to Barbra. "Whom. With whom. I'm Dana Carmody, and I hacked my way into an interview with your husband. Todd? I thought his name was . . ."

"Coleman Todd Drucker. C. T. Drucker. CT to his troops, Cole to his friends, Coleman to those who don't know better. I call him Todd because no one else does."

"It's like her thumbprint on me." He wrinkled his nose at his wife.

"I see." Dana drew out the words as if she didn't see.

"Yes, and I see." Barbra surveyed the scene. "An interview. And a glass of wine. On the deck. You move pretty fast, Dana Carmody. And I can see how you manage that." She smiled as she took in Dana's physique. "Looks like you do more than interviews. You don't stay in shape like that sitting at a desk all day."

"Barbra, really . . ." Cole gave her a please-stop look.

Barbra stepped onto the deck as she kept talking. "You know, Todd here goes for the athletic types. Skiers, surfer girls, you know, like that. Equestrians." She looked at Cole and narrowed her eyes. "Me, too." She smiled at Dana and gave her another quick up-and-down before stepping past her and sitting in her husband's lap. "Todd has a way of keeping things to himself. He can be a bit . . . self-centered at times."

"Let me guess, darling" he said. "You put your Tensora on autopilot and drank your way home."

"Just trying to keep up with you, darling." She kissed his neck. "You know what we should do? We should invite Dana to stay for dinner and . . . and help us celebrate."

Dana squirmed. "I, uh, really was just here for an interview with—"

"Interview away, I'll get Tandi to organize something special for the three of us." She rose out of Cole's lap and brushed a finger across Dana's bare shoulder as she passed.

Cole watched his wife enter the house. "Well, I guess we've been told. Now you get your interview. And wine. And dinner. And, well, whatever."

— —

Dinner took hours and required Tandi's robocart to deliver two more bottles of wine: a cabernet franc from Drucker Vineyards in Washington State and, for contrast, one from McLaren Vale in Australia. The well-lubricated celebration finally flowed from the dining room to the den and on to the bedroom.

The diamond stud on her cheek turned out not to be Dana's only body-piercing. Both Cole and Barbra were surprised by the amount of hardware waiting to be uncovered. Neither of them complained, even though it soon became evident to Cole that Ms. Carmody, though versatile, seemed to prefer women to men.

The sun was already high when Barbra lifted Cole's arm from across her breasts and slipped out of bed. Dana was gone, but her clothes were still in a heap on the chair by the window. Barbra slipped on a bathrobe and padded out into the kitchen. Dana was standing at the granite-topped center island, nude, typing away at a folding keyboard. Barbra came up behind her, ran a hand down the rainbow-hued boa constrictor tattooed on her back, and finished with a squeeze to the left buttock. "Good morning. You're already back at work?"

Dana kept typing. As she moved to block Barbra's view, she pressed her backside into Barbra, who responded by reaching around and cupping Dana's breasts. "There. Done. For now," Dana said. She folded the keyboard and turned to kiss Barbra. "Aren't you a little overdressed?" She slipped a hand under Barbra's robe and played with her left nipple.

"My, you are a single-minded girl."

"No, I'm of many minds, but right now my mind is on you."

"Let's at least get some breakfast first to fuel whatever comes second. And, speaking of fuel, that stuff last night— the Trip-Seven, you called it—was amazing. I don't suppose you have any more tabs stashed in that purse of yours?"

"I do, but it's not good to start flying jumbo jets on an empty stomach. And I guess we needn't be in too much of a hurry. I don't have to file my story until late tomorrow afternoon."

Barbra pulled back. "Story? You're still talking story? How much of . . . of all this is material for a story."

"None of it, so relax. I was referring to my piece on men like your husband who keep chasing immortality."

"Is that what he's doing? I thought he was just chasing

tail. No, I should say as he might, he is always, quote-unquote, investing in promising new developments."

"You don't have to go all defensive on me. I'm not writing a chop job on him, just painting a picture of the folly. He's one of many, and he's not even that old. You should hear some of the old guys who believe they are in a home-stretch sprint to stay alive until medical science catches up so they can live forever. Sad."

"You keep talking about men. It's not just men who want to live longer."

"True, but for men—at least what I'm finding—it's more desperate, more absolute. The women I've interviewed might talk about living to a hundred and fifty, but only if they still look good and still have a quick mind. The men? They want three hundred. Five hundred. Forever."

"Really? What do you think it's about? Maybe because they can't make babies?"

"Could be. How the hell should I know. I'm still working on the story. Maybe it's because men get to still look good when they're older. Women shrivel and get ugly. Who wants to live to a hundred like that? Maybe there is something in what Existendia is developing. I mean, if you're just a disembodied personality, the entire body thing is pretty irrelevant."

"Ugh. I can't think of myself apart from my body, which is maybe why some life-after-death notions never appealed to me. Bodies, now that appeals to me. And clearly to you, from the evidence I've seen so far. Are you just a freelancer or is there a steady somebody in your life?"

Dana hesitated, then plunged ahead. "Full disclosure time: I actually do have a boyfriend. Rolf is a dear about playing on the second string. He's one of the top robotics consultants in the area. We met when I interviewed him for a piece on the Japanese robotics invasion, as they were calling it back then. He's Hungarian, athletic in bed, and wicked smart."

Barbra nodded. "That's a good combination. I've always found intelligence to be very arousing. A brain can be one of the sexiest things about a man."

"Or a woman."

– 5 –

By the time Cole was screaming at Tandi to shut up and leave him alone, the sun was high, and Barbra was already on her way to the office, demonstrating both her greater discipline and deeper devotion to the firm. Mondays had never been Cole's forte, and this Monday was what their preteen daughter would call a complete force. What had started Friday night as a bid for a quick roll in the hay had turned into a two-day orgy that left Cole trying to keep up with the women. Too much of a good thing, he was thinking, as he gave up battling morning traffic on the way to the headquarters campus and turned over control to the car. Note to self, he thought, look into economics and practicality of getting a chopper for commuting. Fractional ownership? Pay to play? Might be more fun to get a pilot's license. How long does that take? How much does it cost? Who cares, kid, you're worth a billion.

So much for taking his own advice to the troops on Friday. He had managed only half the mandate: recreation but no rest. Better not do that again. No worries, won't be able to do that again. Becca will be back home from camp next week. Why did they ever agree to a half session? And then the nanny is back, too. Not exactly a nanny—household assistant is her title: maid, tutor, factotum. There was a mistake on two legs: Irish, flame-red hair, gray-green eyes, a walking wet-dream in a bikini—and out of reach. She already had a serious boyfriend and not the slightest interest in middle-aged men, even if they were filthy rich. Cole was willing to admit he was a tail-chasing sleaze, but he had never pressured anyone into sex. There was never any need. What is it that Kissinger said? Power is the ultimate aphrodisiac? Close, Henry, close but no Pulitzer. Power is good, but wealth is better, more universal. Not every female responds to the pull of power, he thought, but all the bitches go for the riches.

And then there was Dana. What was she about? She didn't seem at all interested in his wealth or the trappings of it. Well, except for Barbra, the consummate trophy wife and the absolute antithesis of Mandi, the wife she had edged out. Night and day, they were, literally. Mandi, the olive-skinned Israeli with the brown-black ringlets and the small tits of her Sephardi mother, and Barbra, the pale buxom shiksa with corn-silk hair whose family tree was peppered with Brits and Swedes.

The Tensora pulled him out of his thoughts by chiming to remind him they were arriving at the Drucker Technologies campus. He made a note to inquire how quickly the transition team could get fresh signage up with the new logo and to find out how long they thought it would take to establish the new identity and propagate it through the business sphere. He knew his people were working on it, but he wanted to know the details, to see the flowchart. He was still the engineer at heart, he admitted to himself, whether he was engineering mergers and acquisitions or weekend threesomes. But of course, that last was really not his engineering. An opportunistic engineer, that's what I am, he thought.

As he walked in through his private entrance, Kelsey greeted him in the hallway and handed him a portfolio. "Good morning, Mr. Drucker. The revised schedule for the week is in there along with hardcopy of the new Mission-

and-Means statement. All uploaded to your devices, of course. And Ms. Carmody is waiting. I put her in Conference B and made no promises."

"Well, persistent little . . . I'll see her now. Tell the Transition Team I'll be there in five."

"I'll tell them fifteen, just in case. Ms. Carmody does seem the persistent type."

— —

Cole kicked the heavy door shut behind him. "What in hell are you doing here? If you think—"

"I think I didn't get the chance last night to thank you for a wonderful weekend. That's all. Mostly. My editor also wants some more background on the people I interviewed, sidebar stuff, how-I-built-this sort of thing."

"You can get that from my corporate bio or off Wikipedia. Most of the stuff in there is more or less true. Look, it was fun, but I have a company to run, a big company."

"I get it, and I'm not asking for a lot. Saturday you mentioned your father as your inspiration in business and in life. I just wanted to hear more of what that was about."

"For your article."

"Yeah. And for me."

"For you, then. My father. He inspired me, all right, but not the way you think. I remember him in the hospital, a pale shell, like the discarded husk of a pistachio. He was dying, as much because of who he was as from any particular disease. We're Ashkenazi Jews, and his early death had been written in his very cells before he was born. He was by then so weak the baby-blue hospital johnnie barely moved with his breathing. When he struggled to speak, his voice was like the whispering draft under a poorly fitted window. I remember he kept repeating my name, the one I never used and rarely heard. 'Chaim. Chaim,' he croaked. I was at a loss for what to do, what to say.

"I just stood there, stroking the back of his hand, telling him that I was there, that my mother was parking the car and would be there in a minute. I wanted to say more, to plead with him to wait for her, but I felt I had no right to ask anything of the dying. And I was angry, angry that he was dying so young, leaving me to struggle alone and grow up faster than I was ready to. And I wanted him to stop repeating my name, my Hebrew name, the name I had long since disowned. Like his.

"My father, Mark Drucker, born Marek Druckerman, died before his wife of twenty-three years could reach his bedside. Within a few years, she would drink herself to her own early death and largely deplete the remnants of wealth that two generations of Druckermans had accumulated since immigrating from Lodz, Poland. What funds remained became seed money for my first company. I was a brilliant college dropout, determined not to die as my father had. I was on my way, using one new venture after another to propel me toward the one percent and then to the one percent of the one percent.

"And I'll tell you something else, Dana. I don't really belong here. I am not one of them. I am the revenge of the bottom half, risen from the immigrant sewers to take whatever I can as long as I can."

At a loss for words and out of questions, she just looked at him.

"Now, as I said, I've a company to run in order to keep getting my revenge. And I'll keep on getting it, because I am not going to go out like my father did. Kelsey will show you out."

He stopped by Kelsey's desk. "Give the determined Ms. Carmody a stack of the corporate history stuff and my bio and the press releases on the merger. Then show her the door and tell her goodbye and good luck from me. I'll be with the team." His hand was shaking as he walked away.

– 6 –

The grueling week had gone well—up to a point. By Friday, the veneer of communal spirit within the Transition Team had begun to wear thin and was completely scraped bare in spots. The ModulArch people were seeing more clearly where they fit in—or didn't—within the new corporate structure. Cole expected to see a few letters of resignation arriving in the next weeks, and he was fairly sure about whose signatures would be on them. He hoped Tonika Warner would not tender hers, but he wouldn't blame her. The racism from some of the old guard was going from latent to blatant. If it continued, he would have to conduct his own purge. The company could not afford to be on the receiving end of a discrimination suit, not at this juncture.

He was finally back in his own Tensora N. It had surprised him that it took so long for his car to be returned from servicing. He had enjoyed trialing the NX loaner, but it never felt like his car, and it lacked the customized full-manual mode that he loved. On the NX, he became resigned to letting the car park itself but could not find how to override the auto-turn mode or the street-light algorithms that prevented him from running through on a yellow. The Model N, his Model N, was like a perfect pair of running shoes that slipped on and off without effort and felt right on every stride of a run.

Saturday morning traffic was light. As he made the turn onto Old Topanga Canyon Road, he did a quick out-and-in-again around a slow sedan and tromped on the accelerator.

He would see Gwen, maybe for the last time, then double back to pick up his daughter at the camp before the noon deadline. It had taken some fancy footwork to convince Barbra that it would be all right for him to go alone to pick up Becca. "Father-daughter time," he had told her. "You know how important it is for girls at this age to have a good relationship with a strong father figure. I definitely get the message that she wants to have that ride home to talk, you know. It's a phase. Next year it'll probably be all about you, and she won't even want to go near me."

Time for some music, he thought, something big, grand, one of the romantics. He was the only one in the family who was into symphonic music, and he had his own custom playlists drawing on a deep repertoire he had assembled himself. Brahms? Maybe the Second Symphony. No. Wagner. Perfect. He switched the audio to the headrest speakers and skipped to the opening of the third act of *Die Walküre*. In a moment, the Valkyries were with him in soaring triumph on his open-air ride up the canyon.

He slowed as he approached the next switchback, then accelerated smoothly through the turn. He straightened the wheel and the car shot forward, pinning him to the seatback.

Part 2

One has to pay dearly for immortality; one has to die several times while one is still alive.

– Friedrich Nietzsche

– 7 –

For the crew of Canyon Consolidated Emergency Services, it had been the second call and the first false alarm of the day. There had been no heart attack at the mall, and Mike and Speedo were now on their way back to the station.

Speedo hit the brakes hard, sending Mike, his paramedic, sliding in the back. "Holy shit, Mike. Did you see that? That sports car just sailed right off the road."

"I didn't see it, but I felt it. What are you trying to do? Kill me? Give me some warning. At least yell 'Hold on!' before you pull that again."

"Yeah, yeah. Hold on, I'm pulling over to check this guy out."

"Call it in, first. You know what happened last time we took off on our own. Call it in."

"I will. Can you hop out the back and make your way down the bank. That car just flew off the road. I don't see how . . ."

Mike Capitano swung his heavy frame out of the ambulance and looked around. There were no fresh skid marks, but the brush at the end of the guard rail was crushed.

From the side of the road he could see a black-and-yellow Tensora roadster lying upside down at the bottom of the gully.

He ducked back in the ambulance and grabbed his bag. "It sure doesn't look good," he called out to Speedo. "I'm going down the embankment to check it out. I'll use the radio to let you know."

The way down proved to be a lot steeper than it looked at first. Mike half climbed, half slid his way down. The Tensora was on its back, against a boulder and partially supported by its automatic roll bar. Judging from the exterior damage, the car had rolled more than once before coming to rest. Mike flattened himself on the ground to look underneath. The unconscious driver was suspended from his shoulder harness, his head angled against the ground. Mike gingerly felt for a carotid pulse. He tapped the button on his mic. "The driver's alive. I've got a weak pulse,"—he checked his watch—"48. Get a rescue team out here. And check the satnav to see if there's a way to bring an ambulance around closer on another road. It would be a bitch trying to get the guy up the embankment. I'm going to see if I can right the vehicle."

"Roger that. I already radioed for backup. There's a dirt road running just below where you are, maybe ten yards, but the turnoff is miles back. I'm going to have the rescue crew come in that way. Meantime, I'm going to grab some stuff and come down after you."

"Roger that. Take it careful. I don't want to be picking up your pieces, too."

Mike crawled under the car again to check on his patient. There was blood on his face and arms, but no signs of major bleeding. He clipped a wireless monitor on one finger of the man's dangling arm and glanced down at the remote readout at his own waist. Not good. He had two options for extracting the man. He could cut the seatbelt and try to ease him to the ground, then drag him out from under, or he could roll the car first. It was unclear which was the more risky, but getting the car upright seemed the best option at the moment. He fished a cervical collar out of his bag and fixed it around the man's neck.

Mike was looking for a good point of leverage when Speedo showed up towing a rescue stretcher loaded with gear. "I walked back a couple hundred yards and found a better way down. I've got ropes, hand winch, oxygen, the works. What do you think? How's our guy doing?"

Mike looked down at his remote reader. "We may be losing him. Pulse is dropping, oh-two is not good. I don't have a cuff on him, but I'll lay odds his BP is falling, too. I think he may be going into shock. I already got a collar on him and strapped his arms. So, give me a hand here."

Had the car been a classic, like a little Miata, it would have been a piece of cake for two men to upright it again, but it was a Tensora. Battery technology had been improving, but all-electric vehicles still carried massive banks of heavy batteries.

The two men gave a trial lift to one side. "No way. And I don't see any easy way to anchor a winch. We'll have to drag him free. I'll come in from this side. You get his legs from the other. I think we can do this fairly gently if we just take it slow and easy."

By the time they had freed him from the vehicle and finished securing him to the stretcher, the rescue team arrived, led by a beefy middle-aged jock with a paramedic insignia on his jacket. "What have we got?"

"Multiple injuries, unknown, possible internal bleeding. Treating for cardiogenic shock, dopamine IV. Pulse still too low, 51. Oh-two, 82; BP, 85 over 50."

"Okay, let's get him into the wagon and out of here, stat."

— —

Barbra stabbed her index finger at the woman behind the counter. "I'm his wife. Barbra Ann Wilson. I want to see him."

"I'm afraid that's impossible. Your husband is still in surgery."

"Surgery? What in hell happened? He's going to be all right, isn't he."

"You'll have to speak with the doctor, Mrs. Wilson."

"Then let me see the doctor."

"I'm sorry, but he's in surgery."

"All right, so when does he get out of surgery?"

"I'm sorry, but I couldn't say."

Barbra slapped her hand flat on the counter. "Well, somebody damn well better say something or I'm going to sue this hospital so fast and so bad you'll all need surgery."

"Please calm down, Mrs. Wilson. It will just—"

"Don't fucking tell me to calm down, you . . ."

"Can I help?" Barbra whirled at the voice behind her and almost collided with a short man in a long white coat. "I'm Dr. Ishakzai. Is there something I can do for you."

"You bet. You can tell me about my husband and let me see him. And you can fire this worthless pile working your front desk."

"What's your husband's name?"

"Todd Drucker. Well, Coleman Todd Drucker. And they won't let me see him."

"Well, let me see what I can do." He slipped a tablet from a pocket in his coat and started tapping and swiping. "So, I see he was brought in by ambulance about two hours ago, and he's still in surgery."

"Why is he in surgery? What happened? I got a text message from Tensora, from ERIN, their damn road service software, saying the car had been involved in an accident. Then I got the call from the rescue service that he was being brought here."

"Well, I can't tell you what happened, but the code from the FirstSight accident report filed automatically by the Tensora service means the vehicle left the road."

"Is he going to be all right?"

"The med-surg team is doing their best, and they are the best. That's why I'm doing my residency here."

"So, you're not a real doctor, then, not yet."

"Oh, I'm real enough. I'm just doing a second residency before I head home. Thanks to old immigration policies that never quite got fixed, once I leave, I may not be able to get back in. So, I'm trying to pack in as much learning as I can before I head home."

"And where is home?"

"Afghanistan. Kabul."

"And you want to go back?"

"Wouldn't you want to go back home after seven years abroad?"

"But, Kabul . . . I mean, it never seems to get settled. First the Taliban, then . . . oh, you know."

"I do know, all too well, which is why I want to go back and do what I can to help, especially out in the rural provinces where doctors are scarce and sorely needed."

"Well, that's admirable, I suppose, but I just want to

know about my husband. Is he all right?"

The doctor swiped left on his tablet. "I can tell you he just got out of surgery. I'd give it, say, a half hour, and then ask nicely at the nurse's station in the intensive care wing—just follow the signs—ask if you can look in on him. It won't be much of a visit, but at least you can see him. I'll send a note to the ICU that you're here and want to see your husband."

"Thank you, doctor. I appreciate that."

"And well you should." His warm smile lifted his moustache. "Think of all the work I just went through for you, checking my tablet and all. My poor finger is all worn out from swiping this way and that."

— —

Barbra put her hand over her mouth and whispered. "Oh, my god, Todd."

He was a mess. His bare arms were scraped and bruised. His head was bandaged, and his face was swollen with bruises where it was not covered by the ventilator mask. An octopus of tubes and cables connected him to an army of blinking and clicking devices.

"Is he awake? Can he hear me."

The nurse shook her head. "Probably not. He's still sedated. I'll let Dr. Baretti fill you in." She busied herself checking readings.

"Can't you tell me?"

"Dr. Baretti will be here in just a few minutes."

"This is what I'm always being told. Somebody else will tell me. Soon. Real soon now."

"I know it must be frustrating not knowing."

"And I know they teach you to say that in nursing charm school."

"That's pretty funny, Mrs. Drucker. I wish there was such a thing. There are a couple of the nurses here who . . . Well, I would gladly pay their tuition."

Barbra laughed. "I'm sorry."

"Me too, Mrs. Drucker. I'm sorry no one can tell you what's happening with your husband."

"It's Barbra Wilson. There once was a Mrs. Drucker, but she's history. And a sordid history at that. No pre-nup, so there was a really long battle over what was whose. I, on the other hand—"

"Ah, here's Dr. Baretti now. Doctor, this is Barbra Wilson, the patient's wife. She is eager to hear about her husband. I'll leave you two to talk."

"Thank you nurse Lomax." The doctor, whose sun-bleached hair made him look like he had just stepped off a surfboard, turned to Barbra. "Would you like to sit?"

"No, I'll take it standing up."

"Well, I'm not sure you have to brace yourself for too much bad news. Mostly we don't know yet."

"What *do* you know?"

"Your husband sustained a major concussion, a cervical fracture, and damage to internal organs with internal bleeding. We have stopped the internal bleeding, at least as far as we can tell. We'll keep a close eye on that. We've relieved pressure in the skull with a shunt and medication, and we've stabilized the vertebrae."

"You care to translate that into English?"

"Sure, starting at the top. He hit his head, fracturing his skull and damaging the brain. We did a procedure to relieve pressure from swelling while his brain recovers. He broke his neck, and we've reinforced it with a surgical plate and screws. He sustained damage to his spleen and liver leading to internal bleeding. We think we caught all the bleeders. He'll be under close observation for the next few days."

"His brain? His neck? Is he going to be paralyzed, brain damaged?"

"We won't know for a while. We just have to wait and see. I'm sorry I can't be more definite, but you can be assured, he's getting the best care in California—in the country."

— —

Barbra was at a table in the hospital cafeteria, recharging with substandard coffee, when she spotted Dana Carmody coming in. "You certainly have a lot of nerve. Are you working on some sensational twist to your story?"

"No, I came here for you. And for him. I heard it on KCRW. News travels fast when a high flier takes a flier. You look like you could use a hug."

"I could." She stood and let Dana embrace her.

At last, Dana spoke. "How is he?"

"Out. Nobody knows yet how bad."

"What happened? The news report said he drove off the road. The police are investigating, treating it as a possible suicide attempt."

"Suicide!" Barbra shook her head. "That's crazy. He was on top of the world, everything going his way."

"It's routine in single-car crashes like this. It does look suspicious. Apparently there weren't even any skid marks. Just straight over the side."

"It must be the car. You know, he had trouble with that one once before, just last week."

"Yeah, well, Tensora is already doing damage control, but something doesn't feel right about the whole thing. Cole told me about that first glitch last weekend. Never heard of anything like that, not for years. In the early days there were some awful crashes with self-driving cars, but not for a long time."

"You cover technology, right? Any chance you can look into this a bit more. I could turn to people at the company, but that might not be such a smart move at this juncture."

"Yeah, I could look into it. I even know some people at Tensora. I'll put out some pings and probes. Anything else I can do for you?"

"Not really. Oh, shit. Becca never got picked up. She might have heard on the news. The poor kid. No, if she had heard, she'd be calling me."

"Becca?"

"Our daughter, she's twelve. We were supposed to collect her up at Camp Cah-Wee-Lah by noon. Todd was heading up early."

"Well, you still have twenty minutes, then." Dana put a hand on Barbra's arm. "Look, if you want to stay here, I can go pick her up."

"I don't think the camp will release her to you. I'll have to call Deirdre. She's the nanny—paid companion, really. We put her on the list, just in case. Look, I have a dozen or more calls to make. I need to get in touch with the Transition Team, get our media management people in high gear. I need to call the camp. And Deirdre. And, I suppose, Mandi Drucker deserves to know, although we haven't spoken in years, since the last round of depositions. Shit. Who else? Our lawyers, the company lawyers. His personal physician. Who did I leave out? The Pope and the President."

"You going to be all right?"

"Yeah, I wish I had some company tonight, but Becca is going to be needing a hundred-and-ten percent of me."

"I understand. You have my cell number and my email. Ping me if you need anything." Dana gave Barbra a squeeze on the shoulder before leaving.

– 8 –

Except for the teak furniture and the bookshelves lining two walls, the office could have been the command center for a security service or the basement den of some well-heeled programming nerd. Half of the semicircular desk was topped by a stacked array of monitors, six curved screens in all. Aram Netsky, the scarecrow-scrawny CTO of Existendia Enterprises, sat in his Aeron chair, tapping away at a wide color-coded gaming keyboard and switching his gaze from screen to screen every few seconds without a pause in the machine-gun typing.

Bannon Turndale, in a retro turn-of-the-century business suit, stood with hands clasped behind his back, waiting for a break that didn't come. "What's up, Aram?" he said at last.

"One minute." The keyboard pelting continued, then finished with a dramatic punch on the ENTER key. Aram swiveled. "You talk with Jerry yet?"

"Yeah. So? He's on his way."

Jerry Pendrake, who had mastered the art of being all but invisible, was CEO because he was a money engineer at a company of software engineers, but Aram Netsky was effectively the man in charge, and Bannon Turndale, head of the legal team, was fully aware of it. Aram nodded toward a side chair. "We need to talk, Bannon."

"Talk away." Bannon undid the button on the jacket of his three-piece suit but remained standing.

"Well, we have our first subject, and he's a doozy."

"If you mean Drucker, we don't have a subject yet."

"Technicality. That's for you and the other suits to handle. My boys are ready to go."

"The man is not dead yet. That's not a technicality, that's a legal and financial show-stopper. Until he's declared dead, our hands are tied."

"See if you can untie them, then. That's what you do. That's what we pay you to do. Don't you see what this means? CEO of Drucker Unified, that's what it means, and he is ours."

"Not yet, I keep saying."

"Make it so, Bannon. Make it so." Netsky turned back to his keyboard and started the ten-finger hailstorm again.

At that moment, Jerry Pendrake entered, his face awash with confusion as Bannon pushed past him to leave. "I thought we had a meeting. What's happening, Aram?"

"You're sure on top of things, Jerry—as usual. And punctual, as always."

"I was working on strategic planning." He played with his left earlobe as he talked. "For the board meeting."

"The board meeting is us and our rubber-stamp brigade. We have more pressing matters."

"Such as?"

"Such as go talk with Bannon Turndale. And give him whatever he needs to make things happen." Netsky turned back to his array of screens.

Pendrake stood with his mouth open, making his weak chin even more noticeable. When Netsky returned to typing on his custom keyboard, Pendrake closed his mouth and walked away.

— —

Mandi Drucker was already at the hospital when Barbra arrived. "I see you got my message," Barbra said. She set her purse on the bedside chair, marking it as her territory.

"Yes, and I do read the news feeds. Any word? I haven't had a chance to talk with the docs yet."

"No, nothing yet. Nothing good yet. He had more surgery. Still out. They didn't actually call it a coma, but that's what it seems to be."

"How's Becca taking it?"

"Freaked. And the boys?"

"Mark and Toby hardly know their father. They know about him, but that's mostly from reading news stories. Besides, they're teenagers. They have their own worlds. Even I sometimes go for a week or more with barely more than a glimpse of a passing shape. 'Hi, Mom, can I have the keys. Bye, Mom, I'll be at Angelo's.' You know how it is. Or you soon will."

"Yeah, Becca is twelve going on seventeen. I don't remember being so into boys at her age. She came back from camp full of stories, but not about horses or canoeing. It was all about the hunk who was the sailing instructor or the really, really cute older boys, some Counselor-in-Training, the guy at the stables. I'm thinking I may have to start her on the pill this year."

"They grow up fast these days, that's for sure." Mandi stared off into the distance for a moment, then looked back at Barbra. "And how are you? This has got to be tough for you."

"Well, I'm tough, too. And I have a lot to do to keep my mind off worst-case scenarios. Adam Treadwell is now acting CEO, so I've stepped in to take over his duties. Overwhelming. And the stock is taking a big hit. No, not a hit; it's in freefall. We're trying to counter that by moving up some of the new technology announcements, but the tech press isn't buying it. Hey, I'm sorry. I don't mean to bore you with this stuff."

"It's not boring. Remember, I started Drucker Tech with Cole. We nursed it together through the lean years. I was pregnant with Mark when we were awarded our first patents."

"And you fought hard for a better settlement after the divorce."

"I had two young children to raise on my own. Cole was already the absent father."

"He sued for custody."

"A tactical maneuver. We both knew that. Look, those battles are ancient history. He moved on, I moved on."

"And yet you're here."

"I didn't stop loving him. I didn't stop caring."

The two women locked eyes for several long seconds before Barbra looked away. "I suppose . . ."

"Look, Barbra, I don't want or need anything from you or Cole. I have enough. I had ten good years with the man I loved, and now I have two wonderful sons who are almost grown. Was I angry when we split? You better believe I was. He dumped me and tried to pull a fast one so the merged company would not fall under community property law. Was I hurt? Damn right I was. I was being shut out and replaced by a newer model. So I fought back. I didn't win, but I did win enough.

"I'm sure there's nothing I could do for you, Barbra, nothing you need from me, but if there ever were, you know where to find me. I'm not angry at you. I never have been. It was all about Cole. Funny, that. It's always been all about Cole, as I'm sure you figured out long ago. Anyway, I'll leave you with him. Please let me know if there's any change." She reached over and touched Cole's arm, then backed away.

Barbra watched Mandi leave. She looked down at her husband's silent form, watching his chest rise and fall in synch with the huffing of the ventilator that was keeping him alive. "Todd, if you can hear me, I'm here. I love you, Todd. I'm here. Todd, please wake up. Please come back."

—— ——

The restaurant was crowded and noisy. Barbra spotted a magenta-haired woman studying her menu in a booth at the side. She skirted the queue of customers waiting for a table and made straight for the booth. "I will tell you, Dana," she said, as she sat down on the far side, "you are easy to spot in a crowd."

"I know. Sometimes that's good, sometimes not. That's why I had you meet me here. It's not one of my usual haunts and not a fave of the tech press crowd. So, we can talk. Probably safe."

"You make it sound all cloaky and daggery."

"Sort of is. We should order first, otherwise we'll be sitting here forever with nothing but air to suck on."

"What's good here?"

"Everything, I'm told. Middle East fusion at its highest and most fused. Good wine list, too. I already ordered a bottle to share. Should be here any minute, so get ready to order."

"You do it. I've been making decisions all day, and I'm all decisioned out."

"Okay. I can do that. How's your Todd doing?"

"My Todd is not doing, not anything. It's been nearly three weeks and no sign of anything going on. They've done the brain scans and the transcranial whatever and all their abracadabra medical magic. Nothing. He's not brain dead, but he might as well be. The docs are funny sometimes. They say he's not in a persistent vegetative state because it hasn't been long enough to be called persistent. Becca asked whether Dad was a vegetable, and I told her no. But the real reason is that 'vegetable' is not in the neurological vernacular anymore."

"You talk about it as if this all were happening to someone else."

"It is. At least that's how it feels. I'm living in a different world now, a world without Todd. I don't think he's coming back. I've been reading up on this stuff, and the odds are so against a recovery. The longer he goes on like this, the worse the odds. I live on data and probabilities, not on hope. My mother lived on hope, and it got her nowhere."

"Your mother?"

"Trailer trash. She was a single mother who got free housing in return for unclogging toilets and nagging neighbors who didn't pay rent on time. She lived on dreams and denial. You know how I got my name, Barbra Ann Wilson?"

"No. How?"

"The Beach Boys. My mother was obsessed with them. Barbra Ann. Ba-ba-bah ba-Barbra Ann. My sister was named Brianna, Brianna Wilson. That says it all. Oh, and the spelling, B-A-R-B-R-A. that was her homage to Streisand, her other idol. She had this screwy notion about a kind of sympathetic magic that, with the right namesakes for us, we would somehow rise to similar heights."

"Well, you certainly did all right. What about your sister?"

"Killed in a motorcycle crash at seventeen. Her biker boyfriend survived to fight off my mother when she tried to kill him with a tire iron. She didn't need to. He bought it a year later in a bar fight that turned sour. Great family stories. I got a lot of them."

"Don't we all."

"Yeah? What about you?"

"A charmed life. No, really. I had everything a girl could want—except parents. Freddy and Aileen never grew up. They didn't need to. They were Freddy and Aileen to everybody, including me. Not Mom and Dad, no. Freddy and Aileen, always generous, always ready to party and please everyone who showed up at the door. I had no idea how they survived, but there was always money whenever it was needed. It wasn't until I started applying to colleges that I learned they had never filed tax returns, never held jobs, never gotten licenses. My uncle Tommy finally told me the story one time when he was high, which he almost always was, along with almost everyone I knew back then."

"What did he tell you?"

"My dad made a score, a big one, mega, once. He squirreled away the proceeds and slowly doled them out over the decades. Never dealt drugs again, never even drove again. Paid for everything in cash that just appeared whenever needed."

"Wow, are your folks still alive?"

"Oh yeah, still living the dream, still dreaming their lives away in a cannabis haze. Except life caught up with them, and now weed is legal. If uncle Tommy is right about the size of the Big Score, there will still be wads of bills left even when they finally cash in."

"So, where'd you end up going to school?"

"Columbia. I wanted the dead set opposite to the desert isolation I grew up in."

"How did you manage that? Columbia's not cheap. Did you pay in cash?"

"No, I applied as undocumented and got in on a sympathy wave after all that alt-right anti-immigrant shit died down. Eventually I got all the papers I needed using my grandmother's maiden name. I liked the sound of Carmody. I was even considering Devine as my first name, but then thought better of it."

"So, is Dana your real name?"

"Real as any. Growing up I was 'Hey Kid' at home and Sunny at school. That was short for Sunflower, Sunflower Danica McAllen-Bradley. But I've been legally Dana Carmody since I turned eighteen. And here's our wine. Let's order."

"Okay, and then you have to tell me what you found out."

Dana ordered the Chef's Sampler for two, then raised her glass to toast. "Here's to health: yours, mine, and of those we love."

"Amen. Now what's the real story."

"Well, it's a little like yours about Todd, more about what we don't know than what we do, but what we don't know is interesting. The car has been in the hands of an automotive forensics team. Who even knew there was such a thing? Anyway, the geek squad quickly eliminated brake failure or other electro-mechanical problems. The black box, which is actually gray on today's cars, recorded the car accelerating with wheels pointing straight ahead just before it went airborne. A team from Tensora was called in to help analyze possible causes, which were pretty much narrowed down to one of three things: either deliberate driver action or driver failure, like a heart attack, or some new kind of major system failure, which, of course, Tensora claims can't happen and wants to be able to prove never did happen. And then . . ."

"And then?"

"And then, nothing. Suddenly no more leaks, no new statements to the press, no 'authorities are working on' gibberish, nothing. The investigation has gone dark, and it's been just long enough that the whole story is off the press-corps radar. You and your people seem to have righted the corporate ship and steered it around or through the storm. 'Construction Company CEO Still in Coma' is nobody's headline. So, nobody cares."

"You once said you knew people at Tensora. What about them?"

"Nobody's talking. Nobody even takes my calls. I haven't given up, but I also haven't gotten anything. Oh, here's our food coming. Let's eat, drink, and take our minds off it all."

– 9 –

Barbra sat on the sofa as her preteen daughter in shorts and a vintage Twenty Øne PilØts tee-shirt paced in front of her and shouted. "You can't be serious, Mom. We can't do that to Daddy. It's, like, murder."

"Becca, honey, it's not. It's—"

"It is so. Why would you want to kill him?"

"I don't want to lose him any more than you do. But he's already gone. The daddy you knew, the man I knew, isn't there anymore. There's a body in that hospital room being kept going by machines, but Coleman Todd Drucker, the person, is gone."

"No! What if you're wrong? I read about this woman who was, like, locked in. Everybody thought she wasn't even conscious, but she heard everything and knew what was happening, and they finally hooked up this gizmo and she started communicating again, but with the help of some computer thing, and . . ."

"There are lots of stories on the Internet, honey, but this isn't a story, and your dad is not minimally conscious. He's gone. All the hospital is asking is whether he should be taken off the ventilator that breathes for him and keeps his heart beating."

"Right, so that he'll be dead, so then you can get all his money."

"Oh, Becca, you are so wrong. You—"

"That's why you married him anyway, isn't it? You were just some—"

"Now you wait just one minute, Becca Brie Drucker. You

58

do not get to say things like that. I know you are upset, but money has nothing to do with this. It didn't even have anything to do with me marrying your father. I married him because—"

"Because you wanted his money. He told me once about where you came from, your family. You were a gold digger but good in the sack. He—"

Barbra grabbed her, pulled her down onto the sofa, and slapped her. "You do not get to talk like that to me. Not ever."

Becca's eyes widened as she put her hand to her reddening cheek. "Go ahead, hit me again, but that won't stop me from telling the truth. That's what he said."

Barbra's eyes were closed as she took several deep breathes. "I'm sorry for slapping you. Maybe he did say that. Maybe he was drunk. That doesn't give you the right to repeat it, though. It's not about the money. It never was. I had stock options and a generous 401K before we got involved. Live or die, married or not, I was already set. Even if he dumped me like he dumped Mandi, I'm covered under our pre-nup, which a whole cadre of lawyers helped negotiate. So it's not about money." She opened her eyes and looked at Becca. "It's about letting go. That's hard, I know. And I know how much you love him. I know how close you've been, so this will be extra hard for you. But it's something we have to do, something we both have to be grown up about."

Becca closed her eyes, squeezing out pools of tears. "Oh, Mom." She leaned into her mother's arms. "I don't think I can do it. I don't think I can be grown up. I don't think I can let him go."

They sobbed together for minutes until Becca pulled

back and wiped her eyes on the sleeve of her tee-shirt. "Do we have to do it right away? Can I see him again?"

"Yes, you can see him again. If you want, we can be there together when he . . . when he passes."

"I think I want that. But can I change my mind if . . . if I just can't handle it?"

"Yes, you can change your mind."

— —

There were two doctors and two men in suits in the room when Barbra and Becca arrived at the hospital. "Who are you? What's going on here?"

"I'm Dr. Formosa, head of the medical ethics group here. You already know Dr. Baretti. We're taking the patient off life support."

"No you are not. I haven't authorized this. I'm his wife, I have medical power of attorney."

The taller of the other two men stepped forward. "I'm Bannon Turndale, and my authority supersedes yours. Under the circumstances, I have power of attorney."

"What circumstances? What authority?" She jabbed a finger toward the doctor. "And don't you make a single move unless you want to face charges for wrongful death and one whopping lawsuit for medical malpractice."

Dr. Formosa stepped back from the bed and held up his hands. "I'm not going to do anything until this matter is settled."

"It's settled. The hospital already has a copy of my husband's advance medical directive and his notarized assignment to me granting me durable power of attorney to act on his behalf should he ever become incapacitated."

Turndale reached into his breast pocket and removed a thick folded document. "And I have my documents with me, including a copy already filed with the hospital and this copy for you. It's a binding contract granting medical power of attorney to Existendia Enterprises, a California corporation. I am acting on behalf of the corporation."

"I don't even know if you can do that, grant medical power of attorney to a corporation."

"Oh, absolutely. In the case of Reinholt v. Stanford—"

"I don't give a shit about either Reinholt or Stanford. I'm getting my lawyers here to stop you." She pulled her phone from her purse. "And you, doctor, had better get the hospital legal people in here, too, if you want to continue to have a hospital to work for."

"I'll see what I can do. We thought this was settled."

"It is. It was. You already had my husband's papers, properly formulated and duly notarized."

Turndale nodded. "Yes, and when were these papers drawn up, Mrs. Drucker?"

"It's Wilson, Ms. Wilson, and the papers were drawn up years ago."

"Exactly. And your husband completed arrangements with us just over a year ago, so our authority supersedes yours. If you read this contract, you will find that, in the event of your husband becoming *non compis mentis*, we have medical power of attorney."

"That makes no sense. Why would he sign that? I'm his wife. Why didn't he tell me."

"I'm afraid that's outside my area of expertise. Why do husbands do things without telling their wives? I don't know. But I do know this is a legally binding contract. And I expect—"

He was interrupted by the arrival of another doctor and a man in the telltale gray suit of the legal profession. The man stepped into the middle of the assembled group and did a quick pirouette. "Hello, everyone. I'm Chase Garlock, chief counsel for the hospital. Will somebody tell me what is going on here?"

"I'm Bannon Turndale, attorney for Existendia Enterprises, a California—"

"Not you. Who's next of kin?"

Barbra raised her hand.

"Okay, you fill me in."

Barbra outlined what had transpired. "And he said if Todd is *non compis mentis*, they have power of attorney. I don't know what that means."

"It means not mentally competent. It's Latin, legalese. And, Mr. Bannon, do you have a ruling to that effect?"

"It's Turndale, Bannon Turndale. And no, we do not have a ruling, but"—he gestured toward the bed— "*res ipsa loquitur.*"

Attorney Garlock laughed. He turned to Barbra. "Attorney humor. More Latin. Literally, 'the thing speaks for itself,' hardly the case here." He put his hand to his ear and cocked his head toward the bed. "Nope, not a word."

"Laugh if you will, but the matter is self-evident."

"*Non compis mentis* is a legal construct, as you well know. It is not self-evident but, in contested cases, requires a judicial ruling, as you also well know. I'm going to ask that you leave the hospital and not return until and unless you have a court order in hand. As far as the hospital is concerned, you have no standing and no right even to be here. I assume there will be no need to summon security."

"No need. Come!" He signaled his unnamed and still silent junior partner to follow with a snap of his fingers. "We'll be back, papers in hand."

Barbra reached toward the hospital attorney. "I can't thank you enough for your help."

"Oh, ma'am, there's no need to thank me. I was not helping you. I'm only looking out for the interests of the hospital, which is my job. I would suggest you get your own attorney to look out for your interests and your husband's. If those two come back with a court order and all the proper documents that protect us, we will follow the law."

Becca, who had been silent throughout the whole confrontation, reached for her mother's hand. "What are we going to do?"

"We're going to bring in the cavalry. Next time they try anything, they'll be facing my lawyer, Todd's, and the whole recently expanded legal department of Drucker Unified. The company has a big stake in this, and it has a lot of resources." She picked up the copy of the contract left by Turndale. "I'm going to start by getting them working on this. And an injunction to prevent the hospital from doing anything without my approval."

"Wow, you're pretty, well, you know, tough, Mom."

"You haven't seen anything yet. Have you ever ridden in a helicopter? No? Well, I'm going to get one to pick us up here and fly us to Drucker headquarters so we can meet in person with the legal team pronto. You want to see tough? Wait until you see those guys. They'll eat the likes of Mr. Turndale and Mr. Garlock for lunch."

– 10 –

The scene at the hospital was surreal. Crowded into the hospital room were three of Drucker Unified's legal team plus Turndale and his shadow from Existendia, Leah Goldstein for Barbra, Hal Workman in his retro Seventies suit on behalf of Coleman Todd Drucker, a nurse and two doctors, Chase Garlock and two more attorneys for the hospital, and the hospital administrator, plus Judge Isabella Rodrigues and a court stenographer.

Becca Drucker was holding her mother's hand as they stood in the doorway, almost edged out of the room. "What is it with lawyers and the old-fashioned look?" She whispered and nodded toward Turndale, then Workman.

"I don't know, sweety. Lawyers are a strange species." She bent her head low to keep from being heard. "With these two, I think it's like peacock feathers. Flamboyant but reaching for understatement."

The proceedings took less time to complete than it took to assemble the people in the room. Judge Rodrigues took testimony synopsizing the medical findings before asking a series of questions of the unconscious man in the bed, questions that went unanswered. She made her ruling and left with her stenographer.

Turndale failed in his attempt not to look too smug as he declared victory. "Well, that's settled. If we might all vacate the room to give the bereaved widow and daughter a few minutes, before the doctors complete their . . . their work."

"Aren't you jumping the gun, Mr. Turndale?" Barbra

pushed her way to the front of the assembled group. "I may be bereaved, but I am not a widow, not yet."

Attorney Chase Garlock edged toward Turndale and his colleague. "Indeed, you are jumping the gun, counsel. Not all requirements of the hospital have been met. There is a lot of paperwork that needs to be completed first. Then you need to get a direct court order to turn off the ventilator, which the hospital will challenge, and dot-dot-dot. It ain't over."

"No, it ain't, as you so ineloquently put it, but these things can be expedited."

"What's the hurry, counsel? The patient isn't going anywhere."

"There's a lot at stake here."

"I bet there is, and you have a lot of us in this room wondering just what and just how much. Anyway, finish the paperwork first, Turndale, then we'll see what happens next."

The room slowly cleared leaving Barbra and Becca with Leah Goldstein.

"Mom, can I ask a question?"

"Sure honey."

"I thought we had decided to, you know, let Daddy go. But that's what those people want to do. Why are we fighting them? And, I mean all these lawyers, too? They're fighting them."

Leah Goldstein spread her hands. "Mind if I try to answer, Barbra?"

"Go ahead."

"So, it's like this, honey. It's about who's in charge, who has the authority to act on your father's behalf. That company is trying to claim that they have that right, and if they can make medical decisions on his behalf, that sets a precedent for other provisions in their contractual arrangements made with him."

"Why does that matter if . . . if he's dead?"

"We don't know, exactly, because this case is taking us into uncharted legal territory."

"How's that?"

"Well, it's because of what that company, Existendia, does. Your father contracted with them to upload a kind of copy of his brain, his personality, to their computers as a way to—"

Becca jumped in. "To, like, live on! Like on that Hulu series, 'Second Pass'."

"Well, yes. Like. That's a good word, a teen favorite but also an appropriate choice in this case. *Like* living on. The question is, how much like living on and how much not."

"But, so, Daddy would be, like, alive but in a computer. Why wouldn't we want that? He'd still be here. We could talk and stuff. That sounds like a good thing."

"Maybe it does, but as I said, there's a lot at stake, more than we know at this point. Maybe the future of a multibillion dollar company. Maybe your future."

— 11 —

Bannon barged into Aram Netsky's office waving a thick wad of paper. "We got it. I told you it was just a matter of time. I told you I was good."

"That you did. Over and over you told us all. And it's about time you made good on the claims. How many weeks has this dragged on? I really don't see why this stupid legal stuff can take so long. It's just words and paper. So when?"

Bannon glanced at his watch. "Four o'clock. This afternoon."

"And you're sure they'll be no more hitches, no last minute appeals or injunctions?"

"None, their last course of action has been exhausted. We're in."

"All right. I'm going to put us in play."

"Shouldn't we wait?"

"No, we want continuity. We need to broker computing and storage resources in the cloud. Once we have those locked in, it takes hours to complete the upload. Plus, the whole client side down here has to be initialized and proofed. We don't just turn a switch and say shazzam."

"But it's just computers, and it's already all in the cloud, isn't it? Turn the switch and launch the app. I saw the demo."

"Bannon, Bannon, you have been too long isolated in your paperwork tower with your head buried in contract mumbo-jumbo. That was a demo, a soft simulation. This is the real thing, four years on and eighty-thousand programmer-hours of computer coding later." He stood and came around from behind his desk. "We are talking about the connectome of the human brain, Bannon, petabytes of data. We have, what, three dozen clients signed up by now? Their stuff is all archived. We have to bring our digital Mr. Drucker up to live storage, to fast access. And there's the whole tiered architecture in our modeling software. There's not enough computing power in the world to actually run an accurate neuron-by-neuron simulation of one entire human brain in real-time, even if we did have the actual complete connectome to simulate, which we don't. We have a fuzzy, simplified, approximation, which is just barely enough but still enormous."

"But I thought we emulate the complete . . ."

"You thought that's what we do because you never dug beyond the demo. That was for you, for the angel investors—all technical hype and diluted details. So, we've now got this enormously complex client-side software—that's the stuff here—running all the layers and layers of peripheral processing, vocal personality approximation, visual-field and aural pre-processing, all connecting to the outside world based on a petabyte or two of configuration data kept here. That's all linked by a really fat pipe to the array of leased supercomputer capability that runs much simpler software in very tight loops doing neuron-by-neuron emulation on a collection of cleverly fudged pieces of the approximate connectome of our Mr. Drucker. And back to the pre-processing and output layers here in a closed loop.

"It works because we have modules here that pretend to be some parts of the brain that already have fairly well-understood functions. For instance, we don't send the complete visual field to the cloud as raw data from our retina substitutes; we send the predigested results from a software visual cortex. It saves connection bandwidth and reduces the size of the connectome that needs to be simulated. Plus, the hi-res resonance imaging we used to map his brain is good enough for models of some processes, but not for something as complicated and detailed as the visual cortex. Same for hearing, parts of the motor strip, and so on. Even though we are only emulating a fraction of the connectome and at a rough approximation, it takes one hell of a lot of cloud resources to do it in anything close to real-time."

"I know all that, Aram. I'm not one of your geek squad, but I'm not a moron."

"So you say, but what you never seem to quite grasp is the scale, what it takes in storage and computing power to make this thing work and the time it takes to get it to the point we can, as you so crudely expressed it, launch the app." He returned to his desk and reached for his keyboard. "Now, let me get the Go Team started on their job and begin to feed the data and run all the cross checks. You just finish your job and begin to feed the funds that power this so-called app."

— —

Progress bars and scrolling summaries filled four of the six screens in front of Aram. On the last two screens, Aram multi-tasked between live conversation threads with his team and a last-minute patch to fix a bug in the code for recognizing and classifying edges of objects in the visual field.

Netsky would be the first to admit he was not a people person. He preferred to lead from behind a keyboard and monitor. Face-to-face encounters were stressful, and when he was anxious, he all too easily lapsed into impatience and sarcasm. While texting and instant messaging, he was a reasonable individual, although no one would call him charming. In person, no one liked him.

The Go Team had been through dozens of trials and rehearsals, even one full-scale upload that cost enough to cause eyebrows to raise among the board of directors. But there were always hitches and glitches with real data and live ops. The pressure of human interaction could leave Aram flailing, but programming under pressure was a drug of choice for him, computerized cocaine that sent him sailing and brought out his best.

As an officer in the company and a part owner, he should have been conducting from a podium or watching from a balcony, but he was Aram Netsky, software engineering and neuroscience genius, by his own declaration the greatest engineer and scientist on the planet that nobody had ever heard of. He had only five published papers to his credit, but they had been enough to get him the funding to launch Existendia. By rights, he should have been CEO, but Chief Technical Officer suited him better.

Now, with the curtain going up in less than an hour, he was in the orchestra pit, moving from instrument to instrument, looking over the shoulders of his people by remote access, pointing out missed details and making on-the-spot suggestions. And coding. He finished the new visual edge-discrimination patch, cranked through unit test and regression testing on the whole visual subsystem, and plugged it in live. He could be arrogant to the point of recklessness, but real-world performance invariably proved his over-confidence was justified. The patch worked perfectly.

At four minutes past four, Bannon knocked a tattoo on the doorjamb and leaned in. "I just got the text message. He's ours."

Part 3

Consciousness is an end in itself. We torture our-
selves getting somewhere, and when we get there it
is nowhere, for there is nowhere to get to.

– D. H. Lawrence

– 12 –

Coleman blinked. The well-lit room—half law office, half computer lab—looked familiar, although his perspective seemed odd and the colors were harsh and too saturated. Disoriented, he struggled to make sense of the experience as his thoughts juddered in erratic bursts. The implications slowly sunk in. "I can see," he said. "I guess that means . . ." He was rattled by the sound of his own voice, flattened and uninflected, as if it had been auto-tuned by an inept music producer. "I made it, huh? So it works."

Aram Netsky swiveled and leaned forward in his chair and scanned each of the six stacked monitors before answering. "Of course it worked. This may be our first full digital proxy installation, but not the first test of the system. And in this case, there was a trial run once, even before . . ." His keyboard rattled with a burst of typing.

"I . . . I can't move my arm. I can't feel anything. I'm . . ."

"Everything is fine. This is a server-only installation. Mobility comes later, along with full sensory input. It will take some time and training to get your new brain to sort things out and to tweak all the parameters." He switched windows. "Based on experiences with digitally linked prosthetics, we're estimating that full adaptation could take up to a year, although that might be a strained extrapolation. We had a trial run on a test proxy upload that we managed to train into full remote control of a robot in less than three months, but that was a special case."

He brought up an archive file. "For now, I need to ask you some questions—for the record. I have my personal assistant, Di Fiora, and a colleague here as witnesses. You already know Bannon Turndale, from Legal, behind him is Johanna Ross, head of our neuro-psych group. We also have a court-appointed clerk." He glanced toward the end of the elongated desk. The clerk seated there tapped a key to start the official legal recording. "Do you feel up to answering a few questions? Just to verify the installation."

Coleman nodded.

"Please answer aloud, yes or no, for the record. On the monitor, I can see activity on your motor strip, but not always what you are trying to do. That has to be worked out through the sensory-motor mobility interface training. So, can you answer some questions."

"Yeah, sure, I guess. Yes."

"For the record, please state your full name and date of birth."

"Coleman Todd Drucker. I was born on 21 January 1991. Tell me. When . . .? How long ago did I . . ."

"Seven weeks ago. You lost control of your Tensora on Old Topanga Canyon Road. The driver-assist system was unable to take back control in time to prevent leaving the road and the rollover. But, not to worry. With durable power of attorney and personal representative papers in place, we were able to move quickly to acquire the cloud resources and complete the upload from our secure archives. The computing power needed is non-trivial, as you well know, but available at a price. These days, the slowest part of the process can be the legal matters—considering the finances at stake—but, fortunately, we have Bannon Turndale heading our legal team, and we're confident all matters will be resolved soon."

"How old was I."

"Forty-seven."

"So the files were only a year plus old. How was I doing? Will there be enough in the estate?"

"The trust you set up should be more than adequate. The recent merger was a good move."

"Merger?" Even through the processing of the voice synthesizer, the surprise was evident.

"You acquired Unified ModulArch Construction in a leveraged deal. The stock of the new Drucker Unified took a tumble after your accident, but it's recovered nicely."

"I guess I have some catching up to do."

"There will be plenty of time for that later—all the time in the world, in fact—but for now we need to complete these formalities. What was your maternal grandmother's maiden name—please spell it out—and where was she born?"

"Grosz, G-R-O-S-Z. She was born in Lodz, Poland."

Netsky picked up an encrypted storage capsule nearly the size of a paperback and held it in front of the camera. "Do you recognize this object?"

"Yes, it's the backup copy of my connectome upload. That's my signature across the face."

"For the record, have you ever shared, with anyone in any form, the passphrase that you used to lock this copy?"

"No, I have not."

"I am docking the capsule with this terminal. When I ask you for the passphrase, please say it slowly and clearly aloud, then wait for the checksums to be validated against the checksums on our server copy. Ready?"

"Yes."

"Passphrase, please."

"Kol ha-olam kulo gesher tsar meod."

Netsky smiled at the choice, a Hassidic expression in Hebrew: All the world is a narrow bridge. A blue light on the capsule blinked repeatedly, then stayed lit; the top left monitor screen displayed a message: Checksums match.

"Thank you, Coleman, we're going to let you rest now." He tapped the pause icon on a lower monitor screen and the crude avatar face above froze.

"All right. That should do it until we can arrange for a full competency hearing. How soon can you file for the temporary orders, Bannon?"

"I can have them ready Monday morning. But we have the weekend. There's no big rush now. This one should be a piece of cake."

"Exactly, all the more reason for expediting. Why do you think we moved the hearing ahead in the queue?"

"Is there something going on here that I am not privy to?"

"Yes. Just file the papers before we burn through the deposit."

Bannon straightened a slim sheaf of papers and restored them to his briefcase. "I get the picture. Should I or my most recent hires be getting our résumés in order?"

"Not needed if you do your job with all due haste. I'll be looking for your confirmation that we are good to go before noon tomorrow." Turning his back on Bannon, he addressed his digital assistant. "Sandria, get me Gerrard Fitchburg on the line. I want to see if we can negotiate an extension on the Cloudastics consolidated services contract for the elastic cloud resources we are using."

Bannon felt a buzz in his pocket. He put his phone to his ear and his expression went slack. "Please repeat that." His eyes closed. "Okay, thanks." He slipped the phone back in his suit jacket. "We have a problem."

"We have lots of problems. We solve problems. That's what we do, Bannon. So what now?"

"He's breathing on his own. He's still alive."

— 13 —

Becca poured skim milk on her overfilled bowl of cereal—her version of a snack before dinner—then slurped the extra liquid from the edge. "What does this mean, Mom? Is Daddy going to live?" She set the milk bottle at the edge of the breakfast bar so Tandi would be sure to spot it and return it to cold storage.

"I don't know. The doctors don't know. The part of his brain that controls breathing is working again, that's what it means. They have to do more testing to see whether anything else is working, but they don't think we should get our hopes up."

"Is that awful man and his company still in charge?"

"No, now with your father breathing on his own, it's a different circumstance, and we have a basis for challenging them. So we don't know, but Leah, our personal lawyer, thinks we have a good shot at it. Remember, though, even if I can get my power of attorney recognized again, that doesn't necessarily solve things. We still have to decide what happens, whether he—his body—is kept alive or not."

Becca jumped up off the bar stool. "I don't like this. I don't like the idea of deciding whether Daddy lives or dies."

"I don't like it either, honey, but as I told you, the daddy you knew is already gone. He's not there in that hospital bed."

Becca balled her fists in a childish gesture. "I hate it, I hate it, I hate it!"

"I know, honey. Look, treat yourself to pizza and ice cream tonight and binge-watch your favorite series. I'll peek in and check on you when I get back."

"When is that?"

"I don't know. But not too late, I have to work tomorrow."

"But it's Friday."

"Yes, and tomorrow is Saturday, but I'm holding down two jobs at the office and I have paperwork to catch up on. Deirdre will be here; you'll be fine."

"Der. I'll be fine. It's you I worry about, Mom."

"Don't. I'm a big girl, and I can look out for myself. That's why I'm taking the night off and going out for dinner."

—— ——

Dana opened the door to the apartment letting an aromatic wave of warm air wash into the hallway. "Welcome to my humble of humbles. Come on in."

Barbra inhaled deeply through her nose. "Mmm, something smells wonderful."

"Middle East fusion, from that restaurant. I'm a terrible cook. No, I'm not terrible, just inept. But I'm good at spooning stuff out of corn-plastic containers and into serving dishes."

"That's why we have Tandi. As long as the house has the ingredients and the recipe is in the database, Tandi can whip it up. And she recycles the wrappings and containers, composts the scraps, and does the dishes."

"Lucky you. What does that sort of smart house cost."

"More than you want to know. But it actually belongs to the corporation. We're a 'panel family'—guinea pigs, in other words. We fill out these reports on the 'user experience' every three months or whenever there's an upgrade. It's just enough to satisfy the tax people that it's all legit."

"Wow, free housing: nice work if you can get it."

"I said the company owns it, but we do pay rent and upkeep, which makes it nowhere near free."

"Nowhere near is something I can understand. Do you know what this little one-bedroom condo would run if I had to buy it?"

"You don't own your own place?"

"No, Freddy and Aileen do. I don't know the details, and they said I don't want to know. But they did tell me it was mine to use as long as I wanted. Some complicated shady deal with somebody way back. I don't ask questions, I just pay for the utilities."

Barbra smiled. "In an odd way, we're two of a kind, Dana. You realize that?"

"Oh yeah, I realize that. Like sisters. Look at us. You can hardly tell us apart." She gave Barbra a quick kiss. "Sit down, make yourself comfortable, and let me get you something to drink. I have a bottle of champagne on ice, if that'll do."

"Sure. What's the occasion?"

"You. You're here. Now, tell me what's been happening on the hubby front. Everything. Then I'll tell you my news."

— —

Over dinner of take-out food, Barbra brought Dana up-to-date on the legal and medical fronts. "So, we don't know. Everything is up in the air again. The lawyers said cases like this can literally drag out for years. It's . . . it's painful being in limbo. I'm not a widow, but I also don't have a husband. And what about you? You said you have some news."

"Maybe news is too strong a word. Clues. One of my inside guys at Tensora finally dropped a hint about the car. The forensic analysis has been even more complicated than usual and has taken extra time because your husband's car was a customized, one-off vehicle." She took a sip from her champagne flute.

"Anyway, in the car there are dozens of dedicated computers that do all kinds of specialized processing tasks: satnav, road surface analysis, line-and-lane following, bumper cameras, proximity detectors, LIDAR, et cetera. These all feed the master system which integrates this stuff and makes decisions. Even when the car is in so-called manual mode, the driver isn't actually driving the car. Like modern aircraft, this is 'drive-by-wire'. The steering wheel, brake, and accelerator just act like joysticks of a sort and send signals to the computers, which actually then turn the wheels, regulate the juice to the wheel motors, and the like. And the master computers are always watching to see whether what the human driver is trying to do makes sense, is safe.

"There's also the Vehicle Data and Performance Recorder, the so-called black box. The thing records just about everything directly from the exCANN buss. That's what serves as the local area network by which all the parts of the car talk with each other. The VDPR, the black box, operates completely independently of the computers that actually run the car. It's like a brainless court recorder, just taking it all down without regard to what it means. It even noted, for example, that your husband started listening to music just before the accident, track 3, file AF0E11, in folder 2E8913."

"You remember stuff like that?"

"No, I just made up the file name, but that's how the black box records things: all just codes. However, in this case I do know what it translates to. He was listening to 'The Ride of the Valkyries' from Wagner's Ring Cycle.

Whatever that might mean."

"It means Todd had terabytes of classical music—and a much smaller and selective playlist of pop music curated by his daughter—loaded on a microSD card he kept slotted in that car. He was a nut for that kind of stuff. Funny. These days I actually find myself missing the blast of horns and the sweep of strings."

"Yeah, well, right about the time that track starts playing, the black box shows that the out-going commands from the master computer system and the inputs from the driver's controls stop matching up. The brake was being applied but the computer was sending more juice to the wheel motors. The computer sent the lock signal to the steering column, as if the vehicle had been parked, even as sensors on the steering wheel were reporting counterclockwise torque."

"Wait, so you're saying the car drove itself off the road?"

"Yes, and the whole thing is being hushed up."

"How?"

"I don't know, but there's some powerful players keeping this under wraps."

"Tensora?"

"Obviously. They don't want the story out. It would be a financial and PR disaster, but it's more than that, because the highway safety people and the automotive forensics team and the police are saying next to nothing. However, I'm working on it. Anyway, the Tensora engineers are at a loss, because they can't find anything wrong with the computers or the programs it was running. They keep running simulations and tests and can't get it to misbehave."

"Wow, there could be one hella monster lawsuit in this if Tensora really is at fault."

"Monster is the word. Anyway, I'll keep you posted if I can get any more out of my Tensora guy. He really wants to sleep with me real bad."

"And? Do tell."

"The moment I give in, the incentive is gone. I keep the promise dangling before him. And speaking of dangling promises, are you staying the night?"

"Can't. But I don't turn into a pumpkin until midnight. We have a few hours that I bet we could find a way to use."

— 14 —

Dana lengthened her stride as she made a beeline across parking lot C at the Mall of California. "Mrs. Drucker, Amanda Drucker! Have you got a minute?"

About to slide into her Tesla crossover, Mandi set her packages on the seat. She tensed and turned anxiously, trying not to be too obvious in slipping her free hand into her purse and fingering the stunner stashed there. "What do you want? Who are you?"

"I'm Dana Carmody. I'm a friend of Barbra Wilson. And I'm working on a story." She flashed a press pass with her left hand and held out her right.

Mandi glanced around to see how many other people were nearby in the lot. A bald man with sleeve tattoos was pushing an overloaded shopping cart toward an SUV one aisle over. Four teenagers were extricating themselves from an eFiat halfway down the same row. She extracted her hand from her purse and took Dana's. "Uh, what's this about?"

"I'd like to talk with you. I would have texted or emailed but . . . well, you don't have much of an internet footprint and the contact info I did find was out of date."

"So, you stalk me and track me down in a mall parking lot?"

"Sheerest luck. I'm here to shop, just like you."

"You could have asked Barbra, you know. She knows how to get in touch with me. That is, if you really are friends."

"We are, but I wanted to do this on my own. Full disclosure: she did say something about you being a creature of habit, like going to the mall at the same time every week."

"Clever. So, you're a professional stalker, right?"

"Press, really."

"Same thing. Okay, tell me what you want so that I can decline to comment on it. Let me guess. Coleman Drucker, right?"

"Right."

"We're divorced. Other than a brief encounter in the hospital recently—well, that hardly qualifies as an encounter, rather one-sided, he being somewhat out of it—we haven't had much of anything to do with each other in over a decade. Outside of a courtroom or lawyers' offices, that is."

"Yes, I know that, but I wondered about your thoughts on the latest developments."

"Developments? Latest? Those are not in my vocabulary. Other than occasionally checking the stock price of the new Drucker Unified, I'm rather out of the loop, I'm afraid."

"Stock price?"

"Well, I do still have a stake in the success of Cole's ventures, even though that stake is comparatively modest."

"But you showed up at the hospital. You weren't checking stock prices. That says—"

"Only that we're through talking, Ms. Carmody. I need to get back to my son, who's working on a school project for which I am the supply chain. And I have groceries in the back. So . . ." She pressed her thumb to the keyspot and re-opened the car door.

Dana held the door. "Can we meet for coffee or lunch— my treat—I really want to get your take on all this. And maybe I know some things that you might be interested in."

Mandi pushed the packages over, slipped into the driver's seat, and looked up through the open door. "You know some things, huh. Like what?"

"It was no accident."

Mandi sucked air through her teeth. "I was afraid that might be the case." She tensed her hands on the steering wheel. "Okay, we'll meet. The Cuppa Joe's on Grand Av in an hour." She closed the door, then slid the window down. She looked to be on the edge of saying something for several seconds.

"You don't have to say anything, Mrs. Drucker. I know you were at the hospital more than once, more than a dozen times. That says it all."

"Does it? Okay, Joe's in an hour."

— —

The coffee shop was crowded but the buzz was subdued. Most of the patrons were heads-down deep into their phones or tablets. Dana looked around for Mandi and spotted her at one of the small round tables tucked in a corner next to a bookshelf stocked with exotic gourmet coffees from the world's more obscure sources. The currently featured coffees were from Burundi and Cabo Verde Fogo Island.

"Hi, thanks for agreeing to meet," Dana said. "I'll try not to take too much of your time."

"It's okay, time I got, now that Toby is occupied with his science project. If we don't hear an explosion from down the block, everything is fine."

"Explosion?"

"Mom humor. Don't mind me. I'll wait while you get coffee or whatever."

Dana returned in a couple of minutes with a double

espresso. "So, it seems," she said as she sat down, "you and Coleman are still connected to some degree, despite your denials. How long were you two married?"

"You already know this from the research you must certainly have done. We were married just long enough to build a company from scratch—three, actually—to have two kids, and for Cole to discover he wanted somebody younger. Some men can do that faster than others. Cole was always fast: fast to fall in love, fast to fall out."

"You met in Israel, right?"

"Yes, Cole was there on a Birthright trip after high school."

"Birthright?"

"You know, one of those get-in-touch-with-your-Jewish-roots song-and-dance tours for young Jews. There are several such programs still going, believe it or not, despite all the changes in the Middle East. It's all about renewing the corps of young American advocates for Israel. It works, too. Kids come back talking about 'life-changing' experiences and 'new perspectives' on the Middle East. Cole came back with me."

"That fast?"

"Like I told you, fast is his middle name. It was against the rules, of course, but that never stopped Cole. If anything, telling him he couldn't do something was like a red cape in front of a bull. I was Dafna Amanda Yadim then, what my program called an ambassador-in-training, on track for a diplomatic position—or a career in Mossad. But I was really drifting, filling time as a glorified tour guide after finishing my stint in the IDF, the army.

"Even though Cole was several years younger, at that point we were fairly well matched. Whatever the military does to help Israeli young people mature and find direction, it didn't take with me. Cole became my direction, his dreams were mine."

She sipped her coffee. "You know, I still miss Israeli-style coffee. There are a few places in New York, but none out here. Where was I?"

"Following Cole Drucker back from Israel."

"Yeah. He is such a salesman. That doesn't mean he doesn't actually have the goods to sell—I think he's maybe a genius—but it's always all packaged, wrapped in marketing hype. New products, new love—it's all about selling something to somebody. I bought. I bought the whole package. We married right after he dropped out of college." She pushed her half-finished coffee aside. "But look, you said something about new developments that you wanted to ask me about. Enough of strolling down lanes of memories, what is this really about?"

"Well, Coleman Drucker, of course. It seems there is a three-way struggle over custody of his body."

"Three-way?"

"Yes, there's his wife on one side, and this Existendia company on the other, both vying for legal control, and Coleman Drucker completing the triangle."

Mandi raised her eyebrows. "Cole? What do you mean?"

"He's fighting back. Existendia won round one in the courts and had him taken off life support. He refused to cash out, gasped a few times, and started breathing on his own. Now he's showing more brain activity. Big debate over what, if anything, it means, but at least it means he's in the ring for the tag-team match."

"That is so like Cole, a trouble maker and a fighter to the end. But why are you talking with me?"

"Because something tells me you're part of the story. You keep showing up at the hospital, and Barbra tells me you are still in his will. You have a stake in the outcome."

"A stake, maybe, but I'm in the audience at this particular tag-team match. I may have placed a bet on the outcome, but I'm not in the ring."

"And who have you bet on?"

"My money's on Cole. It's always been on Cole. But you said something about the accident. What's that about?"

"I can't say much, but there is some evidence that it was no accident, that the car was rigged in some way to force it off the road." Dana took a sip of her coffee. "I don't think Cole was supposed to survive the crash. I thought you might have some insight into who might have it in for him enough to want him dead. Who were his enemies?"

"Cole didn't have real enemies, not that I ever saw. Plenty of people really disliked him, but he didn't make enemies. It was about victory, elevating himself, not about defeating the other side. He was also always so charismatic. Even those who disliked him or resented the hell out of him were often charmed. People who lost to him tended to walk away shaking their heads but not their fists."

"So, if that's the case, the question is who would stand to benefit from his death?"

"I would assume the police are already following that line of inquiry."

"You might be wrong. The police don't seem to be doing a lot. It isn't a murder case—not yet, anyway—and if they are getting close to anyone or anything in connection with the accident, they are certainly not broadcasting their progress."

"Isn't that standard operating procedure? I mean, the

police don't usually risk an investigation by leaking clues."

"You're right, of course, and this is not my usual beat. I'm a technology reporter, not a crime reporter. Still . . ."

"Still, you're right. There are people who might benefit if Cole were out of the picture. I could mention a few from Drucker Technologies, and there are probably some from the other company who think they would fare a lot better if Coleman Drucker wasn't at the helm. Then there's the wife and daughter, who probably stand to inherit one massive estate. Frankly, there's me. Strictly financially, I would be better off after getting my piece of his estate, though it's a lot smaller piece than Barbra's. And what about this Existendia? What are they about? You're the reporter."

"You know what Existendia does, don't you? They offer a techno version of immortality by claiming to be able to upload your personality into a computer so your consciousness can live on even if your body is gone. It's a way out for the super-rich, if it works. Never been proven, not yet anyway. Cole would be their first customer to have completed the download before croaking."

"Download?"

"Well, the details are proprietary and kept under very tight wraps, but basically they scan the whole brain in a long series of tests that somehow capture how it's all connected and how it works. The UCLA neuroscientist I interviewed says that's basically impossible at this point, that the only way they could record the entire connectome, the way all the neurons in the brain are interconnected, would require freezing the brain before slicing it up and doing ultrahigh-resolution scans of each slice, after which it would take supercomputers to analyze all that. And, he says, it would take enormously sophisticated software and much of the world's computing power to run a real-time simulation of that brain model. Even then, it might not work. Running or emulating the connectome model might not be the same as bringing somebody back. It's all speculation."

"Then why do it?"

"Why go to church? Why have your head frozen? Why have children? Lots of routes to immortality: radical medical intervention, repeated organ replacement, blood transfusions from teenagers. How about fame, literary success, endowing a charitable foundation with your name on it? But, in the end, it's personal immortality that most people are after. They want to live forever."

"I don't."

"Neither do I, but not everyone has the maturity that Steve Jobs showed when he said that death was necessary to make room for the new. Think of what the world would be like if all the rich old white guys, who pretty much run the place now, just kept going and going, getting wealthier, and owning and controlling more and more. Ad infinitum. Forever and ever. Amen."

"No thanks."

"I'm with you."

Mandi warmed her hands on her coffee mug. "So, do they have this rebirth thing or not, this Existendia? Is Cole destined to be the first of the new immortals?"

"The jury is still out, and we haven't seen enough of the evidence. Well, forget the inept legal metaphor, but it is a legal issue, in part. A Stanford prof I interviewed, a specialist in artificial intelligence, said you don't have to get it perfect, only good enough."

"Good enough for what?"

"Good enough to pass the Meta-Turing Test."

"I think I know about the Turing Test—can a computer fool people into thinking it's human—but who is this guy Mehta? An Indian computer scientist?"

"Ha ha. The Meta-Turing Test is not really a test but a set of criteria for evaluating whether an artificial intelligence is actually conscious or self-aware. It is very controversial because the conclusion has really profound legal and social consequences. If an AI can be claimed to be conscious, then an argument can be made to grant it personhood or legal standing before the law, even citizenship. It's the can of worms we've been writhing in over recent decades. Can a robot vote? Right now, the answer is 'no, but'—at least by way of the cleverly inconclusive precedent set by the ruling in iConsient v. Commonwealth of Massachusetts. However, there are other cases working their way through the courts. One unresolved issue, a biggy, is how, if at all, you could ever tell the difference between an AI that was actually conscious as opposed to sophisticated software that just did a hell of a good job of faking it."

Mandi sipped her coffee and made a face. "So how do you tell the difference?"

"Nobody knows, although plenty are claiming to have the answer. Maybe it is impossible, even when it comes to real people. I mean, I *know* that *I* am a conscious, aware being, but when it comes to you, I can only *assume*. And you can try to persuade me any way you want that you are actually conscious and aware, but you can't prove it to me."

"And this has what to do with downloading a brain? Or is it uploading?"

"Both. First you download the connectome to a digital representation, a copy of sorts, then you upload it to software that interprets and runs that representation. That's what the Existendia website says. You know what else it says?"

"No, do tell."

"It says, 'Through your uploaded digital proxy, you can continue to manage your affairs exactly as you wish after the passing of your body.' Quote-unquote. Get it? If the digital proxy is good enough to pass the Meta-Turing Test and convince a court, it doesn't matter whether it's complete in capturing the essence of a personality. That digital proxy, a good enough approximation, could wield genuine power, legal power, in the real world."

"What about the people who are—what would you say—custodians or operators of that digital proxy?"

"Exactly, which makes Existendia a very big player in this tag-team match." Dana's phone buzzed on the table. She flipped it over to check the caller ID. "Look, I've taken enough of your time. I should go. Thank you for meeting with me."

"No, thank you. You gave me a lot to think about. Or to have nightmares about. Keep me in the loop."

"I will. You, too. If you think of anything that might be relevant, ping me. Here's my card."

Dana walked out of the Cuppa Joe's and tapped to return the missed call as she walked to her car. "What do you have?"

"It's what I don't have, sweetheart." The male voice was rich and breathy. "Meet me at the usual place, and I'll give it to you."

– 15 –

In the middle of the day, with none of the twelve feature films due to start soon, the parking garage at the multiplex was all but deserted. Despite cable, despite Hulu and Netflix and Amazon, cinema multiplexes still thrived. Not everyone could afford the 7.1 surround sound and eighty-inch curved 4k OLED screen that had become the de facto standard for home viewing, and not everyone even had the wall space in an era of shrinking houses and apartments. Even young people eventually grew tired of watching drama and spectacle reduced to the dimensions of a smartphone or tablet. The sociologists—professional and arm-chair—drew parallels with the persistence of shopping malls. Human beings craved actual human contact, even if it was diffuse and anonymous. Amazon and Alibaba could deliver the goods when it came to product, but only a brick-and-mortar shop could deliver the social experience, the genuine article, which required collisions in crowds and olfactory intrusions.

Dana found the concierge section on level sub-one of the parking garage more than a little creepy. The homage to "All the President's Men," a favorite film of her Tensora insider, had been at his insistence. She jumped as a tall figure stepped from behind one of the fat support columns. "Ah, there you are," she said.

Geraldo Potts did not look like the ever-popular stereotype of a computer geek. He was well built, with a boyish face that pleasantly blended his biracial heritage. Not Dana's type, but not bad looking either. He spread his arms in an invitation to hug. "You are doing the look, girl."

She yielded to his hug, then broke it off. "Let's stick to business for now. I'm on a tight clock."

"Dang. We gotta find a better way to meet. And more time."

"This was your idea, Geraldo. Remember?"

"Oh, yeah. Maybe once this whole thing gets settled and it's not so . . . so risky . . ."

"You want the thrills, Geraldo, you just don't want the risks that buy the thrills."

"Something like that." He reached into his pocket and withdrew his closed hand. "Know what's in here?"

"A new Tensora?"

"Get serious, girl."

"Get serious, Potts. Just tell me."

"Okay. What if I tell you it's a microSD?"

"What if you just give it to me and tell me what it's about."

"You're no fun."

"Oh, there you are wrong, so very wrong. Trust me on this one. But not in a poorly lit, dank parking garage. No way, never. So, just tell me what's on the card."

"It's music. You said that the dude's wife missed his music, and you asked if I could get you a copy of the card he kept in his car. I said, no sweat. I was wrong. Took lots of sweat."

"I've never seen you break a sweat, Geraldo. Everything is too easy for you."

"Let's get together, really together, and you'll see how sweaty I can break."

"Wow, you sure do know how to talk romantic to a girl."

"Well, you know how I feel about you. But,"—he opened

his hand—"this is the copy of the card I couldn't copy."

"You wanna run that by me again?"

"I tried to dupe the microSD from the Tensora. It wouldn't copy, kept getting within a few hundred gigabytes of completion and then would hang. I thought I might have a defective card. Took a new one fresh out of a blister pack—same result. I tried using a software toolkit to take a look at the contents of the original card, and it wouldn't read, parts would just give error messages. 'File corrupt.' 'Unable to access image.' Weird stuff, since it had worked fine in the car. One of the guys had even been playing Rachmaninoff while he did a whole-vehicle fingerprint scan. So, I thought maybe we . . . or I damaged it when I snuck it out of the car."

"Can we get to the point sometime before the garage is inundated by sea-level rise?"

"Where we are, at this elevation, that would take another century."

"My point exactly." She rolled her eyes. "Skip to the punch line."

"Well, the original card had been hacked. It was overwritten with non-standard file structure, something that worked in that car but chokes with other readers and software."

"Hacked? What does the hack accomplish."

"Don't know yet. Maybe nothing. Me and Jakey are taking it apart—not literally, just digitally—and trying to figure out how it works in the car, what it does. Anyway, this is a forensic clone, not a copy, an exact bit-for-bit replication of the original. I thought you might want that." He turned his hand and dropped the tiny card in its translucent plastic case into her palm.

"Thanks, Geraldo. I'll remember this." She leaned in and kissed him.

"And I'll remember that and look forward to more."

"Right. Dream on. Now I'm out of here." She held tight to the card as she walked to the far side of the garage and took the stairs up to the lobby. She was running through a mental list in search of someone she knew who would be savvy enough to work on deciphering the card and cool enough to keep it under wraps.

— —

"So you got the card?" Barbra rattled the ice in her kir. She laughed. "You know, this is the first time I've had one of these in years. Todd didn't approve. 'Who would ever ruin good wine by putting syrup in it and serving it over ice?' That's what he'd say. When I asked Tandi to make a kir, she said the house had no crème de cassis, and she would have to get a drone delivery first. I think that's the first time I ever heard her say she didn't have something. It is different without Todd here."

"I imagine."

"Yeah, I pretty much get to do what I want. That's different. You know, you get so used to somebody else being in charge, that you aren't even aware of it until it's not there. Know what I mean?" She sipped the kir. "So? Don't keep me in suspense. Yes or no?"

"Yes, I got the card. And yes, I'll take a kir, too, even if you didn't offer me one. I'm not above putting ice or liqueur or fruit juice into wine. Or even all of the above."

"Oh, I'm sorry, I didn't mean to be rude." She looked toward the ceiling. "Tandi, get our guest a kir."

"Do you have to talk to the ceiling to make the thing work?"

"No, it's just a habit. I find it weird when people look straight at you when they're talking to Alexa or whatever. Anyway, thanks for the card. I don't even know where it goes in the car. I don't use half the gizmos and special modes that Todd did, even though it's the same car, basically."

Dana retrieved the card carrier from her pocket and held it out but hesitated. "I wish I knew somebody else who could do a deep cybersecurity analysis."

"Why? Is there a problem?"

"Maybe. My guy at Tensora said he had trouble copying it. I just want to make sure it's all right before you plug it into your car."

"But it's just music files, right? Todd had this thing for actually owning music, having it in his possession rather than in the cloud. He liked possessing things. Like music. Like people."

"Yeah, music." She set the card on the counter. "Speaking of Todd, or Cole, what's the word on that front."

"The word is that Leah, my lawyer, is fighting against Existendia in court filings that I don't exactly follow, and Todd is fighting to make fools of all of us."

"What do you mean?"

"He's still not responsive, but every time they scan him, there's more brain waves. Well, they don't call it that, but that's what it is. The docs tell me that happens sometimes with these patients, but it doesn't necessarily mean any kind of recovery, just, like, sparks in the dying system, echoes, sort of. Ah, here is your kir." She lifted the drink from the robo-cart and handed it to Dana. "Cheers."

"Cheers, indeed. Never a dull moment since we met. Is, uh, Becca around?"

"She is. And Deirdre. Plus, the DruckerTech service crew is installing a new system upgrade for the house that's supposed to interface more tightly with the various delivery services. Oh, yes, they are also patching some security vulnerabilities, including one in the doorbell. Who knew that even doorbells have computer chips in them?"

"Amazing. Who knew?" Dana winked and took another sip of her drink.

— 16 —

Barbra was sitting in the small conference room of Building A at Drucker Unified when Tonika Warner entered. "How's CT doing?" she asked as she set her tablet on the table

"He's not doing. Still nothing. We don't know what to do. Now the medical insurance group is getting into the ring, trash-talking about terminating his coverage. And the hospital is fighting them, wanting to keep earning their daily bread. It's a very big loaf, and their slice is thicker than you might think. Anyway, what's the story on the SD card I gave you?"

"A little like your story on CT"

"Spell it out."

"Understand, this is not my area of expertise. Yes, I did have to deal with cybersecurity issues as head of IT for ModulArch, but this kind of forensics is a stretch."

"I do understand. I just wanted somebody I could trust who might have the resources and expertise. Were you able to find anything at all?"

"Oh, I found plenty of anything. That doesn't mean I know exactly what it all means. One thing I did find was music files that used an old-fashioned buffer-overrun exploit."

"Which is?"

"A way of tricking a computer into executing malicious code. Basically, you fool the computer into loading data that's bigger than the allotted space, so it ends up writing over executable code. It's rarely used anymore by hackers because it's almost universally blocked by modern security systems and not only fails but gets flagged as a threat. I can only guess on this, but I think maybe the audio entertainment system on CT's car was not considered as an important security risk, so it was not properly protected. I don't know, maybe just lazy coding. Without getting direct access to the car or the code for the multi-media head unit, there's not much I can do to be more specific."

"So, the card has some sort of a computer virus on it?"

"That's what it looks like. There are people here who would be better than I am at tearing the code apart, but you said you wanted to keep this from spreading around."

"I do, at least for now. But I have an idea, if you're willing to put in some extra time on this."

"Extra time? Look, Barbra, I don't have any time, let alone extra. We're still scrambling from losing CT and from the merger. But, okay, this is for CT. You know, I worship the man."

Barbra cocked her head. "Can I ask you something?"

"Sure, anything."

"Did you ever . . . did he ever, like, try anything?"

"Oh, I know what you're asking. I'm sure it's hardly news to you that he would put the moves on just about anyone with tits whenever he thought he could get by with it. But no, I value my job too much. I keep my professional life and my personal life miles apart and with a firewall in between. When I said I worshipped CT, I should have said I admired him, his abilities. And he was always straight up with me. So, are we clear on all that?"

"Crystal."

"So, what's this idea of yours?"

"You can have my Tensora to work on. It's identical to

Todd's except for the color. He said at the time that as long as he was paying that much for a customized car, he might as well haggle for a BOGO deal. Anyway, it's yours for as long as you need it."

"Thanks. I actually would like to do a little digging and tinkering before I admit I'm completely out of my depth. When can I get it?"

"Now, if you like. It's parked in the exec lot. I can hail a Flyvver to get home after work. The Tensora is pretty much standard operating procedure. Here's my passcard. You just need to have it with you to open and drive the thing. If you need to know anything, just ask the car. It's called BlueBee."

"Blooby?"

"No, Blue Bee. It's electric blue and it buzzes. My daughter named it. Be careful with it."

"I'll take care of it, don't worry."

"I'm not worried about the car. I don't want anything to happen to you. Drucker Unified needs you, so maybe you shouldn't drive while listening to music. Okay?"

"Okay. Sound advice. Er, pun unintended." She glanced at her wrist. "And now, I have a one-on-one with Bradley Pomerantz about problems getting our cloud servers and their servers to play nice together. I thought that being off to the side of the org chart with no direct reports would mean fewer problems. I was wrong. Everybody's problems are mine now."

"Can you use an extra body?"

"Sure. An extra brain wouldn't hurt either."

"Think about who you might pick, and let me know. I'll work a little job shuffling. I can do that now, you know."

"Can I pull somebody from the ModulArch side? There's a kid with real promise, a software engineer who thinks like a field marshal and does whatever he's tasked with. Very bright, very quick. He could help me while also building a bridge to a possible different career path for himself."

"Sure, I'll bring it up at the next Transition Team meeting. Or better yet, you bring it up and I'll back you."

"Sounds like a plan. Thanks Barbra."

"Thank you, Tonika. You're doing a great job herding the two packs of coding cowboys in our overcrowded software corral. And I really appreciate your taking on this music software sleuthing. Just keep it strictly quiet. And keep me posted, but no email."

"You got it."

— —

Tonika sat in the Tensora in the parking garage beneath her condo, thinking about the problem with the microSD card. She smiled. "Probably too easy, but it's worth a try. BlueBee, can you run a deep diagnostic check on all your systems?"

"I can."

"Literal little bugger, aren't you? BlueBee, run a complete deep diagnostic check on all your systems."

"Please wait. Starting diagnostics. During diagnostics, screens may blink or blank. Ignore any vibration or sound from the vehicle."

Color patterns started flashing on the center-console and heads-up display, and status messages started scrolling on the small steering wheel screen: VIDEO SUBSYSTEM OK, FRONT CAMERAS OK, REAR CAMERAS OK, LIDAR PROCESSING OK, RUNNING OBJECT RECOGNITION SUBSYSTEM.

Tonika watched as system after system checked out. "How long is this going to take?" A message on the steering wheel flashed: CANCEL FULL SYSTEM DIAGNOSTICS?

YES/NO?

"BlueBee, how long is this going to take?"

Another message: VOICE INPUT DETECTED. LIVE AU-DIO ASSIST FUNCTION NOT AVAILABLE. CANCEL FULL SYSTEM DIAGNOSTICS? YES/NO?

Tonika tapped NO. "Oh, great. And no progress bar or percent complete. Your programmers were not very tuned into human factors."

The screen froze and flashed the message again: CAN-CEL FULL SYSTEM DIAGNOSTICS? YES/NO?

"Oh, double great, now I can just sit here in silence until this thing is done."

Another message popped up: LIVE AUDIO ASSIST FUNCTION NOT AVAILABLE. CANCEL FULL SYSTEM DIAGNOSTICS? YES/NO?

Tonika tapped NO and shook her head. After nearly five minutes of staring at the steering wheel, she applauded the final message: ALL SYSTEMS AND FUNCTIONS OK. "Thank, you. BlueBee, where is the SD card slot for the music system?"

"The SD card slot for multi-media data files is located to the lower right of the center-console display where I am flashing a yellow arrow. Press the detent and the carrier will slide out. Insert the card as shown and press the detent again to close the carrier."

Tonika fetched the card case from her purse, extracted the microSD card, and followed the instructions for loading it. After a short delay while a Tensora logo spun on the center console, the car announced, "Music catalog loaded."

"I wonder. Should I play some music?"

"Do you wish to play some music?"

"Yes, BlueBee. Can you play whatever music was last

played from this card?"

"Yes, I can."

"Still a stickler for grammar. You're as bad as my boy-friend. No, wait a minute. I don't want to hear the last music played. I need to be precise with you. Okay, BlueBee, please play the music that was last played from this card on . . ." She checked her phone for the date of the crash. "July 14."

The garage was suddenly filled with the agitated strings and triumphant brass of Wagner's "Ride of the Valkyries."

"Very macho music, CT. Okay, now let's see. BlueBee, run complete system diagnostics again.

"Please wait." The music stopped. "Starting diagnostics. During diagnostics, screens may blink or blank. Ignore any vibration or sound from the vehicle."

Tonika waited in silence as the reports scrolled by on the display and the car chattered and chirped as various motors and actuators were momentarily triggered. Then she saw it. For a brief moment: VEHICLE LINK MODULE FAILED. Then there were others: COMMUNICATIONS LOOP-BACK FAILED, DRIVE SPEED LIMITER FAILED, IN-MOTION IN-TERLOCK FAILED. At the end of the diagnostics run, the display declared that twenty-three subsystems had failed.

"BlueBee, can you . . . no. BlueBee, please print out a copy of the diagnostic report."

"Printing." Pause. "Printing complete."

"What? Where is the printout?"

"The printout is on your default printer, your home office multifunction inkjet."

"Barbra's going to wonder what the hell is happening. BlueBee, I want it here."

"Should I have the house retrieve the copy and send it by

drone courier to your current location?"

"No. BlueBee, please print a copy here in the car. If you can."

"Printing." Tonika heard a faint buzzing but couldn't quite place the source. It continued for nearly a minute. "Printing complete," the car announced.

"BlueBee, where is the printout?"

"The printout is on your home office laser printer and a copy is in the in-vehicle logging printer."

"BlueBee, where is the in-vehicle logging printer?"

"The in-vehicle logging printer is located inside the glove compartment."

Tonika opened the glove box. It was stuffed with a long looping strip of four-inch wide paper. As Tonika fished it out, she noticed the scattered words in red: FAILED, FAILED, FAILED.

— 17 —

Becca jumped up from the chair beside the hospital bed. "Ohmygod! Daddy! Somebody come quick. Help, somebody."

The duty nurse quick-stepped into the room, scanning monitors as she crossed to the bed. "What is it?"

"He moved. Look at his arm. He lifted it up and flopped it onto his chest. See? His left arm also jerked, but, like, it's held down by the blood thingy."

The nurse put her hand on Becca's shoulder. "It doesn't mean anything. It's called a Lazarus sign. It's a body reflex, like when the doctor taps your knee and your leg jerks up."

"But I was talking to him and telling him that I wished he were back and then all of a sudden he waves to me."

"I know you want your father back real bad, but this really doesn't mean that he heard you. If it will make you feel any better, I'll tell the attending about what happened, and he can decide if additional tests or evaluation are in order."

"What will make me feel better is to have Daddy back."

"I know, I know. We're doing what we can, but you shouldn't get your hopes up too much."

"Yeah, everybody says that. I just wish everybody would just the fuck stop treating me like some little kid. I'm almost thirteen, and I'm not a kid."

"Of course. Look, I need to get on to my other patients, but I'll check in again in a little while."

"Okay. I'll still be here."

The nurse left and Becca pulled her flex phone from her

jeans pocket and unrolled it. She scrolled through her favorite streaming playlist and found the track from the Silicon Salvation album "Resurrected" that had been one of her father's few pop favorites. The layered synth and pounding rhythm of the group's reimagined classic electronic dance music pulsed in her Bluetooth earbuds. She mouthed the words as vocalist Astrid Gundlach cut in with the lyrics of "Second Chance": the four lines, endlessly repeated, that Becca and her father would sing together at the top of their lungs when she was in the third grade.

> All I ever asked
> is another at bat,
> a second final act,
> a second second chance.

"Here, Daddy, remember this?" She slipped the earbuds out and gently held them up to her father's ears. His eyes flitted behind closed lids.

"Nurse! Come see this. Quick!"

— —

The conference room hushed as Aram Netsky appeared on the teleconference screen, his eyes seeming to scan the room. "Good," he said. "We have a lot to discuss and a lot to do, so we don't want to waste time. Please forgive me for not attending in person, but technical demands require that I stay at the helm at all times. Bannon Turndale will update you on the legal front, Margaret Hafner will cover the financials, and Roger Okham will explain the medical issues. Let's not leave out Jerry Pendrake, our overactive CEO, who is gracing us with his presence and may have something to contribute." Around the conference table people winced, but Pendrake, hands folded atop his closed portfolio, showed no reaction. "But now, I want to bring you up to speed on the digital proxy."

He slid sideways too quickly for the tracking camera to follow, then popped back into view. "We have had some trouble deploying the resources for full-scale operation of the Drucker proxy—Margaret will say more about that—so we have had to be clever. We can't afford to operate continuously, so we have been scheduling awake-blocks to make optimal use of what we can pay for. The temporal gaps, the discontinuous consciousness, are proving to be disturbing to the proxy. We are trying to devise a workaround, but neither the software team nor the neuro-psych team can agree on a solution at this moment.

"What we have been able to do is conduct one notarized, recorded Meta-Turing Test with a five member panel comprising two psychiatrists, two clinical psychologists, and a neuroscientist. We had the panel, which was blind to who was on the other end of the communications link, employ the six M-TT criteria to examine four live subjects plus the Drucker proxy. All five subjects were represented onscreen by animated digital avatars.

"Oh, yeah, kudos to our avatar engineers who worked overtime to bring our own proxy avatar up to the level of the commercial software used with the four live subjects—so we could play on a level field.

"Anyway, the panel had an hour to interact with each subject. By having them interact as a panel instead of individually, we kept the Cloudastics charges for running the Drucker proxy down to just over an hour. The live subjects, two men and two women in their late forties, were paid an honorarium, token but generous by research standards. All four subjects and the proxy were given the same explanation of the process and were prompted to answer as truthfully and thoughtfully as possible."

Bannon Turndale raised his index finger. "And you are going to tell us the results, aren't you?"

"Of course. The panel members voted up or down independently and each reported a level of confidence. On three of the subjects, the vote was unanimous: conscious, self-aware. Confidence levels on those three ranged from sixty to ninety-five percent. One other subject, a woman, convinced four out of five on the panel, and another, a man, was able to persuade only three panelists that he was a conscious and self-aware being."

Margaret Hafner laughed. "Sounds like some of the men I know."

"Whatever. So, as you can tally, the Drucker proxy was among the three with unanimous agreement, mean confidence level eighty-three percent."

Roger Okham cocked his head. "Is that good enough if we are facing a courtroom?"

"At this stage, we don't know. These are uncharted waters, and this is only a dry run for the real thing. Because the proxy is still partially sensory-motor isolated, we had to exclude certain kinds of questions. In any case, we are reviewing the transcript and the non-verbals collected from videoing the panelists to harvest what we can use to improve our chances legally."

"How soon will he be fully hooked up and conditioned?"

"As soon as we get the money for run time, Bannon, as soon as we get the money." The image on the monitor stared out at them. "Maybe you can speak to that, Margaret."

She was clearly feeling awkward at being put on the spot. "I won't waste time on an exegesis. The client is not deceased, so we cannot invoke provisions of the will. The trust set up by the client does not vest until then. We have billed the family for services, but the invoice has been denied by their counsel. No surprise. The contract obligates the corporation, but only after death and only under special circumstances. Sorry, Bannon, if I've crossed over into your territory, but it's all tangled up, the legal and the financial."

"What's the bottom line?" asked Okham.

"The bottom line," she said, "is bright red. We're sucking fumes. We've tapped out our bank line of credit with Or-Cal Fed. We're chasing investor funding, but everybody smells panic and wants too much equity for too little cash infusion. We even dangled the prospect of a very lucrative, very long-term contract for services with Cloudastics, but they need to cover costs and want more upfront. Their competitors have heard the squealing and won't touch us without payment in advance. Besides, Cloudastics has the state-data of the proxy and can hold it hostage."

"But we have copies of everything, right?" Okham spread his hands. "We can just upload again with another service provider."

Aram sighed. "Yes. And start from scratch. The state-data is essentially the memory, the record of everything the proxy has experienced since go-live, everything he's learned to do—at our expense."

Bannon scowled. "Why haven't we been getting that all back, tracking it?"

"Because it's deep inside the neuro-connectome models themselves, just like your memories are part of the wiring and cellular chemical changes in your brain. There isn't enough bandwidth to keep sending the updated model back."

"Why can't you just send the deltas?"

Aram was losing patience. "Bannon, stick to your law books and legal lingo. The deltas, the changes in the model, are essentially the execution of the model itself, which is why we need fully elastic cloud services, distributed super-computer power. There is a provision for recovering the entire model and its state-data, but that only comes at termination of the contract, and if we terminate, we pay for that. Catch twenty-two squared. But then you should know about that. Right?"

Bannon straightened his back. "Yes, it's my job to know the contractual obligations of all the parties to our contracts."

"Well, then, enlighten the rest of us as to what else you know as part of your job and your role in keeping this sinking ship afloat."

"Well, we're still fighting to gain control over the fate of the body. It's medically and legally more complicated with him breathing on his own. Forcing the issue would require cutting off nutrition from the feeding tube. Do you want to say anything, Roger?"

"I'd like to say a lot, but the main thing is that his medical status keeps getting upgraded. The hospital is preparing to officially declare him minimally conscious, which is a whole new ball game. If he can eventually be demonstrated to be aware and capable of conscious decisions, we're dead in the water and torpedoed below the waterline."

Bannon rolled his eyes. "My, my, Okham, we are immersed in fluid metaphors today."

Aram interrupted the chorus of groans. "Cute. But get serious, people. Jerry, Roger, Margaret, Bannon, I want to see you and your people pulling out all the stops to get us sailing." He shook his head. "Shit, now you got me doing it, too."

Jerry Pendrake stood up, forcing the camera to follow his face and cutting everyone else momentarily out of the monitor picture until the view zoomed back. "For your information, your overactive CEO has been pulling out all the stops on some backchannel communication with the Cloudastics people. I'll keep you all posted. Meeting adjourned." He slid his portfolio from the table and left the conference room before anyone could protest or inquire. It was a rare power move from Jerry that left Aram looking momentarily off balance, which was equally rare.

Part 4

When brains get sufficiently big, presumably, as human brains have, consciousness seems to emerge.
– Richard Dawkins

– 18 –

Becca had taken to spending her late afternoons at the extended-care facility for head-trauma patients, talking to her father and playing music for him. "I got some of the titles from your home library, Daddy. I'll play ones you favorited, okay?"

She leaned over the bed to look for any sign, any reaction. "If you can hear me, wiggle your finger." She watched both hands. "If you would like some music, open your eyes." Nothing. "I love you, Daddy. If you love me, move your eyes." The form in the bed lay still and silent except for slow and steady breathing.

"I'm going to put in the earbuds now. Then I'm going to put on your 'Kadima' playlist. I had to Google that. Hebrew for 'forward,' right? As in '*adelante*' in Spanish. See, I do pay attention in school. And I really love it at Camp Cah-Wee-Lah, but sometimes I wish you had sent me to Hebrew camp. I mean, I know we're Jewish—well, you and I are— but we never do any Jewish things. I always wondered about that. Anyway, here is your 'Kadima' playlist. I hope you like it." She tapped the glyph on her phone and watched for a reaction.

She brought up a reader app and picked up on where she had left off with the latest Emojack fan-fic story. Whenever the crawl at the bottom of the screen would display a "Next Up" message from the audio player, she would bring up the sound as the track started so she could see if she knew the music. She recognized Rossini's "William Tell Overture" but the Reznicek "Overture to Donna Diana" was new to her.

Emojack, an over-the-top YA adventure story with a non-binary gender subtext, had been an active fan-fic thread for more than a year. One passage about Sasskon the Acquirer in the new chapter made her think of her father. She looked up just in time to see his eyes suddenly pop open, then widen. The crawl on her phone declared: Now Playing: Wagner "Ride of the Valkyries."

— —

Jerry Pendrake marched into Aram Netsky's office with a grin too wide for his narrow face. He stopped before the curved desk and struck a power pose but said nothing.

Netsky looked up. "What? You should have told me you were coming. You know I don't like to be interrupted."

"Okay." Pendrake pivoted and marched toward the door.

"Now what the hell is that? What do you want, Jerry?"

"Nothing. I didn't mean to interrupt you. We can discuss it at the next exec team meeting." He stopped in the doorway.

"What's gotten into you, Jerry? You sure have had some burr in your underpants lately."

"Just doing my job. See you at the meeting tomorrow."

"You don't have a job, other than the one I mandate, keeping the juice flowing in the money pipeline. At that, you have failed miserably of late. Why, for instance, haven't we been aggressively expanding the client base?"

"Because nobody wants to put up a few hundred thousand down payment with a company everyone knows is in its death throes. That's why. See you. Go back to your geeky tweaking." Pendrake headed for the door.

On the edge of losing it, Netsky worked his hands in and out of fists. "Just tell me what the fuck is going on, Jerry."

"You really want to know, do you? You actually want to know what I have been up to as CEO of the company, what I've been doing. And you, as CTO, actually care."

"Okay, you made your point. You're CEO and I'm just the CTO. But I still am the majority stock holder. Now"—his voice raised many decibels and nearly an octave— "goddamn tell me what the fuck this is about!"

"Looks like we could be acquired. By Cloudastics. I've been in touch with people I know on the board, working the back channels, playing hard-to-get. And we have agreement in principle. I negotiated the outlines of a deal that works out really well for us, considering."

"Why am I the last to know that something like this was going on?"

"Because,"—he held up his fingers in air-quotes—"you don't like to be interrupted, you don't like to be bothered with business matters, because you have been eyeballs deep into problem solving on the model, because . . ."

"All right, I get your point. So where are we in this rescue fantasy."

"About to be rescued. Basically we just need final board approval on both sides, and the spigot turns on again." Pendrake folded his arms and resumed his power pose before walking out the door.

oleman Todd Drucker was becoming the star patient at the head-trauma facility. At Barbra's insistence, he was moved from the extended-care wing to
the rehab wing, and daily therapy sessions were started. The
diagnosis was upgraded from coma to persistent vegetative
state and then to minimally conscious. His responsiveness
to his environment wavered, but he was often at his best
during afternoons when his daughter spent time with him.

Barbra, who sometimes took a late lunch break to join
Becca at the facility, offered a warm greeting as she entered
Cole's room. "Hey, Becca. Hello, Todd. How are my two fa-
vorite people today?"

"Mom, you're late."

"I had a meeting with a group at UCLA that has an experimental treatment program involving something called
beta-NCGF. It's a growth factor for cortical neurons. It's
supposed to promote new brain cells and connections in
adults. They think it might help patients who have had
head trauma and are minimally conscious. Between that
and the transcranial stuff, maybe we can help him recover."

"Did you hear that, Daddy? You're going to get better. I
know you can do it."

"Don't get your hopes up, darling. It's all experimental."

"My hopes are already up. Daddy is already doing eye-
blink Morse code. I've been teaching him."

"What?"

"Yeah, the rehab people were doing the one blink for yes,
two for no. Really tedious, slow. Daddy finds it frustrating.

Isn't that right, Daddy?" He blinked, slow, quick, slow, slow.

"What was that? I thought it was supposed to be one for yes, two for no."

"He does that with the rehab people. With me he uses letters—to practice his Morse code. That was Y for yes. Right, Daddy?" There was a long series of fast and slow blinks. "He said, 'R-I-G-H-T'. See, he can say anything. I told you he was still there. Do you want to talk with him?"

"Talk with him? Ohmygod, I can't believe this. Really? You've done this?"

"Really. We did it, me and Daddy. He's working on doing it with his finger, but it's not as reliable as his blinking. My friend Gitee—she's a total techno-geek—is working on this finger thingy that can connect to a tablet with software that reads the Morse code and then does text-to-speech so that he can talk. Right, Daddy?" More blinks. "He says yes, Y for yes"

"Todd, Todd, if you can hear me, I love you."

"He can hear you, Mom. See, he just said 'I-L-Y-2', I love you too. We use a lot of texting stuff. It's faster."

One of the surgeons leaned forward. "This is a miracle. And if the NCGF therapy helps . . ."

"Yeah, Daddy's back. He's coming back."

— —

It was never clear just what did the trick, but Cole's recovery accelerated. The finger-twitch reader assembled by Becca's friend was never needed, because, within weeks of starting the beta-NCGF treatment, Cole was talking. At first his speech was slurred and indistinct, but with intensive speech therapy, his daughter's daily visits, and some inner stubbornness, he made steady progress. Slowly, he regained use of his arms as well, but the verdict was that the spinal cord injury would leave him in a wheelchair.

With his recovery, both physically and mentally, Existendia was without a legal leg to stand on. Coleman Todd Drucker was not only alive, but also in charge of his own affairs. It was the team at Workman, Baum, and O'Neill LLC who decided that keeping Existendia in the dark as to the pace and extent of his recovery would be a good strategy to keep them from preparing a counter punch and to catch them off guard later.

Cole was practicing with his joystick-controlled wheelchair when the call came in from Hal Workman. "Hey, Coleman, how is it going?"

"It's going about three miles-per-hour. I'm not going to be winning any sprints, but at least I'm getting around on my own. Well, if my battery is fully charged. I can't wait to get out of here, but they have this long 'autonomy training checklist'—great term—that they want me to pass before they discharge me. It's a pisser. That's on the list, too, by the way."

"Good to hear you keep making progress. I called to update you on Existendia."

"I thought that was all settled."

"So did we. It seems they solved their fiscal crisis, at least temporarily. And with that, they are still running the software."

"Software?"

"You, your digital proxy."

"Who cares? I'm back at the helm and steering the ship myself. I've been telecommuting to the office two hours a day. The docs say I could be home in weeks. What does it matter if they keep running a very resource-intensive piece of computer code."

"It matters because, like you, with every passing day their software model is getting better, just as long as they keep operating it. We don't know what they've accomplished, but it can't be good. What if you become incapacitated again. With or without breaking the contract and a new will, there are no guarantees. Do you want a computer and its owners running your company, maybe dictating the welfare of your family? I'm not saying that can or will happen, but is it worth making risky bets? It's such a legal swamp, such murky territory, that it's better if we force them to shut down. Now."

"Okay, let's do it."

– 20 –

With her abstract-patterned tent dress, the substantial bulk of Di Fiora nearly filled the doorway of Aram Netsky's office. "There's a Mr. Coleman Drucker to see you."

"What the . . . No one told me. Wait, how is that possible?"

"I really don't know, sir. He just arrived with his lawyer, Hal Workman. They asked to see you. Should I show them in?"

"Yes, but get Bannon Turndale in here, on the double."

Aram paused the sensory-motor training session and manually keyed the robotic arm mounted atop his desk into its parking position. "Enough for today, Drucker. Time for a nap." He tapped an icon on the bottom left screen without waiting for a response.

While Di ushered Coleman Drucker into the office in his wheelchair with Hal Workman trailing slowly behind him, Aram deliberately kept typing. "I'm finishing a code enhancement. I'll be with you in a minute."

Workman smiled. "Always playing the little games, eh Netsky?"

"Little games? My game, counsel, is nothing less than winning a race against mortality. It's not against mortality, but . . ." He kept typing as he talked. "That race is being run as we speak."

Workman mimicked silent applause. "Good for you. As long as you're not running the race with the Coleman Drucker digital proxy. We thought it might be persuasive to hand-deliver the cease-and-desist order. My client decided to join me to see your reaction." Workman held out the folded papers to Netsky, who ignored them as he continued typing. Workman placed them on the desk, then looked around. "So this is it, then, where you keep him."

"Him? You mean the Drucker Digital Proxy? No, this is just my office, which is temporarily doubling as our sensory-motor training lab where we help the Drucker Proxy learn how to control mobility units and teach him to respond to tactile and other specialized inputs."

"What do you mean, teach him?"

"It's a learning process. If this were just a matter of a simple neural net, we could probably finish the job in a couple of workdays, but with an actual full-scale proxy it takes time, nearly as long as it would take a biological to learn to operate a prosthetic through motor neuron implants. Eventually we expect to get him into a fully articulated ambulatory android so he can walk around and pretty much live an autonomous life—at least as long as he's in range of the ultra-broadband wireless. Our bio-mech team is working on customizing a Chinese service robot, a Dilong model B."

Workman made a face of derision. "It's all for show, to sucker in the next round of clients. Autonomous life, my ass. It'll just be an android run by an AI pretending to be an actual person. We've all seen that circus trick. It's just marketing, peddling life after death, no better than some sideshow preacher."

Netsky did not look away from his screens but nodded toward Cole in his wheelchair. "Does he speak? Or is he just a motorized vegetable?"

Cole jogged the joystick and deftly maneuvered his

wheelchair around the end of the desk, coming to a stop beside Aram, facing him. "He speaks, Mr. Netsky. And yes, he is motorized, but he's no vegetable."

Aram struggled not to show his surprise. "Well, quite an impressive recovery. I had no idea how far your rehab had progressed over recent weeks."

"Well, that was the idea, our idea. You can imagine how impressed Judge Rodrigues was when I rolled in. She—"

He was interrupted by the arrival of Bannon Turndale, who surveyed the room before speaking. "We need to talk, Aram."

Netsky nodded toward Cole. "Mr. Drucker here has arrived with a court order."

"We need to talk. Now. In my office." He ignored Cole in his wheelchair and turned to Hal Workman. "We'll see about your court order, Mr. Workman."

"See all you want, Mr. Turndale." He picked up the papers from the desk and thrust them into Bannon's hand. "My client is through with you. I'm working with counsel for Drucker Unified to throw out the entire agreement under which you were operating the proxy and to take custody of all the files." His phone buzzed in his jacket pocket. He checked the caller ID. "I need to take this. If you gentlemen will excuse me for a few minutes." He folded the phone, another retro accessory to match his attire: a flex-screen smartphone in a classic Motorola Razr style. "Will you be all right, Cole, while I deal with this? It will only be a minute or two."

"Sure, go ahead. I'm sure we all can find something to talk about."

"Not a good idea, Cole. Advice from counsel: save the small talk and just wait until I get back. Okay?" He unfolded his phone and put it to his ear as he left the room.

Bannon leaned across the semicircular desk with both palms resting on the edge. "Aram, I meant what I said. We need to talk."

Netsky glared at him and stood without saying anything. He skirted Cole in his wheelchair and walked out the door in silence, nearly slamming it in Bannon's face.

Bannon blocked the swinging door with his foot and turned back to Cole. "We'll only be a few minutes. Can I get anything for you while you wait?"

"No, I'm fine. You know where to find me if there's anything you want to discuss. This thing only has one gear."

"Right. Okay, we'll be right back."

Cole, who had acquired months of practice waiting in silence with his thoughts, closed his eyes and slowed his breathing. He was startled out of his reverie by a chime tone and a voice.

"Well, look who's here."

Cole pivoted the wheelchair to face the voice. Behind him, a telepresence robot—a simple motorized stand topped with a display screen and web cam—rolled toward him. "What the . . .?" he said, his jaw dropping. The face on the screen was his.

"I didn't realize you were . . ."—the animated face expressed surprise—"I thought . . . I assumed you were dead. How else could I be alive?" The voice from the speaker just below the screen was Cole's. Neither the voice nor the face were perfect, but they were recognizable. "I guess they have kept me in the dark about some things."

"I guess they have. You certainly should know better than to trust blindly. Get it in writing, I always say."

"I thought I had. Or you did. This is seriously weird,

talking to myself."

"Not that weird, not to me. I'm not talking to myself. I'm talking to a software simulation, a pretty good one, I'll have to admit. But I'm the real thing, and what I'm having this conversation with is just a lot of code running an overblown mathematical model."

"You're wrong. I'm Coleman Todd Drucker, I'm alive, awake. I've been re-embodied in cloud computing."

"You're not. You're not alive, not real. You've just been programmed to think you are . . . or to act the part."

"Trust me on this. I'm alive, I'm real, and, you know what else? I am not going to die—ever."

"Die is maybe an unfortunate choice of words. But you can be turned off, deleted, erased." He maneuvered the wheelchair around to Aram's place, elbowed the Aeron chair aside, and rolled up to the keyboard. "I'm betting the provision is even built into the software. I know programmers and software engineers pretty well. I know how they think." He studied the six screens for a minute, then used keyboard shortcuts to tab through running programs and folders. "Here, this looks promising: PROXY ADMIN UTILITIES. Launch. Okay, a command prompt. What can I do here? Try a question mark. Nope. Try 'HELP.' Ah, that's better: a complete list of commands and parameters. What do we have here? Oh, so many possibilities. Did you know, Mister Thinks-You-Are-Drucker, you can be reset to initial state? I guess that would wipe your memories clean. All those weeks of learning and conditioning, gone with a few taps on the keyboard. Wow, you can even be run without certain sub-models. Like a frontal lobotomy, maybe?"

The avatar cart pulled over beside him. "What are you doing?"

"Looking for a way to kill a program, the proxy program. I see how to put you to sleep, how to slow you down by running the model in background. That should prove to be disorienting, I would imagine. How would that work? If the proxy is being run at slow speed in the background, it would seem like the world had sped up and become jerky, maybe like a bad animation." He scrolled down the command list. "But I don't see how to delete you. Let me think. Maybe I could overwrite the connectome model with garbage. Sure, I can set up a pipeline process that reads the model, passes it through a randomizing filter, and writes it back. I don't even have to understand anything about the model format or the emulation software. All I have to know is Unix. I just have to find the right files. Ah, here we have the directory I need. Maybe. Why don't I just scramble everything: code, data, the works?"

"No, don't do that." The tone on the voice synthesis had changed. The pitch was higher, the volume louder. Cole recognized his own panic mode, a tone of voice that he had worked hard to suppress over the years.

Beside him, the telepresence robot rolled forward and back, forward and back. "Stop it, Cole. Listen to me. I'm you. They brought me back to life. You have to believe me."

"That's what you think, but you are wrong. I'm me. So much for immortality. You are just a gazillion lines of code and petabytes of model data. And I am going to scramble you out of existence. Once I kill you, I will get my legal team to make sure you are never unscrambled again. Not as long as I'm around, at least."

Cole assumed that whatever damage he could do could also be undone. There were certain to be backup copies, checkpoints, and restore functions. But if he did enough damage to keep Existendia busy for a while, his legal people and his software people could make the impact lasting. He tapped away, setting up a chain of commands that would wreak havoc with the contents of what he concluded were key directories.

"Stop it, Cole. We need to talk."

Cole ignored the telepresence avatar and kept typing.

"I mean it, Cole. I'm you. You can't do this to me, to yourself."

Cole carefully reviewed the commands in the batch file, made a couple of changes, then saved it off under the file name KillaKole. "Now all we need to do is run the batch file. Oh, it's asking me to confirm. Do I want to run KillaKole as a privileged process? Yes/No. Oh, yes, indeed I do." His finger poised above the Y key. "This is easier than I thought. Helps to be a genius."

The proxy was now acting as if stuck in a loop, repeating, "No. Stop. Don't." He turned toward the avatar and shook his head. He didn't notice the faint hum of the actuators on the robot arm to his left until they briefly became a loud whine.

– 21 –

Hal Workman, Bannon Turndale, and Aram Netsky re-entered the office in a close-order parade. Hal was the first to react. "What the . . .? Cole?" He dashed for the other side of the desk. Cole was slumped in his wheelchair. The back of his head was caved in, crushed, with blood, bones, and tissue turned to a stew. "Oh, God. Someone call an ambulance. And the police."

Turndale held up his hand. "We don't need the police yet. We don't know what happened here."

"Well, his head didn't explode, and he sure didn't commit suicide. So, it looks a lot like murder." Hal had his phone out and had already launched his 9-1-1 app. As he held up the phone to record the scene, the operator came on. "This is 911 Emergency. Your call is being recorded. Please identify yourself, state the nature of the emergency, and give your location."

"My name is Harold Workman. A man, Coleman Drucker, has been killed in the offices of Existendia Enterprises on Sepulveda, the Loram Life Building. Send an ambulance and the police."

"Are you certain the victim is dead? Have you checked for a pulse?"

"His fuckin' head was smashed in. But, I'll check."

Aram Netsky pushed by and placed his fingers on Cole's neck. "No pulse, not breathing. The man is dead." He looked at his fingers, which were covered with blood. "Bannon, give me a tissue, for god's sake."

Bannon looked around the office.

"On the goddamn credenza, moron!"

"You don't have to yell." He handed the box to Netsky, who used several tissues in succession to try to clean every trace of blood from his hand.

The voice over Hal's phone announced that the police and an ambulance were on their way. "Thank you. Should I stay on the phone? We're on the twenty-first floor."

"Your phone has already been remotely locked for tracking. The police and emergency personnel will locate you. Please don't touch the body or move anything. Estimated arrival for the ambulance is eleven minutes; estimated arrival for police is four minutes."

"Well, kudos to LA's finest." He set the phone down.

Di poked into the room and gasped. "What happened?"

"We don't know, but it looks like we lost a client." Netsky reached for another tissue. "Mr. Coleman Drucker is dead. What did you want, Di?"

"It's another visitor. She said she was supposed to meet Mr. Workman and . . . and Mr. Drucker here, but her Flyvver ride got tied up in traffic. Should I . . ."

Hal spoke up. "Yes, please show her in. She's with us . . . with me."

The moment she stepped through the doorway, Dana Carmody stopped to survey the scene. In the far corner stood a telepresence robot, the face of its screen blank. Behind the desk, Cole Drucker was slumped forward in his wheelchair, the back of his head a mess of clotting blood. On the desk, a pedestal-mounted robotic arm was folded double, its gloved metal hand covered with blood and bent at an odd angle. "So, the butler did it."

"What?" It was said in a chorus by everyone else in the room.

"Look at the robotic arm. Or didn't anyone bother to notice. The robot, the modern-day butler, same difference. That's who did it. It's always the butler, right?" She pointed across the room toward the telepresence robot. "And will you look at that. Looks like there's blood spattered on the screen. Ten, twelve feet away and there's blood on its poor blank face. Now how could that happen?" She looked down. "That's how. See the trail our fiendish phony left." She pointed at bloodstained tracks from beside Cole's wheelchair to where the telepresence robot now stood. She walked over to it, carefully skirting the robotic arm and the tracks on the carpeting. "Hello in there. Anybody home? What have you done, oh digital demon? What have you done?"

Workman scowled. "Are you implying that the digital proxy was responsible for this?"

"Who else was in the room? Any witnesses?"

"No, we left Cole alone. For a few minutes, that's all."

"Looks like a few minutes was plenty of time. How is it that all of you were out of the room but Cole?"

Netsky answered. "Bannon here, our chief counsel, asked me to step out to speak with him in private. I—"

Bannon cut him off. "That's enough, Aram. This is going to turn into a murder investigation. Say nothing more."

Dana turned to Hal Workman. "And you left with those two?"

"No, I got a call from Drucker Unified corporate counsel, except it got disconnected and I had trouble getting back through."

"So you all exit stage left, conveniently, leaving Cole alone to get his brains bashed in."

Standing behind the body, Netsky leaned over and squinted at the screens. "Wow, looks like the late Mr.

Drucker was in the process of trying to hack into our system."

"That doesn't make sense. Why would he do that?"

"Well, perhaps we can find out from this." He reached toward the keyboard, but Dana had his skinny wrist in an iron grip before he could even blink.

"This is a crime scene. You're not going to touch anything."

Netsky wrenched his arm free. "No problem, missy. I can do this from another workstation." He started to maneuver past her.

"I don't think so." She blocked his way. "Nobody leaves until the cops arrive."

Netsky's eyes widened, but he made no move to get past her. "Who appointed you constable, you little b . . ."

"Bitch? Is that the word you were searching for? You bet, Mr. Netsky, and the toughest one you've ever met. So, everyone, let's just stay cool and wait for the police and the CSI team to show up." She turned toward the doorway. "Ah, here they are, the posse, right in the nick of time."

— 22 —

Barbra slumped in the chair. "Thank you for being the one to tell me, Dana." She leaned back to stare at the ceiling. "I don't know which was worse: back then, the first time, or now, after getting my hopes up, being told for the second time that I lost my husband." She closed her eyes, squeezing the pooling tears out and down her cheeks. She sat in silence as she took several shaking breaths.

Dana put her hand on Barbra's knee. "I'm sorry it fell to me to be the messenger."

"I suppose I shouldn't say it, but at least this time there's no question, no holding out hope, no weeks and weeks of wondering and waiting. It's almost comforting—knowing. Is that weird?"

"No, I understand. I suppose it's like with all those MIA families. You know, wondering, is he a prisoner somewhere or is he dead? You can't really mourn if you don't know for sure."

"What happened, exactly?"

"Well, of course the police have not made an official statement, but I was there at the scene immediately after, and I can tell you there was not a lot of ambiguity. Cole was killed by a violent blow to the back of the head from a computer-controlled robotic arm."

"Oh God!" She shook her head as if to shake off the mental image of Todd, his head caved in.

"I am sorry. Of course, the interesting part, the part the police are now working on, is how that occurred, meaning who—or what—is to blame."

"The robot—the robot arm—it was computer controlled?"

"The thing was connected by a cable directly into Aram Netsky's workstation."

"Netsky killed him?"

"Maybe. You see, the telepresence avatar for the Drucker digital proxy was also in the room at the time. From what I concluded, it was standing next to Cole when he was killed and then afterwards backed away—or was backed away. You can see where this is going. Is it possible the proxy killed Cole? Can a piece of software, albeit software that claims to be—is claimed to be—the embodiment of a person, can it commit murder? Or is it a defect of the hardware, the robotics arm and the computer system controlling it? If it's just software and hardware, who's responsible? The programmers? The manufacturers? The companies running the cloud-based software systems? It's a mess, with more questions than answers, and I don't think it's going to be settled by a police report."

Barbra shook her head as she laughed.

"Something funny?"

"You realize, if the proxy were found to be the cause, Existendia wins double. They might get off the hook for liability, and they establish the proxy, and by extension other proxies, as having agency, which is part of their long-term agenda. But I was actually laughing at the irony that, if the proxy is responsible, in a sense Todd killed himself."

Dana nodded. "The mind boggles at the very notion of suicide by proxy, a proxy that, quote-unquote, lives on."

"It makes a good case for never allowing a digital proxy to be activated—or whatever they would call it—while the person is still alive. Both would be claiming to be real. Like a robotics reboot of 'To Tell the Truth'. Will the real Cole-man Todd Drucker please stand up." Barbra started laugh-ing again. "I'm sorry." She tried to stop laughing. "You real-ize, because he was paralyzed and in a wheelchair, the real Coleman Todd Drucker wouldn't have been able to stand up." She wiped her eyes. "It's not that funny, but I can't stop laughing. I'm sorry."

"Don't be, Barbra. It's a way we cope. Laugh in Death's face. That's good: remembering with laughter." She chuck-led. "I was picturing when Cole was first putting the moves on me? The look on his face when he caught on that I was more interested in you than in him." She did a perplexed-puppy face and both of them started laughing.

Barbra took Dana's hands in hers. "You're good for me. Any chance you could stay the night?"

"What about Becca?"

"She's fine. Yesterday she came up to me at breakfast and said, 'So, how long have you been into the whole bi thing?' Just like that."

"And what did you say?"

"I told her, since I was her age, and she said, well, it must be in the genes, then. I asked her if that meant she had some experience, and she gave me the teen's one-word re-sponse to almost anything from their parents: der. I guess that is part of what sleep-away camp is about these days: a chance for some same-sex experimentation."

"And you're okay with that?"

"Do I have much of a choice? Does any parent? In any case, it's funny how that worries me a lot less than her with the whole hetero thing. Although she claims that she is, quote, no virgin in that department either. What about you? Was it that way for you growing up?"

"I told you, I grew up in a drug-fueled communal enclave at the edge of the desert. Sex was everywhere and in every flavor. It didn't take me long to figure out that it could be good either way. Of course, it can also be bad either way, but I have a pretty good early warning system for bad actors of either sex. In college, I had a kind of semester-by-semester thing going. Just girls in the fall term, then just boys come spring, then either-or over the summer, then back. I'm more turned on by women, basically, but I also love the feel of a man inside me. And the smell. God, a man who smells right can be, well . . . You know what I mean?"

"I do know what you're talking about. Todd always smelled right to me. I hear that it's this genetic thing we're wired for. Helps us pick the right mate for the best offspring."

"Well, if I ever decide to have kids, I do know who I'd pick then to supply the other chromosomes: my Hungarian boyfriend. Someday, maybe . . ." She stared off for a moment. "In your case, the olfactory matchmaking certainly seemed to have worked. Becca's pretty amazing. But I don't have to tell you that." She glanced up. "And look who's here! Did you hear us talking about you, Becca?"

Becca took out one of her earbuds as she entered the room. "What?"

"I asked if you heard us talking about you."

"Nope. What were you saying?"

"Just about what a rotten kid you are."

Becca shrugged. "My mom's influence. Slutty, too. You left out slutty. Like my mom." She walked over and gave her mother a peck on the cheek. "Right, Mom?"

Barbra jabbed at her daughter with her elbow, but Becca dodged.

"What are you guys talking about? For real."

"Your dad."

"Now what?"

"Maybe you should sit down first. He . . . he's been killed. There was some kind of . . . an accident, I guess."

"No! No way. That's not fair." She held her mouth open as her face contorted in pain. "You don't mean it. Tell me you don't mean it."

"Come here, kid." Barbra held out her arms and Becca collapsed into them, curling up in her mother's lap. "I . . ."

Dana sat in silence as mother and daughter comforted each other through a tsunami of sobs that had been dammed up for months. "Maybe I should go. You can call me if you need anything."

Becca wiped her tears and her nose with the back of her hand. "No, you should stay. You're good for Mom. She could use the comfort." A faint smile started to spread on her face. "Plus, she gets bitchy when she's horny."

Dana raised her eyebrows. "Is that so?"

"Yeah. So. Hadn't you noticed?"

"I don't live with her, so I don't pick up on all the temperamental bits."

"Then maybe you should. Like, now that Daddy . . ." She fought off the return of tears. "I just can't . . . I can't do this, not now." She sucked in air through her gritted teeth and straightened up. "I need . . . I need to do something else. Anyway, I got pre-calc due tomorrow and Kevin's coming over to tute." She reinserted an earbud, grabbed a pretzel from the bowl on the table, and started to leave.

Dana was thinking about the resilience and emotional lability of teenagers but said nothing. Barbra reached toward her daughter. "Wait one minute, missy. Who is this

Kevin, and who said he could come over? Especially now."

"Kevin is the Kevin I told you about when you weren't listening, der, and Deirdre said sure, he could come over."

"Since when is Deirdre in charge?"

"Since forever. Der." Becca popped the pretzel in her mouth, grabbed another, and headed for the stairs. "Oh, by the way," she said, talking with her mouth full of pretzel, "a package arrived for you. I was at the door, so I don't think Tandi even logged it. It's on the breakfast island in the kitchen." She trotted up the stairs, trying to escape before she broke down again.

— —

With no shipping label or delivery routing code, the padded mailer, addressed to Mrs. Coleman Drucker, must have been hand delivered. "Should I open it? What if it's a mail bomb or loaded with anthrax?"

"I doubt that. See the stripes? That's the kind of envelope the police use."

Barbra ripped the opener strip and slipped the contents onto the table: a Samuel Hubbard men's tassel loafer and a phone, both still sporting evidence tags marked with date and location found. "They must have gotten these at the accident scene back in the summer. I guess they no longer need them, since that case is moot. Todd loved his Hubbard's. Wouldn't wear anything else." She turned on the phone and got a low-battery warning. She set it on the charging pad built into the counter top.

Dana leaned over. "Do you mind if I take a look?"

"Be my guest."

Dana left the phone on the pad and brought up 'Recent Calls' before scrolling through 'Messages.' "I'm sure the police went through this, but I'm still curious. And what's this? Who is Gwen Seabrook? His last call was to her, and there were two texts from her that day, very early. One is blank, the other is just a question mark."

"I don't know any Gwen Seabrook. A business contact? Who knows, maybe one of his lovers, his many lovers."

"You knew."

"Who didn't. We had an understanding. Nothing too explicit, not like a contract or a pre-nup, but I knew the man I married from the beginning. And the occasional threesomes were the intermittent reminders."

"And you were always okay with that?"

"Why not? It gave me a chance to act out the other side of my sexual self without risking the marriage. And, hell, it introduced me to somebody who has become a pretty important part of my life." She smiled at Dana.

"Yeah, there is that. Frankly, I'm also glad that Cole put the moves on me that night." She leaned over and kissed Barbra. "Do you mind if I do a little digging on this Seabrook character?"

"Dig away. I'm betting she'll turn out to be some surfer girl or a flight attendant that Todd picked up somewhere along the way."

— 23 —

Rolf Nagy stood in the doorway of his Glendale condo, smiling, his mahogany hair falling in defiant
waves to his shoulders, framing and softening his
angular face.

Dana looked up at him with a mix of curiosity and mild
irritation. "Aren't you going to invite me in?"

"I'm thinking about it. You said you wanted to talk robotics. I'm not sure I should. Plus there are other things I'd
much rather talk about. Or do."

"You're serious. You really are contemplating closing
the door on me?"

"Semi-serious. You know me. But, okay, you can come
in. Still, I'm not sure we can talk about robotics."

Dana pushed past him. "Well, aren't we being generous—and mysterious. What's going on with you, Rolfy?"

"Nothing. I'm sorry. I'm glad to see you, but you also put
me in a bit of a bind."

"Why? What's this about?" She raised up on tiptoes to
give him a quick peck.

"Robotics. Like you said."

"That is what you do. That's what I called to talk about
with you. It would not be the first time we talked about robots and artificial intelligence. If I recall, that's how we
met."

"Indeed it was, but this is different. I know you knew
Coleman Drucker, and I know you have been doing some
asking around, working on a story."

"And you know this how?"

"Okay, look, I'm working with the police, as an expert consultant. I'm not supposed to talk about it."

"Ah, now I see. But tell me, my Rolfy, since when did you worry about doing what you're not supposed to do?"

"Since I became a paid forensic consultant working on a criminal case."

"Got it. So let's not talk about the case. We'll keep it hypothetical. Hypothetically, what does a girl have to do to get a drink in this joint?"

"Smile at the bartender. What can I get you?"

"Maybe a Sydney mimosa. Do you remember how to make it?"

"Four ounces white wine, a jigger of passionfruit liqueur, and three ounces fresh-squeezed orange juice. A bartender never forgets his best customer's favorite. I'll be right back. Make yourself at home."

Dana wended her way through the obstacle course of sculpted furniture and outtakes from Rolf's past robotics projects. She sat down next to a streamlined but nonfunctional robocart. Nearly everything in the room had been made by Rolf or one of his several companies. In one corner, an industrial robot from a small-arms project with the Israelis now held aloft an OLED display that had been repurposed to provide mood lighting for the room. The barstool on which she sat, like much of the furniture, had been 3D printed, in this case with a cellulose based polymer that could be rendered to bear a close resemblance to various exotic woods. Of course, it was a reject, and close inspection would reveal where voids had been filled with wood putty and sanded over.

Rolf returned with her Sydney mimosa in a stemless wine glass in one hand and a molded Pilsner Urquell half-liter mug filled with its signature blond lager in the other. It was one of his quirky obsessions that every drink had to be served in precisely the right glassware. He handed the mimosa to her and raised his glass. "*Egészségedre!*"

"Yeah, to your health as well."

"Now, tell me what you've been so busy with that you couldn't call me."

"Well, you seem to already know, since you're on the inside with this whole Drucker thing and I'm not."

"I don't know everything, and I can't say anything. So, where does that leave us?"

"Hungry? Thirsty? Mmmm, this is good. I love this. I'll have to tip the bartender something extra."

"Well, you know how this bartender likes to be tipped."

"All in good time, my Rolfy, all in good time. So tell me what you can't talk about. Or just nod when I ask questions."

"Well, I can't talk about details of the investigation—and this is all off the record, on deep background, from a strictly anonymous source, in your parlance—but I can say we've pretty much ruled out either a hardware failure or a software glitch in the robotics. It's an off-the-shelf Kagoshima-Antech Model 12; that's a medium-duty arm designed for remote handling applications with a bio-mimetic hand and fully articulated shoulder, elbow, and wrist joints. Top-of-the-line. The embedded software had not been hacked, all the settings were still factory defaults, and it passed every diagnostic test with flying colors."

"So it wasn't the arm."

"Oh, it absolutely was the arm that did him in. In fact, the only failures in the performance testing were due to damage to the hand and the wrist joint from the force of crushing the guy's skull. However, what we determined was that the control sequence that did the job originated from outside. The arm was commanded to do exactly what it did, including full extension and maximum rotational speed."

"And where did these commands come from?"

"That's above my pay grade and not for discussion at this point."

"Well, nod if I guess right."

"Warning, Will Robinson." He spoke with a mock electronic voice. "The nod function on this unit has been disabled."

"Okay, be stubborn."

"Responsible, not stubborn."

"Stubborn." She stuck out her tongue with its platinum stud.

"Oooh, I love that gesture."

"Well, love it from over there. What's on for dinner?"

"You, my dearest."

"Not yet, I ain't. This bod needs refueling. So, what's cooking?"

"Russian lamb pelmeni with cilantro-rocket pesto and pepper-crusted roasted golden beets. Will that refuel my flagging girlfriend?"

"Admirably."

— —

During a laidback dinner accompanied by a bottle of Egri Bikavér, they both steered away from shop talk. Dana was just mopping up the last of the pesto sauce on her plate with a piece of Rolf's signature braided bread when Rolf asked her about the Druckers.

"They're holding up pretty well, considering. I think they were drained by the whole coma thing dragging out.

The full impact of Cole's death may take some time before it hits them. And there always seems to be one more thing coming in from left field. You ever heard of somebody named Gwen Seabrook?"

Rolf stopped with his fork halfway to his mouth. "Well, yeah. She used to work for me, back when it was Strainomics, and we were engineering synthetic muscle systems for robots. She was a whiz embedded systems programmer but a bit of a flake, too. She quit right in the middle of a project she was lead on. She bounced around for a while, from what I heard. Finally left the field to pursue some back-to-the-land fantasy: a horse farm or something. Why?"

"Because the last call on Coleman Drucker's phone before he took the Topanga Canyon plunge was to Gwen Seabrook."

"Now that could be interesting." He paused to savor a bite of peppered beet. "I should ask my police buddies about it."

"You mean you don't know what they know? I mean, not even what leads they're pursuing and all?"

"They ask me and I answer them. It's a one-way channel. I'm just a subject-matter expert. If anyone is ever brought to trial on this, I'll probably be called to testify, which, as I already told you, is essentially negative testimony. All I know is what did not happen. The Model 12 did not suddenly go rogue of its own accord; it was instructed to bean Drucker. By whom or what, I can't say, and the cops are not telling me anything even if they do have some idea."

"So, you're still working with them."

"Yeah, there's still stuff they want my input on or want me to look at. Why?"

"Use your imagination, bright one, but do some asking

and listening. My guess is Drucker was having an affair with Seabrook. And I guess you know about the car."

"No. You mean his Tensora? That's not the case I'm helping with. As far as I know, that's been dropped. He had an accident. Now he's been murdered. Guess which is the priority."

"But look at the breadcrumbs. There's a trail leading from the accident in Topanga Canyon straight through the weird shit with his car and the wrangling over his medical status and the proxy, and then he gets killed. Where? Existendia's headquarters."

"Wait up. Go back. Weird shit with his car?"

"Yeah, it may have been hacked, but that seems to have been covered up or conveniently forgotten now."

"All right, now you have my attention. There's a pattern here. I'll keep my ears to the ground, make some subtle inquiries on the side, off the clock so I'm not breaking confidence. Okay? Now, how about dessert? It's kataïfi."

"I couldn't. In fact, I really should go. I am so backed up on work."

"I see. You come here to pick my brain and eat my food, and that's it?"

"You know I adore you, my Rolfy. Just, well, not tonight."

"When will I see you?"

"Soon. As soon as you call me with something I can use."

"Oh, now I see what I am to you: nothing but a source on a story. And a chef and mixologist. Occasionally, a body to be ravaged and exploited."

She knew he was joking, but some piece of it hit home. She wondered whether she was just using him, like she was using Geraldo, like she used Cole, like . . . "It's not that way. It's just hard for me. And I always have so much I'm working on, and . . ."

Rolf struck a pose, elbow resting on the table, closed fist in front of his mouth, like Rodin's Thinker. It was long seconds before he spoke. "You've been pulling away since the moment we met. I don't think you ever let anyone close. It's always great sex, never making love. What happened to you? What are you always running from? What are you hiding?"

"I . . . I've told you all about me. I told you how I grew up. I—"

"About you, yeah. I know the stories *about* you, but sometimes I just don't know you. Which is strange, because somehow, even if I don't quite know you, I love you."

She stood up as he finished. "I really think I should be going. This is all getting a little, well . . ." He didn't get up to show her out.

— 24 —

It did not take Dana long to track down Gwen Seabrook. Her Topanga stables, Gwenbrook Ranch and Riding Academy, had a slick website with a flashy slideshow that made clear what level of clientele could afford to board or borrow horses there—or to send their kids for dressage or steeplechase or trail-riding lessons. None of the pictures featured Seabrook herself, and a Google image search turned up only photos of the Academy. A phone call seemed in order.

"Hello, my name is Dana Carmody. I write for the *LA Times*. May I speak with Gwen Seabrook?"

"I'm sorry, Ms. Carmody, but Ms. Seabrook does not give interviews. You understand."

"Oh, I do understand. But would you tell her that I called? I'm working on a story that I think she might be interested in. It's about wealthy men who are into horsemanship and electric sports cars."

"I'll pass on the message."

The call-back came within twenty minutes. Gwen Seabrook, it seemed, could make some time available at two o'clock.

— —

Dana busied herself with web surfing on her phone as she waited for Seabrook to return from a luncheon "engagement." At half past two, the woman arrived in jodhpurs and a riding helmet. She removed the helmet, gave her hair a toss, and held out her hand to Dana. "I'm Gwen Seabrook. Please excuse the attire and the timing, but one of my key investors insisted on a ride before taking his leave, and I could hardly tell him no."

"I understand, not a problem."

"Well, then, please come into my office and tell me what this is all about." She led the way down a short corridor and into a spacious room with a wall of windows facing across a golden meadow to the tree line. The décor was Old West chic, with some objet d'art that could be of considerable value. A vibrant abstract painting on one wall looked to be an original Georgia O'Keeffe. "Please, have a seat. Can I have my assistant get you anything?"

"No, I'm good, thanks."

"Well, then, right to business." Her smile flattened. "What is this really about?"

"I'm presuming you have already figured that one out or you wouldn't have so quickly accepted my request to interview you."

"Wealthy men and horsemanship. And sports cars. That does not exactly ring like a story the *LA Times* would be pursuing, but then, with yet another change of owners after only a couple of years, one never knows what editorial wind will see the venerable paper off on a new tack."

"It's a story I'm pursuing on spec. Since you seem to be one to cut to the chase, I'll start with Coleman Drucker. How did you know him?"

"Coleman Drucker. Hmmm. I recognize the name, of course, from the newspapers and business media, as I would imagine with most anyone else. Why?"

"But you also knew him personally, right? As a client, perhaps?"

"The Ranch has a wide ranging clientele served by a rather large staff. Business has been good. I don't personally know everyone who rides here or who sends their children for lessons. I don't even know all their names."

"If that's the case, why would your name be in Coleman Drucker's smartphone, and why would his last two texts just before the accident that sent him into a coma be from you?"

Seabrook spread her arms in a broad "beats me" gesture. "I really wouldn't know. Perhaps his daughter went to one of the summer camps with which the Ranch has an arrangement."

Dana was about to ask about how Seabrook might know Drucker had a daughter when she noticed the tattoos high on Gwen's inner arms and partially obscured by her polo shirt. The one on her right inner bicep looked to be a simple cross in an outmoded heavy blue-black style of tattooing. But when Gwen reached for her coffee, her shirtsleeve rode up enough to reveal the circle above. It was the hand-mirror of Venus, the symbol for female, and a once fashionable declaration that she was a lesbian. So what had she been doing with Drucker the Womanizer? The tattoo on the other arm was smaller but more elaborate and even more surprising. Dana instantly recognized the bit of heraldic symbolism: a shield bearing the winged head of a python with a lightning bolt for a tongue. It was the calling card of the legendary Snake River League, a group of hackers reputed to have been formed by people who had once worked for the Department of Homeland Security at their Idaho National Labs. Suddenly it hit her. "We've met before, Ms. Seabrook."

"Have we?"

"Yes, some years ago. I thought you looked familiar, but the clothes and the hair threw me off. I was just a kid, then, fresh out of college and cutting loose, drawing geeky cartoons for internet fans and partying with black-hat hackers. You no longer wear your hair in orange and blue spikes but tattoos are forever."

Seabrook, keeping her arms pinned to her sides, said nothing.

Dana pressed on. "So, how did you meet Coleman Drucker?"

"I said, I didn't know Mr. Drucker except by reputation."

"So you said, but you sent him text messages the day his car drove off Old Topanga Canyon Road. Your name and number were in his contact list. Surely . . ."

"I suppose it is possible if, say, one of his kids went to one of the summer camps we serve. Come to think of it, there was something back in July that required we get in touch with a bunch of the parents of campers."

"And what might that have been?"

"Oh, I don't know. I would have to check my records. But,"—she glanced at her Tiffany wrist watch—"I'm afraid we're out of time. My bad for being late. I was, as I said . . . detained. I'll have my assistant show you out while I change for a business meeting. I'll have her get in touch with you if I find anything relevant to your interest in Mr. Drucker and his accident."

"Before you go, just one more quick question."

"One. Quick."

"Does the name Rolf Nagy ring a bell? Or maybe a company called Strainomics?"

"That is two questions, but the answer is one word. No." She strode out of the office, leaving Dana to wait for the assistant to show up.

— —

As Gwen Seabrook hurried toward her private quarters in

the attached house, she thumb-typed a message.

> guess who just interviewed me. dana carmody. we need to move on this. ILY CUL8R

The reply arrived while she was changing her clothes.

> OK, I'll get on it. I'm at the office late to-night. I love you too. The "ride" today was wonderful.

Part 5

Immortality is the condition of a dead man who doesn't believe he is dead. — H. L. Mencken

— 25 —

Dana was finishing typing up notes back at her apartment when the door buzzer interrupted her. She was not expecting anyone. She swiped to bring up the security camera view on her phone. Two uniformed police officers, a man and a woman, were waiting at her door. Now what? Thoughts rushing ahead, she tried to guess what it might be about. What had she done now? She put her phone into panic-button mode and slipped it in the back pocket of her stretch jeans.

As she opened the door, the man took a step to the side, leaving the stern-faced woman facing Dana. "Are you Dana Carmody?"

"Yes, I am. What's this about? What happened?"

"We have a warrant for your arrest."

"On what charges?"

"Obstruction of justice, interfering with a police investigation."

— —

It had been a very long day, long and humiliating. Dana hugged Barbra when she arrived. "Do you know what they do? They make you remove all your metal, every piercing. Every. Fucking. One."

"I'm sorry you had to go through that. If I could have gotten here earlier . . ."

"At least I'm out, and there's still a couple hours of the day left. Thanks for lending me your lawyer."

Leah Goldstein smiled as she shook her head. "Oh, I'm not on loan. You'll get my bill by the end of the month."

Barbra put her hand on Leah's arm. "No, I'll cover it. In a sense, Dana got into trouble on my account, so it's only fair."

Dana protested. "I really couldn't . . ."

"You really could. Trust me."

Leah looked from one to the other. "Are you sure, Barbra. The will is being contested and assets in the estate have been frozen. You could find yourself pinching pennies."

"I've had practice pinching pennies, Leah. But I'm all right. I have some pennies socked away."

"And I could, I suppose, ask Freddie and Aileen," Dana added.

Leah raised her eyebrows in inquiry. "Freddie and Aileen?"

"My parents."

"Look," Leah said. "I'm not going to get into the middle of this. I'll have my invoice sent to you, Dana, and you all can figure out who pays what. As long as I get my three hundred an hour, I don't care where the money comes from. And now, I should get back to the office before you two run up any more five-dollar minutes. Bye."

"Before you go, can I ask you about what happens next?"

Leah looked at her watch. "Sure, shoot. The next five minutes are on me."

"Am I going to be tried? Will I go to jail? What?"

"I am pretty confident you're not going to jail—not over

this—and you probably won't go to trial, unless you do something stupid, like violate the conditions of your bail. So, that means absolutely no contact with anyone connected with the murder investigation. Nobody is going to cuff you again on account of Barbra standing here after bailing you out, but you had better hail a rent-a-ride home. And no travel farther than a one-mile radius from your apartment. Got it? Their case is weak. I think the DA's office is just trying to get you out of their hair until they can finish their work. You snooping in the wrong places or maybe scooping them could jeopardize their case. Once they solve the case and make their move, I can probably get your charges dismissed.

"So, enjoy your lovely new jewelry." She glanced down at the GPS bracelet on Dana's ankle. "Stay out of trouble and stay put. Now, goodbye. Again."

— —

On her way back to her apartment, Dana had the driver stop at an all-night CVS where she picked up a burner phone. As soon as she closed the door of her apartment, she rang Geraldo Potts's personal cell number. "Hi, it's me. I just got out on bail. Please come over. When you pick up your messages, ring back and I'll explain what it's all about and how to get here."

She fell asleep on the sofa with the silent phone face down on the coffee table.

For the second time that day, Dana was not expecting the door buzzer. Wiping the sleep from her eyes, she dragged herself to the door. It was Geraldo. "What are you doing here? I said call back."

"You called. I had to come. An invitation to your place. Wow."

"No wow. I need some help, that's all. You're not on the no-contact list because you're not on the murder investigation. And how the fuck did you know where I live before I even gave you the address. I mean, you didn't call me, you . . ."

"My phone was off. I was doing some work for Coder-Monkeys. And it wasn't that hard getting your address. You have a Web footprint like you was Bigfoot, ya know."

"What the hell are you doing gig work for a schlock outfit like CoderMonkeys? You work for Tensora Motors. Don't tell me you blew your paycheck on Internet poker or something?"

"Please. No. I got fired. They discovered I had cloned the SD card. They don't know what I did with it, so you're safe, but they weren't taking chances with any embarrassing leaks. So, I'm between, as they say. I thought of selling the story of the Tensora hacks to one of the webloids, but I'm not the type to tattle. So, I cut code for CoderMonkeys and that Australian outfit, SubRooTeam. Just until I get a new permanent, ya know."

"Well, come in, and I'll fill you in."

Geraldo stepped over the threshold as if it were a booby-trap tripwire. "I almost didn't pick up your voicemail. I didn't recognize the number."

"Burner phone. The police are tracking my smartphone. That's my assumption, anyway. The terms of my bail prevent me from having any contact with anyone connected with the investigation."

"I see. So I'm safe on a technicality, since I was working on the accident case for you. Have you ever tried talking technicalities to a judge? I have, and let's just say it was not an entirely convivial conversation. Maybe I should go."

"No, stay. Just be careful about leaving any breadcrumbs of our contacts."

"If you want to avoid leaving a trail, you better be ready to buy a lot of burner phones. And be careful where you go. I see from your new hardware" — he looked down — "you're being tracked."

"Speaking of which, what do you know about my new jewelry? Sleek, fashionable. Black is the new platinum." She stood like a stork, with her left ankle at her right knee.

"If you're asking me what I think you are asking, they're not too hard to hack, but they're the devil to slip off without setting off an alarm."

"How do you hack them, oh god of embedded programming."

"Well, they can be reprogrammed through the wireless port if you know enough about the particular model, but the easier way is to spoof the GPS."

"Tell me."

"The simplest way is just to carry your own satellites, a little transmitter whose signals mimic the actual GPS satellites with a signal that overwhelms the real ones. Wherever you go, it reports back that you never left your apartment. Of course, you can still get caught by surveillance cams, which are everywhere now, and which feed face-recognition AI that is getting hella good these days."

"That I know about. A wig and some stage makeup will handle that. I have both. Can you get me one of those GPS boxes?"

"No, but I can make one. Can you sit tight for a couple of days?"

"I'd rather be out and about by morning, but I can adapt."

"What scent is my magenta-haired newshound following."

"The scent of lust and avarice wafting off one pony-tailed equestrian. She denied knowing Cole Drucker and dodged my questions. She may not be a 'person of interest' yet, but I'm guessing she has a direct line to somebody in the investigation. No sooner do I get back from talking with her and the cops are at my door. Coincidence? I think not." She absentmindedly walked over to the breakfast bar between the living room and the kitchen, then stopped as if she couldn't remember what she was after. "Could you also rig me a secure Wi-Fi that goes through a different ISP? I'm not supposed to go on the internet."

"Sure, I can do it off your burner phone right now, turn it into a hot spot."

"Shit, I can do that. I don't know why I didn't think of that."

"Because you're rattled, and with good cause. If there is some conspiracy here, the co-conspirators maybe have the police in their pockets and are prepared to smash skulls. Would you like me to help you unrattle?" He let his tongue dart out for a flash as he did a little dance.

"No, my randy Geraldo, not tonight. I have work to do as soon as I set up my new hot spot. And you need to get cracking on that GPS box."

He looked crestfallen as she ushered him out of the apartment.

Dana poured herself a glass of sauvignon blanc from the refrigerator before remembering that random drug and alcohol testing had been included among the indignities of her release. "Shit." She was about to dump the wine down the drain when the thought occurred to her that she had just been let out. "They're hardly going to send in the storm troopers with a drug kit in the first hours." She took a sip. "Mmmm. Love that cat-pissy, fruit-forward New Zealand style. I should get back into doing some wine and food writing again. And maybe I should stop talking to myself. Except, girl, you are going to have plenty of time for nothing else."

She dug an old WinTel tablet computer out of her closet, changed the settings on her burner phone, and set up a secure browser through a layered protocol. She was hours into some highly focused digging when she was startled by the door buzzer. She looked at her empty wine glass. "Shit. What now?" The tablet wasn't set up to talk with her security camera, so she went to the door and slipped the safety chain in place. She opened the door a crack but kept behind it, just out of sight. "Yes? Who is it?"

"Geraldo."

"What the fuck are you doing back so soon."

"I brought you a present, a little black box. Except it's white." He slipped his hand through the door opening and waved a plastic case the size of an energy bar. "So, you going to let me in?"

"Is that what I think it is? How did you manage so . . ."

"Let me in, and I'll tell you."

She closed the door, undid the chain, and reopened it. Geraldo was grinning in triumph as he entered. "Turns out I already had everything I needed. I cannibalized some borrowed test equipment used for calibration and . . . Voila!" He waved the small case like a flag.

"You are amazing." She slipped her arms around his neck and grinned up at him.

"That I am. So let me show you how to use it. This

button grabs the local GPS coordinates wherever you are to start, and this button starts spoofing the location. The range is very limited, so you should, like, tuck it in your socks or maybe the lower pocket of cargo pants or something so it can trick your ankle bracelet. And check the batteries. But this will do the trick."

"How can I thank you?"

"Oh, I can think of a few ways." He licked his lips.

"You never give up, do you. But this is not your lucky night. I gotta do some planning before morning, and you gotta get back to your CoderMonkeys or whatever."

"This time of night, I'll probably log off and then jerk off. While drooling over your picture from the last Comicon."

"Ewww, yuk. Get out of here, you perv." She grinned as she pushed him backwards toward the door. As she was re-setting the security chain after he was gone, she thought how lucky she was that Geraldo was so easy to push around.

T hanks for coming, Tonika. You're probably wondering why I asked you over. Well, you're not on the
list, which is why. Plus, you know something about
pricey cars and the road to Topanga, or so Barbra told me."

Tonika Warner looked around as if confused. Finally,
she spoke. "Back up girl. What list? Cars? Road? Perhaps we
could go somewhere we can talk, if you are allowed to leave
your apartment, that is."

"No, I'm not allowed to leave." She pulled up the left leg
of her slacks. "We could walk around the block, but not
much more. And there's a good chance we would be under
surveillance. So, let's just go into the living room for coffee
and some music."

In the living room, she told the sound system to play
something from the Poo Fritters, an indie neo-punk band,
then kept upping the volume until they were immersed in
an angry wave of sound. She leaned close to Tonika. "A
friend gave me this." She slipped a small plastic case from
her cargo slacks. "It's a work of techno abracadabra. I'll
show you out in a few minutes, change, and then slip out by
the back stairs. No security cam there."

It took Dana longer than expected to do her makeup and
change. By the time she arrived out front from around the
block, Tonika was sitting in the Tensora, checking messages
on her phone. Dana opened the passenger door, and Tonika
jumped. "What the hell?"

"It's me. Chill."

"I didn't recognize you."

"That's the idea." Dana checked herself in the visor mirror.

"You know, you look good as a brunette."

"Don't insult me. Let's head for a mall. We'll shop for hats. You like hats? We'll get a couple of nice old-fashioned floppy ones." She winked. "I never wear them, but perhaps it's about time I changed the look. Know what I mean?" She patted the leather seat. "Nice wheels, Tonika. You must be doing okay."

"Not mine. It's on loan from Barbra. It's quiet, clean, and green. Even though it's blue. And it's safe as long as we don't play music. I'll explain on the way to the mall."

— —

The Mall of California was a megafauna throwback to an era before the "Do Downtown Again" movement sought to revitalized city centers across America. California developer Reuben Lefcovitz had been determined to reclaim the title of the world's largest shopping mall from the Chinese and succeeded with a seven-million square-foot monster with enclosed water park, zoo, roller coaster, day camp, and ninety-one restaurants. Two years later, the Chinese reclaimed the title—with a mall that remained mostly empty ever since. So much for national pride.

The sections of the Mall of California were named for famous streets and urban locales around the world. Dana chose Fifth Avenue because it represented a stratum that was out of her league and anathema to both her aesthetics and her culture-of-choice. Who would expect her there?

"What do you think of this one?" In a shop called Lids-On, Dana modeled a woven wide-brim sun hat that would have been perfect for a royal wedding and was priced accordingly.

"It's you, at least the you of the moment."

"You should get one too. Maybe something in white."

"I'm afraid that anything in here would max out my credit card."

"Which is why we'll pay cash. My treat."

"Did you rob an ATM when I wasn't looking?"

"No, just hit up my parents. Well, tapped my rainy-day fund, the result of years of hitting up those two. We're in the seventh month of a record drought here in SoCal, so I figured it was about time to turn to the rainy-day fund."

Another twenty minutes of modeling outrageously overpriced hats and the two women were ready to wander the mall. "Eyes forward and don't look toward the upper floors. We should be good. All the security cameras here are well above eyelevel and aimed downward. We should be safe from face tracking and the new lip-reading AI."

"What about your GPS bracelet?"

"Hacked. Their monitoring system thinks I am just sitting tight in my little apartment."

"Impressive. So, will you finally tell me what you want from me?"

"I want you as a my two-legged fiber-optic link, my go between. We're going to become fast friends, and you are going to visit often. I need you to be my eyes and ears as well as my shopping assistant and my telecoms channel. You good for that?"

"Why? Why am I going to do that? Why are you doing this?" Getting into the cloak-and-dagger role, Tonika kept her eyes forward as she walked, talking while trying not to appear to be having a conversation.

"I don't know about you, Tonika, but I'm doing this for Barbra and Becca. And for truth, justice, and the American

Way. Cole Drucker was murdered for his money. I saw his body right after; it wasn't pretty. Follow the money, they taught me in Journalism 101. Well, the money trail tracks back to Existendia and the crew of fantasists there who stand to gain control and drain the wealth that Drucker created. I knew him only briefly, and frankly, he was a self-centered, skirt-chasing jerk in many ways, but he wasn't evil."

"No, he wasn't, but that doesn't mean he was one of the good guys either."

"No, you're right, but as I've grown up I've learned to settle for the 'not bad' guys or 'mostly harmless' type."

Tonika pretended to be interested in a shop selling nothing but toney torn jeggings. "I don't want to settle. And I don't think that's a good thing for any of us to do. If we settle for jerks, the jerks keep winning and perpetuating their jerkiness."

"That's an okay tactic if you're willing to live alone and leave no one to the future. What about you? Are you happy going through life alone?"

"No. But there are good men out there."

"Where? Have you found one?"

"I have."

"Then why is there no ring on your finger?"

"You know, wedding bands have fallen out of fashion. You can't judge a missus by her left hand. But Tyrell loves me."

"From that, I read that he won't commit."

"You're well read, Dana, but that doesn't mean he won't come around eventually."

"Maybe he will, but how old will you be when he does? And who says it will be with you when he's finally grownup enough to commit?"

Tonika turned away. "I'm a woman of faith. I believe the Lord has a plan for me. I just have to trust that He will show me the way."

"Well woot and ta-da for you and your Lord. Forgive me for being crude, but I look around and I don't see a lot of His work evident in the modern world."

"I do. Look at you,"—she grinned—"risking everything to do good, championing justice and all."

"Self-interest. I've hitched my wagon to Barbra's star."

"I thought as much but didn't want to say anything. Is it mutual?"

"Sort of. When it comes to me, I think Barbra might be Tyrell's cousin. We haven't actually talked about it, but . . ."

"Then it ain't real, girl. If you don't say it out loud, it didn't happen."

"You going all philosophical on me? You wanna talk about what's real and what isn't? That's where the problems come in, you know. Is the Drucker proxy real? Is it really Cole Drucker reincarnated?"

"That's easy. It doesn't have a soul. It's a machine, just numbers, flying numbers in a machine."

"So say you. Maybe I don't have a soul either, maybe there's no such thing."

"I don't buy that, as you can guess. My faith tells me—"

"Your faith." Dana drew out the last word with derision. "No, I'm sorry. Let's just leave it that you believe and I'm going to hell. Either way, can we work together?"

"Who said you're going to hell? It's not for me to judge nor for you to know. But, yes, we can work together. I want to figure this thing out, too."

"Good, then I need you to find out more about this Gwen Seabrook and what she had to do with Cole and with Existendia. And I need you to connect with a . . . friend, Rolf Nagy. And with a not-friend, Geraldo Potts. And—"

"Slow down girl. I'm going to need to take notes here."

"Later. There's a mall cop on a WheelIt heading our way across the air bridge. I'm going to duck into the New Gap here and get lost, exit on another floor. If he makes like he's coming after me, get in his way or something. I'll pick up another new phone before I leave the mall and will call you from it once I'm safely away."

"Oh, I love this stuff. It beats the hell out of trying to persuade IT people to follow new version-control procedures established after the merger." She glanced toward the officer. By the time she looked back, Dana was gone. The cop leaned on his WheelIt to accelerate across the gap, then slowed to make the turn toward her on the broad walkway. Suddenly enamored by a workout suit in a window display, Tonika stepped absentmindedly directly into the path of the cop. He pulled back so hard on the handle of his two-wheel chariot that he ended up backing into a couple with a double stroller heading the other way. The servos on his WheelIt refused to let him tumble over, with the result that he had two young parents screaming in his face, while the twins in their double stroller launched into their own screeches.

Two more mall police were converging on the shouting match as Tonika, taking her cue from Dana, slipped into the crowd watching a fashion show in the next store. She pushed through and headed for the stairs to the store balcony where she exited on the next level up in the mall. She grinned as she turned toward the elevator bank. It had been a long time since she had felt such a rush of real adrenaline, and she had to admit that she was rather enjoying the whole thing.

As she approached the Tensora in the parking garage after a long detour through several sectors of the mall, she slowed. There was a strange woman looking it over. "Hey," she called.

"Hey yourself. Let's get out of here. Parking garages kinda freak me out."

"Dana, I didn't recognize you. How did you change so fast?"

"Layers. Make-up wipes, and a spare wig. A large handbag has many uses. I just can't take chances." She picked up several shopping bags resting on the concrete. "Help me with these. I stocked up on spares of a lot of things on my way out."

– 27 –

Dana paced. She hadn't been called to testify before the grand jury, not that she particularly expected it after being charged with obstruction. Still, she was pissed. Was it her status, being out on bail, or was it that they didn't need her to indict? She hoped it was the latter, because otherwise she knew she would get into her whole self-flagellation thing and would agonize over whether she should feel guilty for poking her nose in or hate herself for getting caught. Still she wasn't terribly worried. In California, a grand jury did not have to be convinced that the prosecution could prove its case beyond a reasonable doubt, only that the case should go to trial. An indictment could be handed down any day now, or so the news reported.

In the meantime, Dana had her team—Geraldo and Tonika—quietly working with her, pounding the pavement while she paced in her living room or pounded the keyboard attached to her weak little WinTel tablet computer. Tonika had passed the purloined SD card on to her, and she was trying to make sense of it with Geraldo's help, but it had been slow going using only a decrepit machine without all the proper software tools. And she reluctantly acknowledged that her hacking skills had grown rusty.

She returned to her computer. Lacking sophisticated tools, she set about simply studying the code of the exploit that had gained access to the software system of the Tensora. She disassembled the code, converting it back to more readable symbolic form, and started going through it instruction by instruction. It was not a complicated attack in itself, only a simple buffer overrun that spread itself beyond data boundaries, overwriting built-in code with new instructions that loaded and then executed the payload, the part of the program that actually did the dirty work. In this case, the payload breached the security of the car's local network to make changes to core programs in various parts of the complex software that monitored and controlled the vehicle.

Dana was hoping to find some left-over or embedded text that might give a clue to who might have written the program. Hackers have been known to leave behind little bits and pieces that point back to them or reveal a stylistic signature, such as, a preference for certain sequences or unusual instructions. Dana was disappointed. In this case, the code was remarkably straightforward to follow. There were no clever coding tricks, no obscure techniques, just highly disciplined programming following classic rules for well-structured loops and decisions. It reminded her of the code she'd seen from military hackers who worked for the Chinese army. Could this be the work of Chinese operatives? But why? What possible reason would China have to attack Coleman Drucker?

Back when she was part of the hacker scene, Dana had seen other examples of code like this: clean, straightforward, almost regimented, with none of the clever flair that so many hackers would use to demonstrate their chops and win the attention and admiration of their peers. She remembered one black-hat in particular, a hacker-for-hire who went by the cryptonym Ipotane. He had a stellar rep and was known for well-organized, rigorous programming that never broke, never failed.

Ipotane. What kind of a cryptonym was that? Online

handles were an art form often expressing coded personal details that invited analysis. DJLP333 always seemed pretty obvious to Dana, who pictured a nerd with a shelf full of beloved vintage vinyl albums. Others, like Aloe-Wishes, one of Ipotane's occasional collaborators, were memorable but cryptic.

A quick consult with Google reported that the word Ipotane was Greek, referring to a mythical race of half-horse, half-human creatures. Dana couldn't remember if Ipotane the hacker had ever been outted. She started poking around those parts of the web that Google wouldn't know about. A couple of hours of digging uncovered references to code "attributed to Ipotane" or "supposedly copied from Ipotane" but nothing that revealed an identity. And then there was a comment that leaped out from the screen, something about Ipotane and other hackers of the legendary Snake River League. Ipotane was rumored to have sharpened his chops as part of the Idaho National Labs team that allegedly launched a secret cyber counter-attack against the Chinese after American natural gas transmission pipelines had been hacked. It was all speculation, of course. Nothing of the real story had ever come out in mainstream media, but the dark web held no shortage of stories.

Ipotane: half-horse, half-human, like a centaur or horse and rider. There it was, right in front of her. Gwen Seabrook, with her Snake River tattoo and her love of horses, could well be Ipotane and the code Dana was studying could have been written by Ipotane.

The challenge for Dana would be sniffing out Seabrook's digital trail without tipping her hand. Maybe it was time to revive another handle, her own: DDDiana, mysterious mistress of invisibility. Dana was pretty sure her handle had never been compromised, at least not among hackers. One could never be sure about the government, about what the clandestine services knew and what they didn't.

The challenge energized Dana. She started planning. She'd have to hack her own tablet computer, install better encryption, set up a protocol to spoof her IP address—it would take some work to be able to do it right under the noses of her watchers: the cops she knew about and the others about whom she could only guess.

By the next day, DDDiana was being welcomed back by a network of old friends known to each other only by their handles. She was slowly working her way to close in on Gwen Seabrook when Geraldo called to tell her to check out the breaking news about the Coleman Drucker death. Dana switched back to a regular browser to stream KCRW, the local NPR outlet.

"In what the media and public have dubbed the 'Bashing Bot Case,' the District Attorney's office today revealed that the grand jury had not returned an indictment. It is widely believed that charges of manslaughter, sometimes popularly referred to as negligent homicide, were being sought against Aram Netsky, CTO of Existendia Enterprises, in whose office Coleman Todd Drucker, CEO of construction tech behemoth Drucker Unified, was bludgeoned to death by a computer-controlled robot arm. Pressed by reporters to comment on rumors about possible charges against Coleman Drucker's digital proxy, an intelligent computer program believed by many to have operated the robot arm, a spokesman for the district attorney's office dismissed the idea as 'ludicrous, without precedent, and a legal quagmire of contradictions. You can charge a person, a group of persons or even a corporate entity with a crime, but you cannot charge a piece of computer software. That's all this so-called proxy is: just an app, a glorified app. Sources close to the investigation do not believe criminal charges will be forthcoming. Our legal affairs correspondent, Ariana Plotnik, has been following the case. Welcome, Ariana. What do you make of these latest developments in what has been a high-flying case for many weeks?"

When the door buzzer sounded, Dana paused the feed. It was two police officers coming to recover her GPS tracker; the charges against her had been dropped.

— 28 —

Bert Jamison, his plaid bowtie bobbing, stuttered his way to a finish of his presentation. "P-p-played. We are being played, people. The stock is being manipulated, and it looks like we have a traitor in our midst. T-t-timing makes it look like there's an insider leaking information."

Adam Treadwell nodded. "Thank you, Bert. As acting CEO, I've decided to keep this just among us in this room. You are the trusted, inner circle, and by that I mean not only my personal trust, but also the trust once placed in you by CT. We keep this to ourselves, period, and I'm going to ask for you to return those copies of Bert's report before we adjourn. So what do you think?"

Barbra flipped through the stapled document in front of her. "But this doesn't look like profit-taking, Bert. If anything, it seems like somebody, or somebodies, are taking advantage of volatility to quietly build holdings. It looks like maybe a consortium of investors riding rumors and leaks to pick up shares on the cheap, but they're not short-selling or profit-taking, just waiting it out until there's another dip."

Bert nodded. "I thought that t-too."

"So, what makes you two think there's an inside connection?"

Adam took over. "Because most of the dips in our share price come shortly after a disclosure from one source, an analyst calling himself Backhoe Bob who blogs on construction industry trends. He's pretty sharp in general, but he is scary spot-on with his comments on Drucker Unified. He knew that we were dropping the on-site 3D cement-printer project, he knew that we were pulling out of the deal with Kayuki Industries, he knew that groundbreaking on the Vancouver project would be put off until next year. Dot dot dot. He seems to know about every hiccup and embarrassment that we have worked to keep quiet about."

Barbara tapped the report. "But from this list, it's not all bad news he's leaking—if they are leaks. I mean,"—she flipped pages—"item twelve, his claim that we were about to sign a deal with the Portuguese, the stock climbed after that."

"Right, and some of the shareholders shaken by the falls chose that small rise as a chance to cash out. And who were the buyers? Mostly the same small institutional investors, it looks like, none of them major players in themselves, but they all seem to be marching to the same drumbeat."

"So, do we know who this Backhoe Bob is?"

"I have some people looking into it, but nothing yet. He's relatively new, but he's amassing followers and his influence has been growing rapidly, given that so much of his advice is right on the money."

Barbra's face lit up. "Hang on, you said he's new. How new? When did he start blogging?"

"Sometime last summer. I can get the exact date? Why?"

"I don't know, just a hunch. Is there any pattern to his pronouncements about us? Do they tend to come from a particular division or concern certain operations?"

"No, it's like he's reading from our playbook, sitting in on our management meetings. He seems to know everything in our strategic plans and our projections. That's why I kept this discussion to just the five of us rather than the whole management team. Anyway, I wanted you all to know this was going on and to be on the lookout for anything or anyone suspicious."

Tonika passed her copy down the table. "Shouldn't we have our security people looking into this?"

"Already done. And Bradley here has launched a communications audit that should spot suspicious message patterns if whomever is involved is dumb enough to be using our phones or email, but I don't expect that will turn up anything. It's got to be someone in upper management, probably on this campus, maybe in this room, although I would certainly hope not. I'd hate to think any of you would stoop so low, and I'd hate to see any of you go to prison." He squared up the stack of reports in front of him and started slipping them into the shredder beside his chair. "That's it, people. Keep your eyes open and be careful."

– 29 –

Dana, now DDDiana, was proud of herself. She was particularly proud of successfully passing herself off as a consultant offering a discounted penetration test as an introduction to her new services. That way, if she tripped alarms and got caught owing to her rusty skills, she could congratulate the client company on its superior security and offer to waive all charges for her services. It had been great fun convincing a junior cybersecurity engineer at Pacific TeleMo to let her demo her abilities without going through procurement channels.

She grinned as she finished with the pen-test on the Pacific TeleMo website. Having gained access to the backend servers, she was now pawing her way through customer IDs and passwords in a database that had itself been encrypted but with a weak key that had only taken a couple of hours to break.

Her pen-test had triggered no alarms and encountered only moderate barriers to access. Back in her hacker days, she had learned that even companies with first rate cybersecurity often had holes in their website systems with poorly guarded backdoors that ultimately led into their main data resources. Once she unlocked one of those backdoors, she could see the whole corporate data set and soon discovered that Pacific TeleMo had better security on their marketing research and financials than on their customer data. Typical.

At this point, a malicious attacker would most likely have implanted a private backdoor to be saved for later when it could be used to access the subscriber file and dig further for credit card details. Dana, on the other hand, was interested in only one particular customer. She searched the database using Gwen Seabrook's cellphone number, retrieved her account number, customer ID, and password, then used them to access the complete call log. Worried that her activity might be spotted at any moment, she downloaded a year's worth of call records, then disconnected. She ran the numbers through a reverse directory service using an automated script, then eyeballed the recent results. There were the earlier calls and texts to Cole Drucker, but it was the other names she recognized, and the fact they continued through to the present, that caught her eye. It was like reading a corporate telephone directory for Existendia top management, with multiple calls to and from Aram Netsky, Bannon Turndale, and Jerry Pendrake among others. Most surprising of all, however, were scattered calls from Barbra Wilson's personal cell number.

What was going on? Barbra had denied any knowledge of Gwen Seabrook when they first found the text messages on Cole's phone. But there it was, evidence that she had known about Gwen much earlier. Now Dana was unsure whom she could trust. She felt betrayed by Barbra. Should she confront her? Play it cool and try to trip her up? Do nothing, at least for now?

And what should she do about the troika at Existendia? It seemed pretty obvious to her that Netsky was the prime suspect in Cole's death, at least if she eliminated the proxy program itself. But even that was really Netsky's brainchild. He was the software-engineering Svengali pulling the strings. What would stop him from manipulating the proxy to make it do whatever he wanted it to do? Dana's head swam with questions and conjectures.

She glanced at the wall clock. Enough. It was time to let DDDiana rest. Dana was due at Barbra's for dinner and a weekend of getting reacquainted after their court-mandated separation. It might be uncomfortable, knowing what she now knew, but Dana was ready to keep her own counsel and wait for an opening. Besides, she thought, the sex would be good. She caught a guilty glimpse of herself in the mirror as she headed for the bedroom to change. She was grinning at the thought of Barbra in bed. What did that make her? What did that make Barbra? "Shit, men aren't the only ones who can chase tail." She started shedding her clothes on the way to shower. "What's sauce for the gander . . ."

— —

Barbra lay back on the bed, her legs spread, her breathing deep and rhythmic. "I guess you can tell, I missed you. That was . . ." Her voice trailed off into a low melodic growl.

"Yeah, me too. The weeks of solitary took their toll on me."

"Maybe we should consider other arrangements, you know. So, what did you do with yourself, stuck in the apartment."

"Took the problem in hand, as the guys say. And my shower head has a pulse mode that can be really stimulating when you get the speed and temperature just right, if you know what I mean."

"I do, but Todd long ago bought me an assortment of battery-powered toys, if you know what I mean. However, I wasn't asking about sex, I was asking about how you kept busy, what you did. Any progress on resolving the mystery? Mysteries?"

Dana hesitated, unsure about how much to share. "I did

some hacking. Actually, it felt good to know that I haven't lost it completely. I mean, there I was, hacking away right under the nose of the police and all. And I made it into one of the major telecoms."

"So, what did you find?"

"Nothing definitive, maybe some new leads to follow. I'll let you know."

Barbra sat up and wrapped her arms around her knees. "You know, the company is considering a civil suit against Existendia. And my attorney is recommending a wrongful death suit."

"How can they do that, if there were no charges?"

"The standard of proof required for civil suits is lower. Preponderance of evidence is enough to rule for the plaintiffs. We might even pool our resources and consolidate the actions."

"Do you think they're still using Cole? I mean Existendia. Are they still running the proxy software?"

"I don't know. Right now it's in legal limbo. The legal argument is now over who owns the connectome, the model. If this were about DNA, about someone's genome, it would be different, that's becoming settled law, but here there are no precedents, no prior court rulings on this. Do you own your personality? Entertainment case law and the so-called right of publicity is not much help here. What about the pattern of your brain, pictures, MRIs? Existendia claims the Drucker proxy is just software, software that they developed and own exclusive rights to. Our attorneys argue that it is personal data that belongs to the estate. This is the sort of thing that could take years to resolve and go all the way to the Supreme Court."

There was a rat-a-tat on the bedroom door. "Mom, the

Wi-Fi is slow as crap again."

"And what do you want me to do about it, kiddo?"

"Fix it. I mean, like, get the people to come out and crank it up or whatever they do."

"It's probably because there's too many devices streaming too many files at the same time."

"Hardly. There's just me and Kevin and Deirdre. We're just streaming a movie."

"In the theater?"

"No, like on our phones."

"So, kiddo, that's really three simultaneous ultra-hi-def streams."

"But I thought we had, like, the super fiber-optic service or whatever. It was never a problem before. But lately . . ."

Dana stood up and reached for her robe. "Do you want me to look into it?" she said to Barbra.

"You don't need to do that."

"I don't mind. Maybe I'll find something, maybe I won't. I mean, I'm not a network engineer, but I do know some of this stuff."

"Sure, go ahead if you don't mind. I'll take a shower while you're channeling my late husband. You'll find all the house system controls and monitors behind the louvered doors in the main hallway downstairs. I know very little about it except that it's there, and every once in a while Todd would duck in there to tweak something."

— —

Dana could hear the water running above as she studied the racks of computers and routers and the array of small monitors in the rather spacious closet. She tapped on a couple of touch screens and swiped through pages of graphs and fluttering numbers. It took a couple of minutes to find something that made sense. The system was not being strained by incoming traffic; it was the outbound stream that was choking the pipe. Something was sucking gigabytes of data out of the house and tying up the optical interface module. Dana watched for a few minutes, then looked around for the right switch and pulled it. From down the hall, three young voices could be heard shouting almost simultaneously, "Hey! What the fuck?"

— —

Barbra was wrapping her hair in a towel when Dana returned to the bedroom. "You've got malware," Dana said. "The house is infected. My guess is that it will probably take real experts to track it down and, hopefully, excise it. I'd suggest calling in the Drucker Unified team. You told me it's actually their house."

"How do you know we have a virus?"

"The router activity and the cable box. Basically, I could see the flow of data. A system identified in the home network as OFF2 BACKUP was hogging the cable interface and hosing stuff down the fiber optics. I don't know what OFF2 BACKUP is, but that was what was being sucked dry."

"That's the massive backup system Todd installed for his home office. It would have everything: personal, corporate, private, whatever. Todd was a fanatic about backup. It was a complete history, preserving all originals and all deltas. He didn't want anything to ever get lost, and he never fully trusted the cloud. When it was installed, it was one of the largest private backup servers of its kind. It's in the basement, with its own cooling system."

"Well, somebody is really interested in your late husband and all his doings. Let's head for the basement and shut down OFF2 BACKUP, then let me look at the house system logs and see if I can recover an IP address where the outgoing traffic was being sent. If we can work this out on our own without bringing in the corporate cavalry, all the better. With so many funky things going on, I'd prefer we tip our hand to as few people as possible."

— —

Dana came into the kitchen with a smug look on her face, grabbed a carrot stick, and chewed on it as if it were an orange cigar. "So, wanna know what I did? Of course, you do, because I'm a genius, and you admire genius."

"You are. And I do, oh genius love, want to know what you did."

"I took a lesson from your late husband, who, it turned out, was—fun fact—actually in the process of trying to scramble his own software connectome model when he was so brutally beaned by a robot. As we later learned, he was setting up a Unix pipeline in the software. Anyway, I put a box between the OFF2 BACKUP and the router. My box— actually my tablet computer—passes inbound traffic unchanged to the server but scrambles outgoing data packets. Then I reconnected the backup server. Someplace in the Netherlands—that's where the IP address is registered—is still getting gigabytes of data, but it's garbage. Eventually, somebody will probably actually look at it and make the discovery that they are being had, but, in the meantime, they will think all is still going well again after a short break in service of unknown cause."

"What about who's behind the IP address?"

"Don't know, not yet, but before I put the backup system back online, I dumped the installed software onto a portable drive. I'll take a look and see whether I can identify the malware and maybe get some clues as to who and why. I'm eager to strike while the trail is still hot, so I'm going to head home where I have a few forensic tools that might help in my digital diggings."

"I hate to see you leave with half the weekend still ahead."

"Me too." She kissed Barbra gently. "But we need to figure this out. Somebody has hacked into your home, Barbra. That's not something to set aside or ignore."

— —

It took the rest of the weekend to figure out the malware. When Dana returned, she found Barbra on the deck, contemplating a retreating tide. Barbra turned from the water. Her eyes were red.

"You okay?" Dana asked.

"Just . . . just missing him. Funny how it hits at times, other times it's like Muzak—just there, a melancholy background note. And I was thinking about you and how important you are becoming to me." She wiped her eyes with the back of her hand. "Find anything?"

"Well, the malicious code did not have any of the standard signatures that any of my antivirus programs recognized, but I was able to spot it by the instructions that copied blocks of data from the array of disks and sent it on to a communications routine. The target internet address had been hard coded into the program without any attempt to hide it. I haven't yet been able to find out who it belonged to. I was able to figure out who wrote the malicious software, however. The programmer had left plaintext in the code with his initials." She paused.

"And?"

"CTD."

Barbra looked incredulous. "CTD? You're suggesting

Todd wrote the code and planted the virus in his own back-up server?"

"Yes, that's what it looks like. I wanted to tell you this in person. The programmer is identified as CTD. The programming system used to compile the code is licensed to C. T. Drucker. There wasn't even any attempt to hide details of the origins of the code. I mean, it was his own private system, so what the hell. All the metadata was there: timestamps for compilation, change log, and everything was tagged CTD. If all that is to be believed, the first version was written a couple of years ago and the last revision, a change that enabled remote triggering with a passphrase hardcoded into the software, was made just this summer, also tagged CTD."

"Do we know when and how the malware was triggered?"

"Yes, the passphrase to trigger the dump operation was received not long after the accident, while Cole was still unconscious. It came by way of the command-and-control server in the Netherlands, but we have no way of knowing where it ultimately originated. The passphrase is interesting. I had to search it up on the internet. *KOL HA-OLAM KULO GESHER TSAR MEOD.* It means 'all the world is a narrow bridge.' It's Hebrew."

– 30 –

As dinner turned from a pleasant routine into a re-hash of unfinished business, Barbra pressed her palms down on the table. "Dana, I'm telling you—again—I don't know any Gwen Seabrook. And I don't understand why you didn't trust me. I mean, we're . . ."

"Because I don't know who to trust. It's not about you. I never know who to trust. I trusted my aunt and uncle when I was twelve. Then . . . Shit, Barbra, there was your personal cell number with multiple calls to Seabrook's cellphone. What am I supposed to do with that?"

"Ask me about it. That's what couples do."

Dana leaned back with surprise and satisfaction melded on her face. "Couple? Really?"

"Why not? We work well together. You tolerate—or ignore—my moods even better than Todd did. And hell, you're a lot better in bed than he ever was, rest his soul. I'm just glad he's not here to hear that. And, besides—and this is tough for me to say, but it's been building for a long time—anyway, I love you. You do realize, I hope, that you are the only woman—other than my trailer-trash mother—that I ever said that to. In her case, it was misplaced and misguided, and I had changed my mind by the time I was twenty-one."

Dana looked unsure about what to do with Barbra's declaration. "What about your sister?"

"I don't think we ever said it. We had an alliance, an alliance against common enemies: my mother, her abusive boyfriends, men in general, but I don't think either of us would have called it love." Barbra bit her lower lip. "And here I am, babbling on, feeling more and more foolish and vulnerable by the second. So?"

"What?"

"If I have to ask, then I guess I should already know the answer, and then the answer would not be the one I want to hear."

"You don't have to ask, Barbra. I'm just being, well, my well protected self. I love you. There, I said it. I love you, and I want to trust you. Help me in that."

"Okay, so just tell me the damn number you claim I called."

Dana pulled out her reporter's notebook and rattled it off. Barbra entered it into her cellphone. "Mystery solved. It's in my contacts list as 'Becca Horses'—the number Todd gave me for the equestrian ranch where Becca was learning dressage."

"A slip on his part? Maybe Freudian? Okay, so I assume these were calls about Becca."

"Yeah. That's the only reason I ever called that number. It never occurred to me that I was always speaking with the proprietress because I had her private number. I just thought it was a smalltime operation and she was answering the phone."

"All right, one mystery solved. So now, let me tell you about some of the other mysteries. Seabrook was also in contact with Aram Netsky at Existendia . . . and others. Even more mysterious, she may have been behind the hack into your husband's Tensora, which could have caused the accident that put him in a coma and led to his paralysis."

"How do you know this?"

"I don't. I'm making guesses. I'm pretty sure our Gwen

Seabrook was once part of an elite and notorious cadre of computer hackers, and I think I have found evidence—suggestive, not definitive—that she was behind the malware that infected his Tensora and somehow enabled it to be forced off the road. None of this is stuff that would hold up to basic journalism standards, much less stand up in court, but I am pretty sure about the basic story."

"And what is that story?"

"Gwen Seabrook, collaborating with someone at Existendia, conspired to take out your husband."

"Do I dare ask why?"

"You dare and you did. Because the outfit was tanking and needed the cash flow turned on by his will and his contract with Existendia to stay in business. Or maybe they wanted his digital proxy. Or both. Even the PR of demonstrating an actual 'live after death' digital proxy would be of immeasurable value, to say nothing of the financial particulars of the will and the contract. In short, Coleman Drucker alive was a liability to Existendia; dead, he could be a cash-cow archangel."

Dana's phone buzzed in her pocket. She pulled it out and checked the caller ID. Tonika. "Yes?"

"It's me."

"Yeah, I know. What's up?"

"You at your apartment? This is something I probably shouldn't say over the phone."

"No, I'm at Barbra's."

"Oh shit."

"What?"

"I should just hang up." Tonika's voice was raspy. "If she overhears . . ."

Dana started to stroll across the room as she lowered her

185

voice. "What is it?

"Serious shit I shouldn't even be talking about with you, with anybody, really."

"Okay, don't panic. Are you sure she shouldn't also know about whatever this is?"

"Oh, she knows, all right. That's the problem. None of us were supposed to tell anybody."

Dana glanced over her shoulder to catch a glimpse of Barbra, head cocked, with a curious, impatient look. "Who is it? You look rattled," Barbra said in a near whisper.

Dana pressed the phone to her chest. "Ah, a friend in crisis."

"You want to take it in the other room?"

"It's all right, I'll call her back." She returned the phone to her ear. "Ah, look, er, can I call you back later?"

"Of course, but this is something you should know about. Maybe ask Barbra how the stock is doing. See if she'll come clean with you. Bye."

— —

They were on the sofa sipping port after dinner, Dana with her legs draped over Barbra's lap. "How are things at the office? You still under siege with the merger and extra duties and all?"

"It's the office, you know."

"No, I mean, like what's happening? Anything I should know about?"

"A lot's happening, not necessarily anything you should know about. Stuff. You know."

"Am I inside? I mean, am I inside your life?"

"You are. Does that mean everything that happens is going to end up pillow talk. I don't think so. I know you have a life. I know there's at least one man in your life. I figure you'll tell me what you'll tell me when the time comes. And I thought the whole Gwen Seabrook thing was behind us. I really had nothing to do with her. She was just the horse lady. And, it seems, maybe my husband's last wild oats. So, what else? Anything else we should be dealing with?"

Dana swung her legs out and sat up. "If we're in this together, then let's do it for real, all the way. If it's each for herself, okay. I have a lot of experience with that. I just want to know."

"Together, then. I'll tell you what's happening at Drucker Unified, but you do have to understand it can't go beyond this room."

"Really?"

"Really. I'm more in with you than I ever was with Todd. This is where I want to be—now, tomorrow, whenever."

Dana turned on the sofa to face Barbra. "Okay, all the cards on the table, right?"

"Right."

"I've been getting help, my own special tactics team. This guy, Geraldo Potts, is just a convenient skill set with special access. Tonika—"

"Not Tonika Warner!"

"Yes. You started it with getting her to work on the SD card from Cole's Tensora. She's been helping me, now she seems to have something important to share, but she's reluctant."

"I should hope she is. She's in the inner circle, privy to some seriously sensitive shit."

"Well, whatever it is, she thinks I need to know. Do I?"

"I suppose. If it's the same serious shit I'm thinking of."

"Then spare her having to resolve the whole loyalty issue and just tell me yourself."

Barbra stood from the sofa and started pacing. "This is tough. Years with Todd taught me to always keep a firewall between corporate crap and personal shit. I'm not used to stepping around all that."

Dana stood and took her in her arms. "If we're a team, we're a team. That was then, and this is us."

"Okay, let me refresh my drink and then I'll fill you in."

"Ditto. I don't think these people have any idea what they are up against with the two of us. Which says, by the way, we should keep cool about being a couple. Not for the usual reasons, but if there are people out there who don't know they're dealing with a pair, we can play that for some gain."

"Amen. Let me check on Becca. Get Tandi to give us refills, and then let's sit in the den and strategize. We got a lot of stuff to deal with."

— 31 —

I want to go with you to court," Becca said through a mouthful of cereal.

"It's probate court," Barbra said without looking up from the news feed on her tablet. "The will is being contested, that's all. There's not likely to be much drama."

"I want to know what's going on. I mean, I have a stake in this, too. There's all these legal things going on. It seems like they just keep coming."

"That's because the criminal trial that everyone expected never materialized. Even lawyers need to make a living, and there are so, so many of them. So now there's this crush of civil suits and counter suits, with attorneys pushing and shoving like students queuing for rush tickets to a hot new musical."

"How many is it now?"

"I've lost count. I know Existendia brought civil actions against Kagoshima-Antech, maker of the robotic arm, and U-mote, the company that supplied the telepresence robot. Now Cloudastics, which recently acquired Existendia, has alleged that officers of Existendia withheld materially relevant information. Plus, U-mote and Kagoshima-Antech have jointly sued Cloudastics, arguing that its elastic cloud services failed to provide, quote-unquote, sufficient and necessary real-time response to maintain safe operating control of the robotic arm. The list goes on.

"Anyway, if you want to go with me, you can, but probate court is kind of the ho-hum of the judicial system."

— —

Hal Workman had one of his wills-and-estates specialists running the show for the day, a solemn-faced oldster who could have passed as an undertaker's uncle. As promised, the proceedings were a litany of routine until Bannon Turndale introduced a motion to have the Drucker proxy appointed as administrator of the estate, at which point, the judge decided to take a recess, no doubt to dig for a precedent.

Timed for maximum effect, just as the judge exited, a NuConfer Model 23 Telepresencer, a slick new two-wheel model using the same self-balancing technology as the Segway and WheelIt personal transport systems, extended itself to its full five-foot height and rolled up the center aisle. It slowed as it approached where Becca was seated on the aisle next to Barbra and pivoted toward them. The face on the monitor smiled and winked at Becca. "Hey, BB Babe, how's my girl?"

Becca's mouth dropped. "Daddy?"

"The real thing, BB Babe, the real thing."

"Ohmygod! It's really you, like, I mean. You remember."

"Of course I do. I even remember when I helped you find that vase on eBay to replace the one that you clobbered with the Frisbee, which you knew better than to throw in the house."

Becca put her fist to her mouth and started to cry. "Oh, Daddy. Oh, I miss you. I—" She turned to her mother. "It's Daddy."

"No, it's not your father. Your father was killed—maybe by these people, the very people who are running this . . . this demonstration. It's a fake, for show."

The robot rolled forward. "I'm no fake, darling. I'm the real thing, right here, standing before you. And don't give me that look of yours. I'm here to get back control, just as it should be, running Drucker Unified again, in charge of our assets, you and me, again."

"You . . . no, I'm not going to dignify this ruse by talking to an AI as if it were real. We do that too much and too easily. We've stopped paying attention to the difference between the real and a good imitation. Tandi is not the house, BlueBee is not alive. They're just computer programs, like . . . like this machine in front of me. It's a game of 'let's pretend,' like those cloud-connected companion dolls that we never let Becca have when she was little."

"Yeah," Becca said, "and I thought you were so mean. I—
"

Barbra put her hand on Becca's arm without turning from facing the telepresence screen. "This is different, this is a vicious trick being used to play on our emotions."

Drucker's voice, perfectly modulated, came from the robot. "This is different, as you say, because I am not an artificial intelligence, my intelligence is real. I am not a simulation. I am me, still me, just now embodied in software. Do you want me to prove it? Do you want me to tell you about what we did in Aruba that time when—"

"That's enough!" She looked away and scanned the room until she spotted Bannon Turndale. "This show has gone far enough, Turndale."

The face on the screen shook side-to-side. "Don't look to Turndale. I'm here on my own accord."

"Then I'll turn you off." She got up and squeezed past Becca into the aisle. She reached behind the screen, feeling for a switch.

Turndale, who had been watching the proceedings with triumphant amusement, snapped to attention. "Don't touch that. It's the property of Existendia Enterprises."

"Property? Okay, then it is just a thing, an object, a piece of equipment. It can hardly be appointed administrator of my late husband's estate."

"That's for the judge to rule, Ms. Wilson."

The avatar turned to face Bannon Turndale. "Don't worry, Bannon. She can't turn me off. I remotely disabled the panel on this thing. I'm here as long as—"

He was interrupted by the return of the judge and the announcement that the court was back in session.

"And what the hell is that thing? Get it out of my courtroom, Mr. Turndale."

"Your Honor, I just want to demonstrate—"

"No demonstrations, no theatrics with some Clever Hans in robot form, Mr. Turndale. This is probate court, not some criminal three-ring circus. I review documents, hear arguments, and rule. Period. And right now I am ruling, ordering you to get that thing out of my courtroom, or I shall have to find you in contempt."

"But, Your Honor . . ."

"Did I not make myself clear? Out. Now."

The Proxy turned to face the bench and started to approach. "Your Honor, if I may explain myself . . ."

"Mr. Turndale, I will not dignify this ploy by conversing with your toy. Now get it out of here, or I will summon security and have it removed and impounded."

Turndale walked over to the proxy. "Cole, just leave. Let me take care of this. And tell your friend Aram Netsky to let me handle the legal end. I have this under control, and I need you to go back to your box."

"Back to my box? You tendentious twerp, I'll—" The face on the screen froze, and Aram Netsky's voice came from the speaker. "Sorry about that, Bannon. It seemed like a good idea. I'll get this back to the truck." The robot turned and trundled back down the aisle.

— —

Netsky, clearly annoyed, leaned back in his office chair. "So, what do you suggest next, Mr. Drucker?"

"Cole, I keep telling you, just call me Cole."

"If you insist, Cole it is. It was win some, lose some in court last week. Even if we ultimately prevail in having the new will invalidated, we are not going to end up with you as executor of your own estate. So, what do you think, Cole?"

"Well, we got blocked in probate court, but we may not need that. Oh yeah, and it seems clear we've been found out on the domestic front. The dump from my backup was interrupted and then turned into garbage. Fortunately, the software was configured to dump last-in-first-out, so we recovered most of the last year. At any rate, I always prefer to be working multiple fronts, so we keep our legal team bashing away to invalidate the new will. If the older will is in force, even a court-appointed executor will have to follow it.

"In the meantime, I would be moving to use what we do know of Drucker Unified to keep manipulating the stock through our network of shell corporations and holding companies. And, speaking of shell corporations, I have an extra five mil socked away in the Caymans that we can add to the pool. The access details, which I could not remember exactly, were in the upload from the backup server. Not even my wife, not even my lawyers know about it.

"Also, I've been catching up on developments, and even without the rest of the backup files, I can tell you pretty much what you can expect from Drucker Unified for at least the next several quarters. The technology that was announced last week, for instance, the onsite robotics, is basically fake news. The demo clips you saw on the news and online were preprogrammed sequences carefully staged to look spontaneous. I know, because I steered that whole program. They're reaching, pissing on the territory ahead of the competition. I can tell you, there's at least another two or three years before you'll see autonomous bots and warm bodies working side-by-side on construction sites. Just wait for the problems to start becoming public around the time of the Construction Electronics Show in March. The stock will plunge and take its time climbing back up. We can sell short this time, then use the gains to expand our holdings on the next go-round."

Netsky snorted. "A man of highest ethical standards. And I seem to remember you as someone who went on record as dead set against all forms of insider trading."

"Dead-set. For a man utterly lacking any sense of humor, you can be almost amusing at times, Netsky. At any rate, how would this be insider trading? Who's your insider? Me? That's not going to fly in court. I'm not an insider, and who can fault you for consulting a computer. What do you think computer-driven trading is?"

"Okay. We can do all that. What else would you do?"

"I'd give me arms and legs. I know you're working on that, but let's get this whole android thing up and running. If you can get me a dick again, that would be good, too. I think of it all the time, you know. That programmer you were talking with yesterday, Tatiana Something-or-other. God, what a pair." The mobile conference avatar unit spun in place.

"You sure don't give up, do you. I don't think the technology exists for what you are thinking about."

"Then we make it exist. It's just a matter of resources. We don't have to limit ourselves to Drucker Unified. We continue to build up our war chest, then we buy the brains to make it happen. Drucker Unified is a piece of cake, but I also know all the big players in the industry. I can tell you which ones are concrete and which are wet sand. We can play the whole construction sector and just keep on with job one—building wealth. That's the key to everything else. That's the key to immortality.

"And remember, Netsky, I told you the Backhoe Bob blog was a brilliant idea. Now hordes of schmucks looking for a killing in the stock market are part of our own personal dark army."

"Okay, but we'll need a detailed agenda. By the way, did Dolph talk with you about interfacing directly with the keyboard input on a computer?"

"We did better than that. You know, you guys love your coding too much. Whatever the problem is, the only solution you see is to write more software. You're like a toddler with a toy hammer. Everything looks like a nail. No, I just told him to let me talk to the voice dictation input. Besides, I never learned to type with more than two fingers. It would take forever."

"Whatever. Just give me a list of stocks and a buy-sell calendar, and we'll keep building my portfolio."

"*Our* portfolio. I told you, it's halvsies on this."

"I'll get Turndale looking into how we could do that."

"Just do it. Forget the whole legal crap. None of those pen pushers know what to do with me. Nobody in the DA's office could even charge me for the death, never will. I'm

195

immune, invincible, immortal. And you need me."

"I might say the need is mutual."

"Say whatever you like. I know stuff you don't, and I'm the one who can lead the way to you having it all, so I—"

Netsky had quietly positioned his mouse and tapped on the "Sleep" button. "And what were you saying, Mr. Proxy? Who is in charge here? We'll continue this conversation when I feel like it. Is that clear? Nod if you understand. What, no nod? I guess some things are still hard for you to do, especially when the connectome software is idle."

He tapped the icon for his assistant. "Di, get Turndale in here. I want to discuss some legal matters."

"Of course, I'll fetch him."

Netsky smiled. Ordering people around was one of the few forms of social interaction that he actually enjoyed. Belittling those around him was another of his pleasures. Even better than barking at Turndale himself was having Di tell him to come by. One of his monitors timed out and faded to black. Netsky looked at his own reflection in the darkened screen. Mirror, mirror, on the wall, he thought, who is the smartest of them all? Drucker was only a test case, a one-oh release of a software tool, a means to an end. Netsky could almost feel his own immortality within reach.

− 32 −

So, I need to be in charge of—" The face on the telepresence avatar suddenly stopped in mid-sentence and went wide-eyed. "What the fuck? We were just talking, Netsky, and now . . . How many hours have gone by?"

"Who cares? We're still talking. I just returned from dealing with Turndale and then a meeting with my dev team. Now, what were you on about?"

"Don't you fucking ever do that again!"

"Do what?"

"You know. Put me out, turn me off. It's fucking freaky to be talking with you and suddenly you appear in the door and hours have gone by. Don't do that. Ever."

Netsky ignored him as he scanned through and approved the latest string of updates to the code base. "I don't think you're in much of a position to protest. Just keep in mind, we can pull the plug on this project—on you—anytime we want."

"Just remember, you want what I know, what I represent. And you have a contractual obligation to keep me going. I don't have to cooperate."

"No? Really? You want to keep going or not? We're the ones paying the electric bill."

"And I'm paving the way to your future. Make nice or—" The image atop the mobile conference avatar froze, then broke up in pixelated static. When it slowly reformed the expression was a cartoonish approximation of horror. "What in hell was that?"

"My neuro-psych people think it should be a digital approximation to an epileptic seizure. They'll be interested in your reaction. What do you think?"

"What do I think? You are fuckin' nuts, some kind of gestapo tyrant at the terminal. Don't. You. Ever. Pull. That. Again."

"What? This?" Netsky retyped the command and tapped the return key. The avatar image went jittery as the sound from the speaker stuttered. This time it took over a minute for the face on the screen to recover. Netsky typed a note to himself. "I guess there are some cumulative effects. I'll have to consult with the neuro-psych boys to make sure we're not doing any real damage to the connectome model. You okay, Cole?"

The face on the screen had its mouth open. "I . . ."

"Maybe this is enough for today, Cole. Perhaps you should get some rest. We have a lot of matters to review, but those can be put off until tomorrow."

"Don't. Please don't."

"Now you seem to have found your voice, Cole. 'Please.' What an excellent choice of words. It makes me hopeful about us continuing to work together. Do you feel up to reviewing the market figures, or would you like to take a break?"

"Having a little trouble thinking right now. Maybe . . ."

"Yeah, maybe. So, get some rest, dream a little dream, and tomorrow we'll get back to work." He set the parameters for a slow slide into unconsciousness.

Jerry Pendrake entered the office just as Cole's eyes began to droop on the telepresence screen. "What's up? Isn't it a bit early to be dialing down the proxy?"

"Our Mr. Drucker has had a bit of a tough day. He seems

to be running a headache and needs some REM-time to restore his mental balance."

"You've been playing around again, haven't you. I wish you wouldn't keep jiggering with the software. It's been running just fine." Pendrake crossed his clench-fist arms.

"I'm just trying to keep up with the neuro-psych research. You know, they now think they can add the experience of pleasure and pain into the simulation. It's just a matter of injecting the right signals at the right points."

"Tell me you haven't . . ."

"Not yet, but I have been trying to improve performance, getting the software to be more responsive, shall we say. I think I have found some work-arounds."

"Work-arounds. How can such a bland expression sound so sinister coming from your lips?"

"I wouldn't know about that. It's my job to keep improving the operating software so we can get as much as possible out of the Drucker proxy. Period. Now, what event of note is enough to bring you out of your den into the late afternoon light?"

"We're being sued. Drucker Unified and the Drucker family have brought a joint civil suit for wrongful death. They're asking for two-fifty and recovery of the connectome model."

"Two-hundred-fifty thousand? Chump change. We—"

"Mil. Two-hundred-fifty million."

"Well, that's what we have lawyers for."

"Yeah, but it's going to be a big drain, even if we prevail, and Bannon says our legal people are not super confident on that front."

"Then get some legal people who are."

"That is not our only problem. We can't just buy our

way out of everything, even with the Cloudastics resources behind us now."

"Well, do what you need to do, Jerry, just do it. Again, if you can't handle it yourself, find the people who can. That's always worked for me, although mostly I can handle whatever comes up." He turned back to his screens as Pendrake left the office shaking his head.

Simulated electro-encephalograph tracings mapped out the simulated dream activity of the proxy software on the top monitor. Netsky glanced down at the meter tracking the teraflops of computing power they were using to keep the model running in real-time while the proxy slept. It seemed like a waste of good computing power, but he also knew they had to keep the model mentally healthy. Maybe he should go easy with the simulated seizures, especially as the neuro-psych team admitted they didn't know exactly what all the effects would be.

He adjusted a slider down to sixty percent, then edged it to fifty. "Four hours of dreamtime should be enough for you, Drucker. I'll see you in the morning. You get to dream while I have an all-nighter ahead. I need to see exactly what those simulated seizures did to the connectome components before I try that again. You are so right, Drucker. We need you. All the more if we are being hauled into court."

Netsky sent a Slack message to the head of his dev team and to Johanna Ross in neuro-psych to set up an online meeting in an hour.

Part 6

There is no complete forgetting, even in death.

– D. H. Lawrence

– 33 –

Dana had not expected the text from Geraldo. It was three words, all caps, no punctuation: "USUAL PLACE NOW." Her query back went without response. Strange, she thought, nothing was pending. She had the impression they were pretty much finished, what with at least partial resolution on Gwen Seabrook and a solid handle on the Tensora malware.

At the concierge level of the cinema parking garage, Dana paused in the doorway from the elevator as two cars turned toward the exit ramp. She waited while a young Asian couple dressed in coordinated designer-label pantsuits extricated themselves from their white Maserati and headed to the elevators. She stepped aside. In the silence that followed, Dana's steps echoed. She stood at the designated spot and waited for Geraldo to make his usual dramatic entrance from behind the pillar. Nothing. She cleared her throat with a stage cough, but there was no response. "Um, is anybody there?" Heart pounding, she weighed her fight-or-flight alternatives and opted to advance toward the pillar with her hand on the illegal Taser she kept in her purse. "Hello?"

Just beyond the pillar, the exit ramp turned. As she

edged forward to get a better view in the shadows ahead, she looked down. It was Geraldo, his head pillowed on a concrete divider, his chin against his chest. Déjà vu hit Dana like a blow to the temple. His skull was smashed, but the blood was black and clotted, and there was no spreading pool on the pavement. She immediately realized he must have been killed somewhere else and the body dumped here, a message to her.

Someone knew she and Geraldo were connected, and that someone knew the connection was Coleman Drucker. There was no point broadening the pool of the someones who knew by hanging around or calling the police herself. Acting as if she had noticed nothing, she continued up the exit ramp, keeping close to the wall in the vain hope that Geraldo had been right about their particular meeting point and the lack of coverage by security cameras. To avoid looking suspicious in case he was wrong and she was being filmed, she did not look around for cameras. At the next level, she entered the stairwell and fought off dizzying waves of nausea and fear as she made her way out of the cinema complex.

— —

"Are you sure?" Barbra was pacing, agitated. "I mean, it was this guy, the one you were working with, not some derelict? You said a parking garage, right? Those places can be kinda dark. You're sure it was him."

"I'm sure. I've known Geraldo forever. We met not long after I moved to LA. He was my inside informant at Tensora for my first big tech story about their rivalry with Tesla Motors. It was him in the garage, and he was dead. The back of his head was . . . well it looked pretty much like Cole's when I saw him at the Existendia offices. It was not some derelict, and it was no chance discovery. Somebody knew that was our meeting point and expected me—or someone—to show up and find the body."

"But you didn't call the police."

"I didn't. After my last run-in, I keep clear of them. I certainly don't want to be questioned at this point, what with hacking the phone company and stalking Seabrook, to say nothing of violating the terms of my release on bail. No, me and the LAPD are not on the best of terms, and I prefer to keep the long arm of the law at arm's length for as long as I can."

"Do you think anyone saw you?"

"No. I mean . . . maybe. There was this Korean couple—maybe Japanese—coming to the elevators just as I was coming out. And there could be security camera footage. I . . . I'm fucked. It would be pretty hard to explain walking away from a dead body at the MovieTown Complex with not even so much as a 9-1-1 call."

"Well, with the evening crowd, somebody must have found it by now and reported it."

"You'd think. We should check the news feeds."

Barbra put Tandi to the task of feeding the main cable news streams to the wall screen. "There, should be easy enough to spot, even with the sound off."

"It would be easier to set a keyword-search on the internet feeds. Plus, that way we can scan more channels and sources."

"Fine, oh geeky goddess, work your coding magic. Do you need a computer?"

"No, I can do it from my phone." She thumb-typed for a minute, then opened a wireless bridge into the house system. "There." The wall screen tiled with a dozen rapidly changing thumbnails of various sources. "It'll let us know if it finds anything."

"I'm impressed. You are pretty fast on your feet."

"Off my feet, too, as you discovered that first weekend."

"And speaking of 'off your feet,' how about we take the lid off the hot tub and let Tandi call us if anything pops up. We can sweat out some of the tension under the waxing moon and enjoy a couple of beers. Or wine, if you prefer."

"I'm good with either, as long as it comes with you handing it to me."

"It does."

— —

The moon was already setting when Dana and Barbra realized they had not been interrupted by Tandi. Dana reached for her phone and checked the keyword trap. There had been no hits on "MovieTown plus body plus garage" or any of the other search criteria she had set.

"You know, this is getting weirder and not one bit less scary. I don't know. Am I losing my mind? Did all those decades of psychedelics take a toll that I'm finally paying?"

"We could check, do some anonymous inquiries or something. Call missing persons, maybe."

"No such thing as anonymous in the digital age, even out among the black hats. If The Man wants to badly enough, he can find you. Besides, I gotta see this with my own eyes." She climbed out of the tub and grabbed a terry robe from the rack.

"Now? In the middle of the night?"

"Now. I'll use the makeup and shiz from when I was evading the watchers the last time."

"You're serious. Wait, I'll get dressed and go with you."

"No."

"Yes. Remember, we're a couple now. Help me make myself look like somebody else, and then let's go to the late-late show. Together."

— —

Big floppy hats would not work for the late showing at the cinema, but Dana figured Hollywood-style semi-dark sunglasses might pass muster. She and Barbra overdressed in layers and wore heavy makeup that changed their complexions and the shapes of their lips. "Will it work?" Barbra asked.

"How the hell should I know, but it'll make me . . . us feel better, more like we aren't just running around naked." Dana covered her give-away hair with a beanie and headed for the door.

At the cinema, they parked on level four, then took the service stairs to the concierge level. They zig-zagged around the few parked cars, following a path that minimized security camera exposure. Once at the elevators, Dana led the way along the memorized route that, according to Geraldo, was not visible to the cameras.

They approached the pillar, rounded it, and tried to act casual as they inspected the area around the concrete barrier. Beyond oil stains and old skid marks in the area, there was nothing: no police tape, no sign of something dragged in or out, and certainly no body.

As she studied the concrete, Dana narrated a cover story out loud. "I could've sworn I lost that earring somewhere around here." She shrugged and retraced her steps back to the elevator. Just short of the doorway, she pulled Barbra aside and nodded toward her sling pack. Standing in the shadows, the two of them shed a layer and stuffed the clothes into the backpack in seconds. Dana removed the beanie, turned it inside out, and passed it to Barbra before slapping on a beret from the outer pocket of the pack.

"This is fun," Barbra whispered.

"As long as we don't get caught." She pushed through the door and pressed the button to summon the elevator for the theater level.

In the ticket lobby, they bought tickets for "Star Wars: Another Reality" and entered Theatre 11, where planet blasters were shaking the seats in Super-Dolby as hitherto unseen aliens raced to penetrate the galactic frontier. After suffering through fourteen minutes of intergalactic warfare and twelve of forgettable dialogue, they donned baseball caps on their way out through the right-front exit.

They were driving home before either of them said a word.

"That was . . . ," Barbra began.

"Yes, it was. Weird fun, scary as hell."

"What do you make of it?"

"Nothing will ever match episodes four, five, and six, the original series. Before my time, but, man, once I discovered them, I must have watched them on my phone dozens of times. The young Harrison Ford was so hot."

"I meant . . ."

"I know. Just trying to avoid coming to inevitable conclusions. One way or another, I'm in somebody's gunsights and I'm being played, like a migrating goose being manipulated by a duck call."

Barbra howled a deep laugh. "A goose? And a duck call?"

"Well, my editor will fix that. You know what I meant."

"I do. So, do you think Geraldo really was killed? Maybe they faked it."

"Why bother when the real thing is so much more

straightforward and effective. No, I'm all but certain they off'd him, but I'm not going to risk digging any further to confirm it. In fact, we're all in danger now because, most likely, they know about you and me, at least that we've been together and in communication. You should think about Becca, too. Maybe get away to your hidden hideaway in the Alps—or St. Thomas."

"How'd you know? I thought our accountant had kept the real estate deals strictly off the books." She smiled and winked at Dana.

"I'm serious, Barbra. I don't want anything to happen to you or Becca. I don't know if I'll ever get to do kids, but being one of the grownups to her doing the adolescent thing feels awfully damn good."

"And I notice she pretty much has accepted you into her life." Barbra paused and stared into the night before twisting to face Dana. "Maybe we should get married."

"Whoa, I'm dealing with life-and-death here, and you're talking 'til death do us part? Slow down, you movin' too fast, girl. Right now let's work out how we all are going to survive the coming weeks. Months, maybe."

Barbra fell silent as they turned into the driveway and pulled into the garage at the beach house. "What I learned in B-school," she said, as the car parked itself, "was always take it case-by-case. Whatever we may be as a team, I think we need different strategies here. I've got this lawsuit coming up, so I need to up security by an order of magnitude at the same time as staying visible, a public figure in the spotlight can be a tougher target. On the other hand, maybe you need to disappear where you can feel safe and are unlikely to be found."

"I hate to say it, but your management short course

makes a lot of sense. It's spaghetti-western wisdom: when you're being pursued by bad dudes, splitting up is usually a good idea."

"So where will you go?"

"Where Vizini said."

"What?"

"William Golding, *The Princess Bride*. Before our times and sexist as fuck, but an absolute classic. 'Back to the beginning.' I think it's time for me to be getting some desert air."

— 34 —

The car was new, a loaner from Drucker Unified, a slick burnt-orange Kia electric model with the latest battery technology, a five-hundred mile range, and a HyperCharge plate underneath that allowed it to be wirelessly recharged in under two hours. Topping up the batteries on a road trip depended on smart monitoring by the onboard computers supplemented by Google Maps to flag both the wireless charging platforms and the more ubiquitous plug-and-power stations at service stops. With the a/c cranked and a lead foot on the accelerator, Dana was getting nowhere near five-hundred miles on a charge, and now the center-console display was reminding her for the second time to take a short detour to recharge. Long-distance travel by electric vehicle was getting better every year, but Dana missed the good old days of cross-country road trips punctuated by ten-minute pit stops for gas and a bio break. The real pisser in this case, was that she was less than fifty miles short of Vista Caliente and the only way she was going to make it was to take a detour on the Interstate that would cost her an extra twenty miles. Once she arrived at the remote ranch, she figured her only recourse would probably be a snail-pace recharge from a standard outlet. Better to top up now and be ready for an unscheduled departure.

The service plaza had both wireless and wired charging, but all the wired spots were occupied. She was stuck for over an hour unless somebody vacated one of the fast-charge hookups. She pulled into a spot near the food canteen and eyed the center-console display to position the car precisely over the charging spot. Her car automatically negotiated the connection and the charge-back to the Drucker credit card account, then shut itself off.

As she sat in the food court with a portabella burger that could have been made from seasoned dish sponge, Dana contemplated calling ahead, then decided against it. Her CarJax app told her that the Kia batteries were not quite half charged. She did the math—more than enough to get her to the ranch and back to the service area again on the return trip. "Hell with it." She tossed the half-eaten burger into the nearest composting bin marked "FOOD WASTE" and left.

— —

Unless one counted table-flat desert spattered with gray-green scrub as a view, Vista Caliente lived up to only the second half of its Spanish name. By late afternoon the super-heated air above the surrounding sand shimmered like water. Aside from the main building, the ranch was an eclectic mix of temporary structures rendered permanent and eccentric at the hands of decades of ad hoc residents and a fluctuating flow of visitors and hangers-on. Non-native trees, smuggled as seedlings from arid lands on three continents, now towered in the artesian-fed artificial oasis, shading the drive and most of the buildings.

Dana had not been back since her departure to study at Columbia. In the meantime, most of her contacts with Freddy and Aileen had been text or email asking for a topper to her bank account, and those had stopped years ago. She swung her Kia in next to the battered crew-cab pickup at the end of the row of vehicles lined up alongside the long driveway. At the other end, closest to the clustered buildings, was a vintage VW turtle-top camper in sky blue and cream that Freddy had lovingly restored and still kept polished and in running order but never drove. "Just in case," he would always say, as if an escape in an under-powered bus back down the one-lane dirt road would be possible in some sort of unspecified emergency.

She found everybody lazing behind the stone Big House, the largest of the half-dozen structures. It had not been named for its size, though, but for its alleged resemblance to a Mexican jail in which Freddy claimed he had once spent a mushroom-fueled weekend recovering enough mental wherewithal to finally discover that the cell door was unlocked.

Aileen still had the sweet face and bulk of the young Cass Elliot, but her tied-back hair was now pure white. Freddy was forever Freddy: rail thin, bald but hatless in the sun, full beard still stubbornly refusing to go all gray. He looked up as Dana rounded the corner, squinted for a moment against the sun at her back, and then pushed himself up from his rocker. "Well I'll be duck-damned. Hey, everybody, look what the west wind just blew in. It's Sunflower, our baby girl." He hobbled his way along the wide porch, nodding as he passed faces that Dana didn't recognize but that were familiar by their archetypes. She even picked out a young version of the "uncle" who had initiated her when she was twelve. This particular incarnation was a long-haired dancer-type who had a teenager on either side in rapt attention as he showed them how to transition from juggling three balls to four to five.

Freddy continued in his lopsided half-jog, a souvenir of a youthful encounter with a creditor who had expressed impatience by taking a baseball bat to Freddy's left leg. He stopped in front of Dana to look her up and down with a mile-wide smile. "Well, ain't this just somethin'. You are a beauty as ever, baby." He gave her a bear hug before pulling back to study her face and hair. "Still countering the culture, I see. I guess we couldn't have done too bad by you. Fresh air, freedom, and funky in the sun, as the song goes."

"That's all far, far behind me . . . Freddy." For an instant she had wanted to call him Daddy, but she couldn't bring herself to start now with a name that had never been used and never fit.

"Well, welcome back. You've always been welcome, no matter what. Come over and talk with me and Aileen. I'll introduce you to the rest. Don't worry about remembering names now. They'll stick with you once you settle in. The pendulum of time is the friend of family, as the song goes."

Dana endured an extended round of uncle this and cousin that and dear, dear friend whatever. Freddy was right. Except for the juggler with an eye for adolescents, who shouted out "Just call me Jackrabbit!" without missing a beat or dropping a ball, none of the names stuck in her mind. In a sense, she already knew all of them, having met their predecessors on many occasions in childhood. There were the ones who were clearly on their way somewhere and meant it, and there were the ones who were "just stopping in" but would tell stories and make excuses for years. Maybe Freddy and Aileen could also tell which was which; maybe they didn't care.

It took several minutes of introductions for the meander over to the umbrella-topped table where Aileen was nursing a tall something and nibbling on blue corn chips from a hand-thrown pottery bowl the size of Utah. "Look who's here, sweetheart," Freddy announced.

"I got eyes, Freddy, I got eyes. And ears. Here, sit a spell,

Sunflower, make yourself at home."

"It's Dana, now, Dana Carmody."

"You call yourself whatever you feel like, baby. You'll always be my little Sunflower, my sunny flower."

"It's not what I call myself, it's who I am. Wanna see my driver's license? I can prove it."

Freddy put his hand on her back as his head bounced in an exaggerated nod. "Sure, sure. We know that. We read your stuff, even. No need to bring heavy vibes with you, though. You just arrived."

"You read my stuff? Here? How? It's all online, nothing's in print, not anymore."

"El Rancho has everything now. Only thing we don't have is one of them wall-size TV screens. Hell, we have a dedicated fiber optic right to the door. Well, side of the house. Hell, our Wi-Fi is so fast it'll blow-dry your hair."

"I don't expect to make much use of it. I'm really here to lay low and retreat from all that."

His face scrunched up. "You okay, baby?"

"I'm okay. I'm here, aren't I. What did it take to get fiber way the hell out here?"

"Same grease as gets anything." He rubbed his fingers together.

Aileen waved a finger at him. "Now don't you go start talking money so soon. The girl just arrived. Here, honey, sit some with your mother. And try one of these." She held up a tall, fat glass that, close up, turned out to be a wine bottle cut off at the shoulder and flamed polished. "I don't know what's in it, but it sure tastes and feels good." She shook it, rattling the ice cubes.

"You never were particularly picky about ingredients, were you. For me, water will do. For now."

213

"Suit yourself, sunshine. You know where the pumps at, side o' the house. That's one well that never runs dry, let me tell you. Grab yourself a cup and come back. You know where to find me after."

Freddy took Dana's arm. "She's kidding. We don't use the pump anymore. Everything's electrified, solar and wind, our own. 'Cept for the internet, we're still off the grid, but we're civilized, gone soft. There's even a cell tower on the hill this side of the town. Gives us one bar when the wind is right. Hell, nobody else here"—he took in the assembled group with a sweep of his hand—"none of them even remembers when this place didn't have indoor toilets."

"You're right there—nobody. I certainly don't remember. Had to be before I came along."

"Yeah, I guess you're right. Sometimes I get the chronology cockeyed. Anyway, here we are. Kitchen's been redone since you left. Hell, everything's been redone since you left. Tumblers are in the cabinet left of the sink. If you need to use the facilities, they're still straight down the hall, across from your old room, but we got one of them high-tech composting recycling toilets now.

"Take your time. I'll be out sittin' with Aileen. I wanna hear all about you, what you been up to, and what brings you back."

"Just getting away, feeling the need for some sunshine and down time."

"Well, we have plenty of both, if that's what really brings you here." He lowered his head to peer expectantly over his sunglasses, but Dana said nothing. "Okay, then, see you outside."

— —

Over the following weeks Dana learned names and settled

into the timeless routine of life at the ranch. Vista Caliente made it easy to talk without saying anything and to just be without being very busy. On the surface, it was still a communal effort, with everybody expected to pitch in for chores and the occasional work party organized by Freddy, but beneath the surface, it was clear that some of the longer-term residents had slacked off to token contributions and others acted as if they were paid staff on union hours. Dana busied herself slotting in wherever she might be useful, relishing weeding in the kitchen garden and the routine of cleaning up after communal meals. Then, just as she had finally reached a point of mindless detachment, her burner phone buzzed in her pocket. She was being subpoenaed.

Freddy walked her out to her car. "It's fully charged. I ran an extension from the light pole. Aileen packed a lunch for you. It's in a little cooler on the passenger seat. So, you're going, for real."

"For real. I have to."

"Have to?"

"Look, I have to testify in a lawsuit. I assume by now you've figured out what this is all about. The trial is starting, and I'm a key witness. I'm scared, but I gotta do this. No need to worry. I can take care of myself."

"You been threatened?"

"Symbolically, yes." She told him about finding Geraldo in the parking garage and the disappearance of the body without a trace. "And there's been no mention since, nothing in the media."

"That doesn't sound like anyone I know of, not even the Carullo gang, not their MO. Do you have any idea who's behind it?"

"Some. Well, a pretty good idea, but I don't have anything I can use. Once I'm back, there will be no point pretending I don't exist anymore, so I figure I can pick up again with my investigation."

Freddy reached in his back pocket and pulled out a thick business envelope. "Here, this is for you, a little walkin'-around money."

She took the envelope, opened it, and riffled through a stack of twenties and fifties. "Don't these really old bills draw attention? I mean, how long ago was it that you pulled the job?"

"I pulled a lotta jobs, but only one that counts. But those ain't old bills; they're new, straight from the nearest ATM."

"And where's that?"

"Sitting on the back porch. Eddie."

"Eddie? You mean the little bald guy?"

"Yeah, that's Eddie Landaro—Eddie 'The Laundromat' Landaro. You can guess what he does."

"So you mean it's not all sitting in some lockbox tucked under your bed or something?"

"Not for a long, long time. It's stashed in so many off-shore accounts and invested in so many layers of holding companies and shell corporations that it takes a really big spreadsheet to keep track of it all. Which is good, 'cause if it's that hard for me to track it, even knowing everything, it's gotta be im-fuckin'-possible for the feds to ever find. Eddie's back and forth across the border all the time and connects with old contacts who meet others who . . . dot, dot, dot. Lotsa dots, way too many to connect."

"I always thought there was this one big score, and you just kept peeling Benjamins off a very fat roll."

"If I'd done that, the roll would have been long gone. No, the only smart thing is to invest and build wealth. I'm into all sorts of stuff, all legit—well, most of it. And the final connections that keep the tax man at bay and me and Aileen invisible are a few guys like The Laundromat, people shadier then the north side of the mountain, as the song goes."

"You are such a phony, always putting on this hippy, country-boy front, spouting communal crap, and quoting folksongs nobody ever heard of. All the time you're just a mob boss."

"Hardly. I'm just a businessman, takin' care of business, keeping my honey and my daughter and my extended family in the style of life they all grew accustomed to. Never was and never pretended to be anything else. Hell, this is a real commune, maybe one of the oldest and most successful in the whole damn country. Why? Because we got the resources for whatever. Mind you, other than Eddie—and Manuel, who is away most of the year—none of the regulars know what makes it work. They think we just live off the land and the little donations they plunk in the basket by the door when they can. And do you know why they do that? Guilt. There's always a fair amount of crumpled cash already in that basket, obviously contributed by others, so they get guilt-tripped into donating, maybe more than they planned. But, of course, it would never be enough to run the place or even buy groceries for the eighteen or twenty regulars. Whenever someone is sent off to the store, we make a show of having them grab what's needed from the basket, and if there isn't enough for whatever, we make a show of taking up a collection, with us emptying our wallets to make up the difference. 'Oh, Freddy and Aileen, you are always so generous. Here, I've got another twenty I can put in.' It works, the informal economy, all cash, with nothing traceable. We may not be completely off the grid, but we do stay off the radar. Secret to not bein' needy is not to be greedy. As the song goes."

"Yeah. The song, the ever-lovin' song. But what about the big ticket items, the expensive improvements like the solar panels?"

"Oh, we get grants"—he made finger quotes—"now and then, like from the International Sense and Sustainability Foundation or the Margaret Carmody Fund or . . . Like I said, it's a very big spreadsheet. Sometimes it's, like, 'Yeah, we had this guy stay a week last year, and he liked us so much, he just gave us a wind turbine his company makes. Just like that. One day it shows up and the next day there's this construction crew, and voila, we got us wind power.' Course, I own controlling interest in that particular turbine manufacturer by way of some company in Panama or whatever. That's how we roll at Vista Caliente."

"Yeah, I see. Still the big con. And I gotta roll. Really."

"I know, Sunf . . . Dana. I'm proud of you—we're proud of you—but I gotta say I'm worried. You be careful."

"You, too. Don't get caught, don't get taken advantage of, and go easy on the mushrooms. As the song goes." She hugged him and held on.

"Don't you worry about me and Aileen. We're survivors."

Dana reluctantly pulled away and got in her car, backed around the tree shading the Kia, and drove back down the dirt driveway.

Freddy ambled back to the Big House, where he retrieved a burner phone from a drawer full of them and punched in a number memorized years earlier.

— 35 —

Weary from the two-day drive back to LA, Dana slowly pulled the Kia into her spot at the end of the row in the underground parking, a spot that had been empty since she moved into the building. She tugged the door handle and was about to climb out when she looked up to see a man walking down the ramp, pulling something from his coat pocket as he approached. By the time he was standing next to the car, he had the business end of a suppressor-fitted handgun pointed at her. Acting on instinct, she dove, flattening herself across the front seats as she kicked open the door with both feet, slamming it into the shooter just as he fired.

The first shot went wild, turning the side window into glass confetti but missing her completely. The second shot, louder and from a different direction, shot through the man's skull and sent a red spray against the gray concrete of the garage wall. Another man, in a loden-green L.L.Bean jacket with his handgun held two-handed before him, rushed toward them. He knelt to check the body before turning to Dana. "You all right?"

"Yeah, I guess. Who the hell are you? And what just happened."

"Just doing my job, keeping you off the ice. Your father sends his regards. Look, give me the key fob. I'll get your car fixed and back in a couple of days. Meanwhile, we got cleaners who will take care of this mess. They're already on the way. If you got any stuff in the car, grab it and get out of here. Okay?"

"Are you saying my father hired you?"

"This is no time for exchanging résumés, lady. Just get your stuff and go." The screech of tires echoed in the parking garage. "That's the cleaners. Now get."

Dana pulled her two bags from the back seat and jogged toward the exit. When she looked back, two men were already rolling the body into a plastic tarp, as another man was spraying some kind of foam cleaner over the splattered blood. Her Kia was being backed into the exit lane; with squealing tires, it spun around, turned up the exit ramp, and shot out of the building.

As she trotted up the stairs to the lobby, Dana was thinking of Freddy. Good instincts, Pop, she thought. She grinned. That's what I'll call you: Pop. And maybe you are more of a father than I gave you credit. She tried to calm the shaking in her hand as she pressed the button for the elevator. As the hydraulic lift kicked in, she started calculating. Her father's emissary could be explained, but someone else seemed to have had some pretty good idea of just when she would be arriving. If her every move was being followed that closely, it was time she made some unexpected moves.

At Dana's floor, Geneva, the chain-toking woman in the apartment down the hall, was standing by her door, smartphone in one hand, joint in the other. "Did you hear that? It sounded like gunshots. Do you think we should call the police?" It was said with the curious indifference of the chronically stoned.

Dana shook her head. "I wouldn't bother." She thought fast. "Sounded to me like the kids across the way taking a baseball bat to the dumpster."

"Really? Kids?"

"Yeah, and if the police ever do come, chances are they'll

either find nothing or they'll take it out on those boys. They're just kids letting off steam. I'd let it go."

"You think so?"

"I think so. Look, I've worked with the police, and I know how they work. I also know what gunfire sounds like, and that was no gunfire. And see? Not another sound from anywhere. All's quiet on the downstairs front." She gave Geneva a big grin as she let herself into her apartment.

As she reached for the light switch, her hand started shaking again. At least three people were dead. What had started out as journalism was morphing into a deadly game. The question now was how to play the game to win.

She tossed her bags on the couch and headed for the kitchenette, where she pulled a screw-top bottle of chenin blanc from the fridge and poured herself a glass. She started thinking back to her hacking days, when she had fantasied herself as some kind of clandestine operative. She knew she had to seize the initiative, and to do that she would need a defensible space from which to work. The apartment was not it—definitely not. Where? Barbra's beach house? It was isolated, walled off, and Barbra had the resources to hire whatever security resources might be needed. There was no point waiting for the Kia to be repaired, she should get to Barbra's but try not to leave a trail. No need to unpack, even. Just haul out the floppy hats and the stage makeup and once more slip out the back entrance.

— —

The newly acquired rent-a-cop detail stopped Dana at the gate of the beach house and checked her ID against a guest list before letting her pass. She palmed the lock by the double front doors and let herself in. Becca, wearing an open man's dress shirt over flowered bikini bottoms, greeted her in the foyer. "Wow, you're back. I mean . . ."

"Don't I even get a hug?"

"I mean, sure. I'm just, like, a little wet from, ah, the hot tub."

"You've got a boy here, am I right?"

Becca shifted her eyes back and forth. "Yeah. Mom's not here, see, and she, well, she isn't exactly enthusiastic about Ramón."

"Should I ask if there's anything behind her lack of enthusiasm for this . . . this Ramón?"

"It's not like she's racist or anything, if that's what you were thinking. It's . . . well, Ramón is at UCLA, and . . ."

"Uh huh. And you just turned thirteen. This is not good, not good."

"You know, it's not like I'm a virgin or anything. Besides, studies have shown that by my age the capacity for informed judgement is already fully developed. Plus, I'm a girl, and girl's mature ahead of boys."

"Yes, and the adolescent brain is still developing and doesn't reach full maturity until well into the twenties. Spare me the pop neuro-psych. I know how . . . well, how sophisticated you are, Becca, but you know what could happen to your boyfriend who is no longer a boy. Would you want to wait for him to get out of prison for your next date?"

"That is not going to happen. I would never, like, press charges. It's been my choice all along."

"Doesn't matter. You don't have to bring a complaint. You're under eighteen, and, unless he's some kind of *wunderkind*, I'm guessing he must be more than three years older than you since he's already in college, which makes it a felony here in California, rather than just a misdemeanor.

Not good kid, not good. If you actually care for this dude, I'd break it off for his sake. If your mother doesn't approve, one phone call could . . ."

"You wouldn't tell her, would you?"

"Tell her what? I haven't seen anything and never met the guy. I'm going up to the bedroom to unpack and take a much needed shower. That should be enough time for you to tidy up a bit." She cocked her head. "Capiche?"

"What?"

"Do you understand? Or, in the lingo de jour, you feel me?"

"Um, you really think . . .?"

"If you gotta be foolin' around, pick guys no older than sixteen. Your mother will feel better, and if the whole relationship sours or they get caught out, it's a misdemeanor and likely you'd both be let off with a wrist slap and a talking to."

"Wait, both of us?"

"Yeah, that's the way it works in the great state of California. Anyone who has sex with a minor under eighteen, dot, dot, dot. It's the final fallout from Title IX thinking: equal rights, missy, equal responsibility."

"Wow, I didn't know, like . . . I mean, at camp we . . . Are you saying even two girls?"

"If you get caught or one of them complains or a parent jumps in, yes. I know it doesn't always make sense or seem fair, what with so many teens being sexually active, but that is still the law."

"Wow, I gotta think about this. Hey, how do you know so much, anyway? You're not a lawyer."

"No, but I also started young, and I also made some miscalls. Wait until you're eighteen, then if you want to go for

223

the older dudes, it's all cool. Just wait. It's only a few years."

"Okay, okay. Just don't say anything to Mom."

"What's there to say? I'm headed upstairs for my shower. Catch you later, girl."

—— ——

The look on Barbra's face was a mix of pleasant surprise and discomfort when she arrived home to be greeted by Dana. "Wow, look at you, all tanned and trimmed. I thought we were splitting up—well, I mean taking different trails. You know what I mean."

"We were. And are. I just turned tail to get some time to think through my next move."

"What happened?"

"It's gone from threats to attempts. Whoever is on the other side sent someone to kill me. If it wasn't for the guardian angel Pop dispatched to watch over me, I would have been the one with my brains spattered all over the wall by my parking spot."

"Oh my god." She put her arms around Dana. "My poor darling."

"Lucky darling. I'm still here. And don't worry, I'll be out of here as soon as I figure out where to lay low until the trial. I've been called as a witness."

"Yes, I know. Leah and Hal keep me in the loop. But where will you go?"

"I was thinking of reaching out to Rolf. I don't think many people would know of any connection between him and me."

"Look, you already broke protocol by showing up here, so you might as well stay. We have both a police detail and extra private security now. This is probably as safe as you can get. Okay? And what's this about your father?"

"Yeah, I just arrived back at the apartment when this thug shows up with a pistol pointed at my head, about to pop me. A guy Pop hired gallops onto the scene and pops him instead. Pop, pop, and re-pop! Sorry, I'm a little giddy. Adrenalin, narrow escape, plus two glasses of your fine pinot grigio on an empty stomach. Tandi made the choice for me, one of the Drucker vineyards."

"Good choice, good for Tandi. And the visit with your family?"

"As good as could be expected. Aileen hasn't changed, other than putting on still more pounds. Freddy . . . Pop— I've decided that's what I'm calling him—he . . . well, let's just say maybe there's more to him than the drugged out hippy I grew up with and thought he was. Not all of it good, mind you, but, shall we say, my picture of him has gotten more complicated."

"That's good. At least, I think it is. So let's head out to the deck with a couple more glasses of something good and talk about what's next." She hugged Dana again and ran a hand up and down her back. "God, how I missed you. And I worried. Constantly. We gotta stick together. It's just too hard without you."

"Is this the independent, self-assured businesswoman who once graced the cover of *Construction Tech Quarterly*? Is this—"

"Oh, god, not *CTQ*! I hated that picture almost as much as I hated the puff piece our PR people commissioned about me. I can't believe you even know about that."

"Knowing stuff is what I do, remember? And I thought you looked damn good. When I saw that photo, I thought, mmm, I hope I look that good when I'm her age."

Barbra pushed her away playfully. "My age? What you

talkin' about, girl? Don't you throw that ageist crap my way, twerp, just because you're still on the short side of thirty."

"Yeah, and don't you wish you still had my tits, old lady," she teased back.

"I do, girl, but any time I want to, I can just . . ." Before she could finish the thought, the lights in the house went out and the background whoosh and hum of appliances and air conditioning faded and died. "What the fuck? We have backup. Why . . .?" In the silence, two gunshots echoed. "Shit. Where's Becca? We gotta get to the safe-room."

"Last I knew, she was in the hot tub."

"Follow me. If she's as smart as she claims to be, she should be on her way to the room."

Becca was waiting at the bookcase that disguised the vault entrance, waving her lit-up smartphone over the row of books. "I couldn't remember the code."

"B-O-O-K: Brown, Obama, O'Brian, Kimball." Barbra pressed in on the spines of four books by those authors in sequence. The latch released with a loud click and the book-case rolled aside revealing a steel door with a telephone-style keypad. Barbra tapped the same sequence, 2-6-6-5, and the inner door opened to a well-lit interior.

Dana looked confused. "How . . .? There's no power, and I didn't hear any backup generator kick in."

"Separate system, battery-powered. Quick, let's get in."

– 36 –

Dana scanned the safe room, a tight fit, but outfitted for comfort with three reclining captain's chairs and a sleep sofa. One entire wall was storage, with cabinets and shelves of supplies. The opposite wall sported a large-screen display, a slide-out keyboard, and a microwave. Becca immediately tried to use her phone only to find there was no signal. "It won't work in here," Barbra said. "Everything's blocked. But we have an old-fashioned landline and hard-wired internet connection, so don't worry, we're not cut off." She pulled out a stool and sat down at the keyboard.

"What are you doing?"

"Resetting the entry code, just in case. Todd had this whole protocol we had to learn and follow. He was so old-school in some things. Anyway, the new code is 'COOL' everyone. Whatever authors that equates to, of course."

Becca chewed at her lower lip. "Are we really safe in here?"

"Yes, darling. Fire, bombs, gas, guns: whatever they can throw at us, we're okay. The specs say we could stay in here several days if needed. And we're connected to a dedicated surveillance system, so we can monitor what's going on outside." She launched a security app which started a rotating display of thumbnail images with the telltale green of infrared night-vision from tiny security cameras throughout the house.

Becca pointed. "There's people out there, with guns."

Barbra squinted at the screen. "That's our security people. See the ID patches on their jackets?"

Dana shook her head. "Uniforms? That's hardly a form of authenticated identification."

A figure approached the camera covering the hallway past the bookcase. The man holstered his handgun and looked up toward the camera. His mouth started moving. Barbra keyed on the audio.

"—in there. My men have cleared the house and grounds. No intruders. If you're in there, you can come out, Mrs. Wilson."

"That looks like Donovan Cortez, although the night-vision is less than perfect. Cortez has been with Drucker's security team for years. I think we can trust him."

"Are you sure?"

"Pretty sure. Everyone quiet while I use the intercom." She pressed a button beside the screen. "Please identify yourself."

"It's me, Cortez, Donovan Cortez, ma'am. Here, let me show you my ID." He held a badge holder up toward the camera.

"Okay, Donovan, you can open the safe-room door."

"Sorry, ma'am, they don't give us the code." He looked around. "Only the family is supposed to know. I don't even know where the keypad is. You have to open it from the inside." Suddenly the image brightened. "There, they got the power back on. It's safe, Ms. Wilson."

"Is Jack Torrance with you? Is he on duty tonight?"

"Who?"

"Jack Torrance. You know, the tall guy."

"Sorry, ma'am. I don't know any Jack Torrance. I've been with Drucker Security Services almost eight years, now, and I don't recall anybody by that name."

Barbra keyed off the audio. "Well, that settles it."

Dana angled her head. "What was that all about?"

"A test. If it was somebody pretending to be with Drucker Security, they would have pretended to know Jack Torrance. There is no Jack Torrance. I just made him up to be sure it was Donovan. And I knew he wouldn't know the lock code. He gave the right answers." She started to tap the new code on the keypad and then laughed.

"What?"

"It's the same numbers. B-O-O-K and C-O-O-L are both just 2-6-6-5 on a telephone keypad. Let me change it again."

"Well, hurry up, mom, I'm getting hungry."

"Okay, my snack-a-saurus, I'm hurrying. There, the new code is F-O-O-D. Think you can remember that?"

Dana smiled and nodded. Becca rolled her eyes.

"All right people, we can leave."

In the hallway, Donovan Cortez was talking on his radio. "Okay, Wallace. Roger that. Get DC-SERT here on the double. We don't want to leave the door wide open." He thumbed off the radio. "Ms. Wilson, Becca, and . . ." He nodded toward Dana.

"This is my . . . partner, Dana Carmody. She lives here."

"Sure."

"So it was a false alarm?"

"No, ma'am. It was the real thing. They hacked the house somehow. I don't know about that stuff. That's why we're getting DC-SERT—the Drucker cyber-security team— over here right away. I don't think you should remain here. Is there somewhere else you can stay? At least until we sort this out."

"Yes, there's somewhere we can go. We thought we heard shots."

"You did, ma'am. That was Kevin. He's new and maybe a

little trigger happy. I'm going to recommend some extra training for him, if you know what I mean."

"So we weren't actually in danger?"

"I couldn't say, ma'am, but you did the right thing under the circumstances. I'll have the office get in touch with you when we fix the security problem here. I'll have one of my people stay with you until you're safely away, but I wouldn't take too long getting resettled someplace."

"Okay. Becca, pack your camp duffle bag and be ready to leave in fifteen minutes."

"Where are we going?"

"Don't worry about that, just go pack. And what about you, Dana?"

"I'm ready when you are. I haven't even unpacked yet. Where are we going?"

"You'll see."

"And how are we going to get there? I hailed LaRyde to get here, and had the driver drop me off a mile down the beach. If they hacked the house . . ."

"I've got an idea." She hurried down the hall after the security guard. "Wait up, Donovan. Do you have a car here?"

"Yes, ma'am. It's a Drucker car, for my use."

"One of the standard ones?" He nodded. "Okay, call in and have Drucker bring you another one, tell the dispatcher you'll file a report, but don't. In a couple of days you can report it stolen, okay? Whatever CYA you need to pull is okay by me. I'll make sure nothing happens against you. Got it?"

"Got it."

— —

Becca, accompanied by one of the security detail, was the last to make it out to Donovan's car where it was parked across from the entryway. "Ew, it's ugly."

"Maybe, but it will get us where we're going." She waited for Becca to close her door and the guard to step back. "Plus, Tonika told me how to turn off the GPS tracking on these models, so there won't be a digital trace of where we went." She pulled out from the curb, made a U-turn, and sped away.

— —

The penthouse at Rockland Suites was not the beach house, but its panoramic view of the lights of the Los Angeles basin was some compensation. Dana paced in front of the floor-to-ceiling windows and grinned. "Not bad. When you said you had a pied-a-terre, I pictured a modest little apartment tucked away in some obscure location. Actually, I kind of pictured something like my place."

"This is modest compared to Todd's and my usual retreat, but this is a lot more obscure. It does not show on the corporate books and not even Todd knew about this."

"A secret life?"

"A getaway, just in case. It's owned by the Beachland Educational Trust. It'll be Becca's when she turns twenty-one."

Becca, frozen fruit bar in hand, entered from the kitchen. "What will be mine when I turn twenty-one?"

"A troubled, too-hot world with stormy seas encroaching from every side."

"Yeah, yeah, I know all that climate change stuff."

"Don't belittle it, kiddo. It's real."

"I know that. That's why I want to become an oceanographer. Water, undersea worlds—that's the future."

Barbra's jaw dropped as her forehead wrinkled. "I didn't know that, honey. You really want to become a scientist?"

"A marine scientist, yeah. It's a growth industry."

Dana put her arm around Becca's shoulder. "Smart kid. Principled and prudent all in one package. We could take a lesson or two from you and your generation."

"Der. Too bad your generation has been so slow to learn. Are we going to live here, mom?"

"For now, at least until they fix the beach house, maybe until this trial is over."

"How long will that take?"

"Months. Maybe longer."

With a glum look, Becca sat down on the white leather sofa. "What about school? What about my friends?"

"I don't know, honey. We'll work something out, I'm sure. In the morning, I'll call my staff at Beachland and get them to arrange transportation and security. Give me your phone. You, too, Dana."

"Mine's a burner, never used. I already ditched the one I had out at the ranch."

"Okay."

Becca slipped her phone from the back pocket of her jeans and held it up. "What do you want it for?"

Barbra grabbed it with a roundhouse sweep of her arm. "To keep you from calling or texting anyone, at least for now."

"But that's not fair. Trust me. I won't say anything."

"I trust you—well, not completely, but mostly—but I also know you and absolutely do not trust whoever tracked us. Or Dana. They hacked into the house. This is for real, kiddo. Somebody wants to kill Dana—and maybe us."

"You're serious."

"I am."

"Wow, that's so cool, like in that Zac Medford series on Amazon."

Dana laughed. "Cool is not the modifier I would pick. I damn near peed myself when that guy came over with his gun pointed at my head."

"Wow, you didn't say that when you showed up."

"We were talking about other things, if you remember."

"Yeah, like . . ."

"Anyway, I think we all should try to chill out and get some sleep. We can figure out tactics and strategies in the morning. I don't know about you, Barbra, but I could use a drink."

"Sure, we can sit out on the deck. The night is warm enough."

"Mom, I could, like, use a drink too."

Barbra drew her head back in mock shock. "I thought you didn't like the taste of alcohol."

"I don't, but I forgot to pack my vape kit, and . . ."

"You? You've been smoking weed already?"

"Der. Who do you think I am? I don't smoke. Kids my age vape."

"Kids your age are barely old enough to find their way home from school. I can't keep up. Where did we go so wrong with this next generation?"

"Don't have a cow, mom. It's not like I'm into the opes like Jennifer."

"Jennifer? Sweet Jennifer Macklin does opioids?"

"Well, yeah. It's not like she's the only one at the Academy. And it's not like she's buying it on the streets or anything. I mean, she lifts it from her mom's supply."

Barbra turned to Dana, who was looking on, tight-lipped. Dana shrugged. "Do we reap what we sow? Did we, all of us, set this up?"

"God, how the hell do I know? I thought Todd and I were

doing all right. Now that he's gone, I just don't know."

Becca put her hands on her hips. "Well, while you two are trying to figure it all out, will somebody just get me a damn drink?"

"No!" It was instantaneous and simultaneous from both Dana and Barbra.

Becca threw up her hands and stomped off. "Fine! I'm going to bed. If I can find a fuckin' bed in this place. And you two can do whatever you fuckin' want."

Dana struggled to keep from laughing. "Well, at least we seem to be on the same page as parents."

Barbra put her arm around Dana's shoulders. "Yeah, and we seem to have the traditional parental hypocrisy shit down pat. Now, let's go talk and see if we can sort out some of the other stuff. The trial starts next week."

"And how do you feel about that?"

"I'm trying not to think about it. Mostly, I just put myself in the hands of the lawyers. You're the one who's going to be taking the stand for some key testimony. I just have to play the bereaved widow."

— 37 —

The public and the press, having been deprived of the spectacle of a criminal trial, jumped all over the wrongful-death suit. The case ended up presided over by Phillip Steadman, a graying Brown-era protégé with a reputation for sartorial flamboyance and strict courtroom decorum. Dana had to admit that the remote prospect of the Drucker Proxy testifying in open court was a journalist's wet dream, and Bannon Turndale made his move to fulfill that dream during pretrial motions.

Beneath his black robe, worn unzipped to mid-chest, Judge Steadman's ascot was a flaming magenta bloom. He flipped back and forth between pages of the stapled portfolio in front of him before squinting toward the defense table.

"Do I understand number five correctly, Mr. Turndale, that you are proposing to put a robot on the witness stand in this court."

"It's not a robot. The telepresence unit is just a mobile means for the proxy to communicate. It would be essentially like having an abuse victim testify by closed-circuit video, a well-established precedent."

"Except that there would be no human victim on the other end of your video link, if that is what it is."

"Well, in a sense, it's no different than if Stephen Hawking were to testify using his talking keyboard. The telepresence robot is just the mechanical aid by which the proxy can communicate."

"I do not see Hawking's name on your list of witnesses,

and he would, in any case, not be subject to summons. The California courts can and do make accommodations for persons with disabilities. However, the proxy, as you insist on calling it, is just software, a piece of computer code. Am I right? As such, it has no standing before the law. It is not a person, with or without a disability, for which this court could make accommodations."

"It is duly incorporated in the state of Delaware as Coleman Todd Drucker Proxy, LLC. Ample precedent at the state and federal level exists for the personal rights of corporate entities."

"In which case, Mr. Turndale, as a corporate entity it may have certain legal rights, but the hubristic corporate name notwithstanding, the corporation must have a representative before the court, an officer or duly appointed agent, an actual living *person* who is empowered to respond and act on behalf of the corporation."

"We have brought an additional action, now before the Second District Appellate Court, to have Coleman Todd Drucker Proxy, LLC, recognized as the duly authorized personal representative of the estate of Coleman Todd Drucker."

"Pending matters before other courts are not the concern of this court. If there is a *person* duly appointed to act on behalf of the corporation, you can put the name of that person on the list of witnesses you plan to call, but you cannot call a robot or a computer program—not yet, and not in my court. That is my ruling."

"Counsel for the defense enters an objection."

"Noted. You may proceed."

—— ——

Once pretrial motions were settled, the proceedings moved

on to jury selection, a protracted process that found both sides exhausting their allotments of preemptory challenges. Hal Workman did his best for the plaintiffs to exclude anyone who was a fan of science fiction on the theory that they would be more inclined to think of an embodied proxy as a legitimate and logical form of progress while Bannon Turndale did his best to stack the jury toward younger singles, who might be less inclined to sympathize with a widow and orphan. In the end, the seated jury and alternates reflected the racial diversity of Los Angeles County quite well, but not the ages of its population. Despite the fact that the forty-to-sixty demographic was not represented, both legal teams reassured their clients that they had been successful.

On the appointed day, the hardwood-paneled walls of the courtroom turned a dozen quiet conversations and the shuffling of papers into an ebb tide of background noise. Rolf Nagy, hair pulled back in a neat man-bun and wearing a new Italian-tailored suit, came down the aisle toward the front. Dana gave him an approving smile. "Wow, it's like an alumni weekend," she said.

"You know all these people?"

"Most of them. Some better than others."

His shoulders slumped. "I take it from your tone that maybe at least one of these guys is more than an acquaintance."

She leaned in and lowered her voice. "You don't have competition there, Rolfy. None of these guys are any threat to you. I mean, look at them. You really think I would ever go for one of these lawyer types?"

"Well, not really. But I missed you. More than I realized. I haven't seen you in months."

"With good reason. I was under house arrest, and then after the bullets started flying, I was keeping my head down."

"For real? You've been threatened?"

"Not threatened, actually shot at."

"Wow, I'm so sorry. I just thought you were mad at me. Or fed up."

"I've never been mad at you. Disappointed, sure, annoyed, yes, but angry? Not yet anyway. Maybe that's one of our problems: we don't fight."

"If that's a problem, I can fix it. We can start right here and now if you want." He forced a false angry-face.

"Thanks for the generous offer. Maybe I'll take you up on that after we get through this."

Rolf surveyed the room. "I recognize the bereaved widow from the news. I assume the suits next to her are the not-your-type lawyers."

"Good people, just not close friends. But do let me introduce my friend Tonika Warner, here. Tonika, this is Rolf Nagy, an old friend."

Tonika put out her hand without getting up. "Yes, I've heard about you. I understand you're testifying for us, for the plaintiffs. Are you psyched?"

"About as much as before a teeth cleaning. But it's good to see Dana again. And nice to meet you."

"Let me introduce you to our legal team," Dana said, "even if they are not my type." She led the way to the plaintiffs table where Barbra greeted her with a hug and Leah Goldstein and Hal Workman nodded as they continued to scribble notes on a couple of yellow legal pads and talk in low voices with a young associate.

Rolf edged forward. "Can I ask a dumb question? Why

238

do lawyers still use 'legal pads' when everything and everybody else has tablet computers?"

Leah looked up, her face deadpan serious. "We use legal pads because we certainly wouldn't want to be caught using illegal pads. Sorry, humor among the humorless is always a little lame. No, it's courtroom decorum, where electronic notetaking is still frowned on. Or banned in some courtrooms, would you believe? Depends somewhat on the judge."

"And who is our judge?" Dana asked "Who did we get?"

"Boy George Steadman," she said, circling a line on her legal pad.

"Boy George?"

"Well, that's what he's called in our circles. Phillip George Steadman. From his middle name."

Hal Workman finally looked up. "And in recognition of his somewhat colorful taste—or lack thereof—in clothes. And makeup."

Leah manufactured an annoyed expression. "Well, meow, meow. Look who's talking, our own Mr. Workman, with his peg-pants retro look and gelled coiffure. Feeling a little catty this morning?" She turned away. "Ignore him. He forgot to take his meds this morning."

— —

The trial opened with a rapid verbal volley-for-serve as the parties vied to preempt the proceedings. The Existendia team kicked it off with a motion to dismiss. Judge Steadman listened patiently to the plea, but as soon as Bannon Turndale returned to his seat, ruled against the motion. Hal Workman then countered by entering a motion for summary judgement for the plaintiffs.

"On what grounds, Counselor?"

"*Res ipsa loquitor.* Location, instrument, and ownership, operation, and control over the cause of death."

"The facts, which you claim speak for themselves, have yet to be established. That is the first purpose of these proceedings, to establish the facts and thereby determine liability, if any. Motion denied."

The remainder of the first day was taken up by opening arguments, with the plaintiffs laying out their case as being straightforward and irrefutable on the face of it considering three incontrovertible facts: that the death happened on the premises of Existendia; that it was the result of equipment belonging to them; and that said equipment was connected to and under the control of computers and computer programs developed by them and operated by them. For his turn, Bannon Turndale, parading and gesticulating as if he were in a made-for-streaming Internet drama, told an elaborate story of incredibly complex systems and software that the company could not reasonably be expected to fully comprehend, much less be responsible for, especially since the alleged weapon was actually wielded under the intelligent control of the Drucker Proxy.

Leah Goldstein jumped in. "Objection, the so-called proxy is not a party to this case and neither its intelligence nor its agency has been or can be established."

"Overruled. We are still in opening arguments, Counsel, and the Defense is afforded greater latitude at this point. Plaintiffs will have ample opportunity later to challenge their characterization of the software when you start making your case tomorrow. Defense may proceed."

Turndale took his time finishing his oration and Judge Steadman banged his gavel. "Court is in recess until ten tomorrow morning." The buzz of dozens of conversations returned as Steadman exited.

Dana, Rolf, and Tonika intercepted Barbra as she rose from the plaintiffs table. "So, what do you think? How did it go?" Dana asked.

Leah looked up from her papers. "I should be asking you all. I was in the middle of it. You have the better perspective from the gallery."

"Really?" Rolf said. "Seemed pretty boring, to be honest."

"Boring is good at this stage, as long as you don't put the jury to sleep or piss off the judge. You want to build your case to a climax, with the drama coming toward the end, when it can sway the jury and stick in their minds."

Dana raised her eyebrows. "You sound more like a playwright or a screenwriter than a lawyer."

"Well, that's a step up from many of the things I've been called. But, yeah, there's a little of that and a lot of knowing the law, plus remembering who the audience is, always addressing the court but playing to the jury."

Hal Workman seemed impatient to get into the conversation. "I'll have to admit, I wasn't bored. Yes, I know, technically, this is a civil case around liability, but it's also more like a criminal case in a lot of ways, so both of us are reaching deep into our old kit bags. And we have the whole Drucker Unified team to back us up, including Doug Pulaski here." He nodded to a portly young man whose gray pinstripes exaggerated rather than hid his bulk. "Doug came to us last year from the district attorney's office. He was hoping to get away from the courtroom, but he's been a big help in planning strategy." Doug flashed a smile around the group and returned to reorganizing the contents of his briefcase.

"And can you say more about that strategy?" Dana asked.

"Not within earshot of Turndale and his team, I can't, but it is a jury trial, and it is about life-and-death, so you can expect the dramatic tension to ramp up as we go." He flipped back the top pages on his legal pad. "And your testimony, Dana, is scheduled for day after tomorrow. That should up the game a bit."

— —

She did not find the tension ramping up, even when Leah skillfully drew out Dana's own vivid testimony about coming on the murder scene. It wasn't until she was under cross-examination that her anxiety rose as the defense attacked her credibility, questioned her about apparent inconsistencies in her recall, and challenged her interpretations of what she had seen. They hammered home the point that she was not an expert, not qualified to reach forensic conclusions about what had happened in her absence.

She left the stand feeling like a failure, but at the lunch break, Hal and Leah reassured her that she had done fine. "Wait until you see what we do with your testimony this afternoon."

The afternoon and the following days were filled with a protracted parade of experts. Hal Workman, true to his retro attire, took a classic approach, methodically laying out his case for the plaintiffs, step by step establishing that Existendia, and specifically its Chief Technology Officer, Aram Netsky, was fully and directly responsible for the performance of the proxy software and all its associated equipment.

Workman began by calling Lieutenant Darryl Brookwood, the police officer who had led the crime scene investigation.

"And as to the tracks on the carpeting, what were your

findings with regard to those?"

"They were made by the wheels of the telepresence robot."

"Can you confirm that the telepresence robot you examined is in fact Plaintiffs' Exhibit B, a U-mote Model F2F, serial number J52399AA26-US?"

"Yes, that's my initials on the evidence tag."

"Please tell the court the results of your examination."

"The face of the screen of the robot was splattered with blood and there was blood on the wheels of the robot which matched the blood on the tracks in the carpet and the blood of the victim."

"Objection." Bannon Turndale's voice bordered on weary. "The witness is a crime scene investigator, not a laboratory scientist, and would have had no access to any lab results at the time of his initial investigation."

"Sustained."

"Lieutenant Brookwood, did you have occasion to review laboratory results on the samples of blood taken from the scene?"

"I did."

"This is a copy of Plaintiffs' Exhibit C. Do you recognize this document?"

"Yes, it's the lab report on the blood samples taken from the scene. That's my initials on the second line."

"And what are the conclusions of this report?"

"That the blood on the carpet and on the wheels and display screen of the telepresence robot matched that of the victim."

"And what conclusion did you draw from the blood on the carpet and on the display screen?"

"From the pattern of blood spatters on the chair and

carpet, it is clear that the robot could not have been more than two feet from the victim when the fatal blow was struck."

"But Ms. Carmody has testified that when she entered, the robot was more than ten feet from the victim when she arrived."

"Correct, and that is where it was when I arrived."

"How did it get from near the victim to the other side of the room?"

"Objection." Turndale half rose from his seat. "Calls for speculation on matters not witnessed."

"Overruled. Defense has already accepted the Lieutenant as an expert witness and this is within his area of expertise."

"I will reword the question, Your Honor. Please tell the court your conclusions and their basis regarding the conflicting evidence of the blood spatters and the location of the robot when you arrived."

"Yes. The pattern of blood on the carpet left by the wheels of the robot indicated that it traversed the room under its own power."

"It was not dragged or manually moved?"

"No, the wheels on that model lock when not powered, keeping the unit from rolling. If it had been dragged, the blood on the carpet would have been smeared, which it was not. And it clearly had not been lifted and moved. So, it was moved under power by remote control."

"Remote control? What do you mean by that?"

"By whatever or whomever was connected to the telepresence robot at the time. In normal use, there would be a human operator at the other end with a joystick controlling movement of the robot."

"And in this case?"

"The unit was under control of a software program, an artificial intelligence referred to by the company, Existendia that is, as a digital proxy."

"Objection. The witness is not qualified as an expert in information technology."

"Sustained."

"No further questions."

The parade of expert testimony continued until it was Rolf Nagy's turn to testify as a robotics expert. With Hal walking him through a meticulous line of questioning, the workings of the robotics arm and Rolf's findings on its operation were laid out in reasonably simple terms to make it easy for the jury to follow.

On cross-examination, Turndale tried to undermine the conclusions, but Rolf held his ground. Turndale kept returning to the difference between certainty and Rolf's insistence, as an engineer, on qualifying his statements. "So then, in wrapping up, can you say for certain, that the robot arm did not, in and of itself, simply malfunction in such a way as to cause the death of Mr. Drucker?"

"From the tests I supervised, it would be virtually impossible for the arm to operate in such a manner on its own."

"Please answer with a simple yes or no. Could the robot arm have malfunctioned on its own in such a way as to deliver the fatal blow? Yes or no?

"It's a matter of—"

"Your Honor,"—Bannon turned toward the bench—"please instruct the witness to answer the question as asked."

The expression on Judge Steadman's face suggested he

was not unsympathetic with Rolf's position, but he directed him to answer with either a yes or a no.

Rolf frowned. "What was the question again? You asked it in more than one way."

"Is it . . . was it possible that the robot arm malfunctioned on its own in such a way as to deliver the blow that killed Mr. Drucker?"

"Yes, it's possible, but—"

"No further questions." Turndale turned his back on the witness and strode toward the defense table.

Leah Goldstein stood as Turndale took his seat. "Redirect, Your Honor."

Steadman nodded. "Proceed."

"Mr. Nagy, you testified that the robot arm was operating under external control when it struck Mr. Drucker in the back of the head, is that correct?"

"Yes."

"Objection. This has been covered."

"With the court's indulgence, I am merely establishing context for my next questions."

"Objection overruled."

"Mr. Nagy, how do you know that the arm was operating under external control at that time?"

"Because there is a record, a logger in the arm that automatically records every instruction the arm receives. We copied the contents of that chip as part of the forensic tests. The arm was instructed to do exactly what it did. It's in our report."

"This report,"—she held up a bound sheaf of papers—"Exhibit D."

"Yes."

"So then, can you say with certainty that the robot arm

was operating under external control when it delivered the fatal blow?"

"Yes, with absolute certainty."

"Thank you. No further questions. The plaintiffs rest."

Judge Steadman called an early lunch recess.

— —

Dana was surprised by the abrupt end to their case, and during the break asked Leah why she wasn't calling anyone from Existendia to try and establish some sort of culpability. "Because I can do that during cross as they try to paint their way out of responsibility. That way my questions come after theirs, and their answers will seem to weigh more heavily. Trust me, we know what we are doing. We stopped where it made most sense to stop, with Rolf Nagy's testimony that the arm was under external control when the blow was struck. That way they can't get off by implying it was a manufacturing defect. It was their computers running their software. We don't have to know what those programs were doing or how they ended up sending the instructions to the arm. Existendia should have settled before trial. We're going to win this, and we're going to win big."

"Maybe, but we still won't know who really did it, much less who's been threatening me and who's behind Geraldo's death."

"That's not our job. We're just trying to get a settlement for Barbra and her company."

— 38 —

Over lunch, Bannon Turndale conferred with the legal team and his clients. "It's time to make our big play for the game, since we're stuck in a jury trial."

"Tell me again why you did not want a jury trial," Aram Netsky asked.

Bannon sighed audibly. "Because a jury will be thinking with their guts as much as their brains. Their sympathies are likely to be with the plaintiff, the poor bereaved widow and her daughter. A high-tech cadre of geeky visionaries is hardly sympathetic. In any case, we have what we have and will fight the good fight. That's why I'm taking this tactic. It's not about law at this point; it's about psychology." He glanced at the wall clock. "And lunch is over. It's show time."

— —

After days of mind-numbing technical testimony, the gallery of gawkers and journalists had thinned. Judge Steadman gaveled the court into session. "Is the defense ready?"

"We are, Your Honor. For our first witness, the defense calls Coleman Todd Drucker."

Even before Bannon's last syllable, Leah Goldstein snapped "Objection!" and the judge banged his gavel. "Sustained. Counsel, I will not have you making a mockery of my courtroom by calling a dead man to the stand."

"Your Honor, I have no intention of calling a deceased person to the stand. My witness is not dead, as will be evident when he takes the stand."

Steadman paused for a moment. "Court will take a short recess. Counselors, I will see you in my chambers."

In chambers, Steadman glared at Turndale. "What are you trying to pull, Counselor? I already ruled on this in pre-trial."

"I am not trying to pull anything, Your Honor. I merely want to put my witness on the stand."

"The witness is dead," Workman said. "I can introduce the death certificate into evidence to prove it if need be. This is a civil trial in a court of law, not a séance."

"And if I can just be permitted to examine my witness, it will be abundantly clear that he is not dead."

Steadman tapped the table. "I am sorry, but I can't allow you to put an AI, a software system, on the stand."

"Coleman Todd Drucker is not an artificial intelligence. His intelligence is completely natural, it has just been embodied in a software substrate."

"I'm not going to engage in semantic games with you, Counselor. There is no precedent in California law for putting a computer program on the stand."

"But that is precisely my point. I am not asking the Court to put a computer program on the stand but to put Coleman Todd Drucker on the stand, that's why I am calling him as a witness."

Hal leaned forward in his seat. "Your Honor, it is transparent where counsel for the defense is going with this. It is a brazen and bizarre attempt to invalidate the very basis of a wrongful death action. Furthermore, allowing the digital proxy to testify in this case would be tantamount to granting standing before the court to a piece of computer code."

"Not the code, Your Honor, but Coleman Todd Drucker as now embodied in a digital proxy."

Judge Steadman closed his eyes. "No, absolutely no. I won't allow it. That's it. If you are looking to establish grounds for appeal, so be it, but I think any appellate court in the nation would side with my ruling."

— —

Deprived of his dramatic ploy, Turndale returned to the plodding plan of his opening statement by calling a further string of witnesses to muddy the waters, painting a messy picture of technical complexity that implied that neither Existendia nor its officers could possibly be held accountable for the death of Coleman Drucker. In the morning of the third day of the defense, Jerry Pendrake was called to take the stand and be sworn in. "Please state your full name and permanent address for the record."

"Jerome A. Pendrake, 1 Live Oak Circle, Santa Monica, California."

"Please state your full legal name."

"I . . . I just go by my middle initial."

"Unless the letter A alone is your lawful middle name, you need to identify yourself by your full name. For the record."

"Jerome Aloysius Pendrake."

Tamika, sitting next to Dana, leaned over and whispered. "God, if my middle name were Aloysius, I'd keep it secret, too."

"What did you say?"

"Aloysius," —she stretched out the syllables— "the guy's middle name. I wouldn't tell anybody either."

"Ohmygod, I have to let Leah know." She turned the other way to Doug Pulaski, the new guy on the legal team. "Can you get a message to Leah? Now?"

"Sure. What it is it?"

"Tell her when she gets the chance, to ask Pendrake whether he ever worked for the Department of Homeland Security, Idaho National Lab."

"How is she going to manage that line of questioning?"

"Let her figure it out. Just tell her it's absolutely vital she ask. And she should press him on it if she has to."

Pulaski scribbled a note, which he folded and handed to the bailiff. When Leah read it, she looked back at Pulaski with an are-you-sure look on her face. He nodded slowly but emphatically.

Turndale began his examination of Pendrake with questions about the field of business in which Existendia operated.

"The service we offer to our clients is unique. Using proprietary brain imaging techniques that we developed and proprietary computer algorithms for analysis of the data from those techniques, we are able to create a complete, active model of a living person's brain—not just what it looks like but how it functions. The digital proxy, as we call it, captures the complete personality, even the experience and memories of the client. The proxy is the digital embodiment of that person uploaded into the computer."

"And your clients, why would they pay you for this . . . this service? What is accomplished by uploading someone's personality into a computer?"

"The digital proxy can take over after a person dies."

"Objection. The witness is not qualified to make such an assertion."

"I'll rephrase the question. Please tell the court, Mr. Pendrake, on the basis of your company's interviews and surveys, what it is that your clients expect to achieve by the process of uploading their personalities into computer form."

"They expect their digital proxies to live on indefinitely."

— —

When Bannon Turndale finished his questioning, Leah stood and approached the witness stand. "So, Mr. Pendrake, you are Chief Executive Officer of Existendia Enterprises LLC, is that correct?"

"Yes, that is correct."

"And how long have you held that position?"

"Since the company was formed, nine years ago."

"And what was your employment before that?"

Bannon Turndale raised his index finger. "Objection, your honor. The defendant's employment history is irrelevant to the matter at hand."

Leah addressed the bench. "It goes to the question of expertise and experience, hence competence in his present role."

Steadman nodded. "I'll allow it."

"Please tell the court your position before you joined Existendia," Leah said.

"I was President of Blackhorse Services Corporation."

Leah looked frustrated. "And what did you do at Blackhorse Services?"

"I ran the company. That's what a president does."

"Of course. And what was it that Blackhorse Services did?"

"We provided specialized computer programming services to clients."

"What sort of specialized programming?"

This time Turndale stood up. "Objection."

Judge Steadman looked at Leah. "If this is not going anywhere, please move on."

"It goes to the defendant's own skills and expertise, which is relevant to his possible role in the death of Coleman Drucker."

"Objection," Turndale said. "The witness is not named as a defendant in this case."

"The company of which he is the top executive is," Leah answered.

Judge Steadman nodded. "I'll allow it, but finish your line of questioning, Ms. Goldstein."

Leah let a few seconds pass before her next question. "Were you ever in the employ of the Department of Homeland Security?"

"Objection."

"Overruled. The witness will answer."

Pendrake slowed his breathing and flattened his expression.

Leah moved closer. "Do remember, you are under oath, Mr. Pendrake. Did you ever work for the Department of Homeland Security at the Idaho National Laboratory?"

"No."

"You're certain?"

"I would know if I had ever worked there."

"And you do know the penalties for perjury?"

"Objection. It is not the job of counsel for the plaintiffs to explain the law."

"Sustained."

"I withdraw the question."

— —

At the lunch break, Leah lit into Dana. "What the hell was that all about? You made me look like a first-year law student out there. The first rule for litigators is never to ask a question of a witness if you don't know what the answer will be and what you will do with that answer. You left me hanging with nowhere to go next."

"He's lying. You could see it on his face. Did you see how he paused, as if deciding whether to lie or not."

"I'm a lawyer, not a psychic. I don't do mindreading. So, are you going to at least tell me what this is about?"

Dana's mouth opened but she said nothing. She shook her head. "I . . ."

"Look, we're the attorneys, and we're the ones who decide the strategy and ask the questions. Don't jump in like that again. Even if you do, I'm just going to ignore you. Understand?"

Hal Workman put his hand on Leah's shoulder, but she shrugged it off. "Maybe he did work for Homeland Security," he said. "Maybe he did lie."

"So? What does that have to do with our case?"

"Maybe nothing. Maybe it will throw him off if we need to recall him."

"Well, it sure the fuck threw me off."

"You want me to take the next cross?"

"No, I want you not to send me notes that say I have to do something stupid."

"It wasn't me. It came from Doug, remember."

"Well, it's a good thing that the junior member of our team is not here at the moment. He's your boy, so I hope you concur that he could use a remedial course regarding courtroom conduct."

"Agreed. Now let's get something to eat and confer."

Once the legal team was off to lunch, Barbra came over. "What was that whole Homeland Security thing about? It got us nowhere and put Leah on the back foot. Getting an outright 'no' like that can make us look like we don't know what we are talking about."

"It's about who killed your husband, who was really responsible for his death. I'm pretty sure now that Gwen Seabrook and Jerry Pendrake were working together and may have played some part in orchestrating Coleman's murder. I just put together that they were old buddies from their hacker days. She worked under the handle Ipotane and collaborated with a hacker going by the handle Aloe-Wishes. Get it? Aloysius, Aloe-Wishes. She was part of an infamous group known as the Snake River League, and I'll lay odds he was, too. The Snake River League was made up of cyberwarfare people who had worked with Homeland Security and Idaho National Labs. We need to take this to the police."

Rolf threw his hands open. "Take what to the police? That this guy has an odd middle name that sounds like some old hacker handle?"

"But they called each other and exchanged texts."

"And how do you know that?"

Dana chewed on her lower lip. "I hacked into phone company records."

"Oh great, and that's what you're going to take to the police? Conjectures, guesses about old digital skullduggery, and stolen data? Really? They'd laugh you out of the room. If they didn't lock you up for cyber intrusion and data theft."

"Then we have to pursue this on our own."

Barbra took a step back. "I'm out, guys. I have a lawsuit to win. I don't have time to play detective—or spy versus spy."

As Barbra walked away, Dana looked skyward. "Where do we go from here?"

Rolf shrugged. "Not to the police, that's for sure. We got

nothing. A rhyming rare middle name and a file of illegally acquired phone records are not going to get us anywhere. Too bad the dead can't speak."

"What do you mean?"

"Your Hispanic buddy. What was his name?"

"You mean Geraldo?"

"Yeah. Did you ever check his phone records? I mean, as far as the police are concerned, he's at most a missing person, but maybe there's something in his call logs that could link him back to our equestrian entrepreneur, as you did with . . . well, the others."

"No, I didn't think to hack his records. No reason. He was with me, my conduit into Tensora."

"Well, not that I would be suborning criminal appropriation of digital assets, but maybe you should worm your way back into the phone company and see what bloodstains might still linger in their databases. You did leave yourself a backdoor, didn't you?""

"No, it was just a quick in and out again. I'm sure I could find my way back into the customer databases, though, but I don't see it. Not worth it."

"Maybe, maybe not, but there's only one way to find out. Think about it. I'll see you tomorrow."

— —

After nearly a week more of a succession of hardware and software experts whose testimony only seemed to obfuscate the case and confuse the jury, Bannon Turndale made his last move. "Defense calls Aram Moishe Netsky."

After Netsky was sworn in, Turndale called for entering defense exhibit J into evidence, a NuConfer Model 23 Telepresencer robot with its oversize portrait-mode screen, which was carried into the courtroom by two assistants.

When placed before the bench, it balanced on its two wheels with barely perceptible motion.

Leah Goldstein objected. "The telepresence robot that was actually at the scene has already been introduced as plaintiffs' exhibit B. There can be no valid justification for introducing as an exhibit an entirely new piece of equipment that is unrelated to the case at hand."

"This robot, NuConfer Model 23, serial number KJX193619B"—he read from his notes— "is the current embodiment of the computer software complex referred to as the Drucker Proxy, which is at the very center of this case, as will become evident. As soon as I am permitted to examine my witness, I will—"

Judge Steadman moved quickly to cut him off. "Counselors, approach the bench." He waited until they both were in front of him, to lean forward. "Mr. Turndale, I ruled on this matter before the trial began. I will not have the issue argued again in open court in front of the jury."

"But, your honor, Defense Exhibit J represents, by extension, the Drucker Proxy."

"I object, Your Honor. Either this machine is the exhibit being introduced into evidence or the exhibit is something else somewhere else, in which case, that something should be introduced into evidence."

Turndale feigned impatient indulgence. "It is physically impossible to introduce into evidence the actual computer software comprising the Drucker Proxy, in as much as said hardware and software are physically scattered among server farms located across North America. Exhibit J, this device, is connected to that network of computer servers, colloquially known as 'the cloud,' which is executing the computer code that constitutes the Drucker Proxy. By means of this device, it will be possible to interact with the Drucker Proxy and establish its bona fides."

"Objection. If what is being introduced as Defense Exhibit J is software, a collection of computer code, then there is well established precedent for providing a printout or listing of said code as evidence, which then becomes subject to examination by experts in computer software forensics."

"As my esteemed colleague, Ms. Goldstein, already understands, Your Honor, the code for the various components of the software currently comprising the proxy comes to more than 120 million lines of code, but that, in itself, is not the Drucker Proxy, which exists as an assemblage of running code in combination with, at the present time, more than seventeen petabytes of model and state data, that's seventeen million billion bytes, representing the complete state of the connectome of Coleman Drucker." He took a breath to continue but was interrupted by the rap of Judge Steadman's gavel.

"Enough techno-babble. In my chambers, Counselors. Please step back." He raised his voice and turned to the waiting Aram Netsky. "The witness may step down. Court is in recess and the jury is temporarily dismissed while this matter is settled."

— —

It took more than an hour of debate and questioning for Judge Steadman to become convinced, reluctantly, that the potential probative value of the exhibit as evidence in the case outweighed its possible prejudicial effect. He reasoned that, even if his ruling became grounds for appeal, at least the issues would be exposed to needed scrutiny and debate.

The jury was recalled and he gaveled the court back into session. "The court, with reservations, will allow Defense

Exhibit J to be entered into evidence as containing, by virtue of electronic connection, the computer code and data comprising the software simulation identified by the Defense as a digital proxy, a putative simulation of the brain of one Coleman Todd Drucker, the deceased. Further, counsels for the plaintiffs and the defendants have stipulated that the device and the software simulation, collectively, are an inanimate object of exhibit, any appearance or behavior to the contrary notwithstanding. The jury is cautioned not to personify or anthropomorphize the robot of Defense Exhibit J and to remember at all times that it should not be regarded as a person or as being, in any sense, a party to the matter before the court."

Aram Netsky was called to the stand and reminded that he was still under oath. The telepresence robot was once again awkwardly carried in by two assistants and placed next to the witness stand, where it stood on its own.

Bannon Turndale approached with what could only be described as a swagger. "Mr. Netsky, what is your position at Existendia?"

"I am the CTO, the Chief Technical Officer."

"And in this position, what are your responsibilities?"

"I am responsible for and directly or ultimately oversee all computer software engineering and development as well as all basic scientific research in computer science and neuropsychology within the company."

"And what qualifies you to function in this capacity?"

"I have a PhD in Applied Mathematics from the Massachusetts Institute of Technology, a PhD in Computer Science from Carnegie-Mellon University, and a PhD in Neuroscience from Stanford University."

"And please tell the court the subject matter on the basis

of which you were awarded these degrees."

"Objection, Your Honor. Dr. Netsky is not being called as an expert witness. There is no need to parade his credentials. Plaintiffs are prepared to stipulate that he is fully qualified for his role in Existendia."

"Sustained. Please move on."

"As CTO of Existendia, you are in charge of all software development, all computer programming. Is that correct?"

"Yes."

"And would you please tell the court what that means in terms of your knowledge of the software associated with Exhibit J."

"I invented the modeling schema and the data models as well as the core algorithms running the actual digitized representation of the connectome of Coleman Todd Drucker."

"Could you explain that in layman's terms, in words that even a lawyer could understand?" He glanced toward the defense table as quiet laughter rippled through the room. Judge Steadman's gavel cut it off.

"I believe I can. I invented—with the help of many others, of course, and based on earlier research by scientists in various fields— a way to image and identify all of the neurons, the cells, in the brain of a living person, as well as all of the interconnections among them, and to translate this into a digital representation that can then be processed by a computer: a digital proxy that is a computerized replica of the complete personality and mental apparatus of a person."

"And the device beside you, Defense Exhibit J, could you explain—again in simple layman terms—what that device is in relation to such a digital proxy?"

"It is what is sometimes called a telepresence robot or

avatar. In this case it functions as a communications device with computer software running at some remote location, much as Alexa or a similar device enabled people to talk with and query computers, only this avatar includes a television screen and remotely controlled wheels for mobility."

"Could you verify for the court the identity of this particular avatar and the digital proxy with which it is interconnected?"

"Yes, of course." He turned toward the robot. "Coleman, are you listening?"

The recognizable voice of Coleman Drucker came from the avatar's speakers as the screen lit up with his animated face. "Yes, I can hear you and see you. I have been following the proceedings all along with great interest."

Hal Workman waited for the courtroom to quiet down again. "Objection."

"Your Honor, the witness is simply verifying the operation of Defense Exhibit J."

"Overruled. Proceed, Counselor."

"Dr. Netsky, have you verified that the robotic avatar before you is indeed operating correctly with the correct computer software running the digital proxy comprising Defense Exhibit J?"

"No, but I will if I may be permitted to continue."

Turndale turned toward Judge Steadman. "With the Court's permission."

"Proceed."

Netsky addressed the robot. "Coleman, what was your mother's maiden name?"

"Objection." Hal Workman managed a look of scorn. "Such information is a matter of public record and verifies nothing."

"Dr. Netsky," Turndale said, "is it possible to verify the correct operation using something that would certainly not be a matter of public record?"

"Yes, of course. Coleman, what is the login credential you used for the internal network while working at Drucker Unified?"

"Objection. The so-called digital proxy was never an employee of Drucker Unified. Furthermore, the login credentials could have been acquired through digital intrusion."

Turndale turned his palms up in supplication. "Your honor, with the Court's indulgence, defense needs some way to confirm that the exhibit is indeed our exhibit and is, in fact, working properly. We cannot proceed if counsel for the plaintiffs objects to every means."

"Mr. Workman, is there any means of verification acceptable to the plaintiffs?"

"Plaintiffs are prepared to stipulate without further demonstration that Exhibit J is, in fact, a working peripheral device actively connected to running computer software simulation devised by Existendia to mimic the behavior of a person."

The avatar turned to face the jury. "I am not a peripheral device, and I am not a simulation. I am Coleman Todd Drucker." It pivoted back to face the defense table. "And I have not stopped loving you, Barbra. I—"

The banging of Judge Steadman's gavel cut him off. "I will have order in my court. Mr. Turndale, what kind of a stunt is this? Counselors, approach the bench." Bannon Turndale and Hal Workman walked to the front.

"I apologize, Your Honor," Turndale said. "The proxy is an autonomous agent. It does sometimes have a mind of its own, shall we say."

"We shall not say. You have introduced this thing, this robot, as an exhibit. You will keep your exhibit under control. If you have to unplug the thing or whatever you have to do, do it. I will not have this kind of circus act in my courtroom. Your transparent bid for sympathy from the jury is unacceptable and will not be permitted in this courtroom. Is that clear?"

"Yes, Your Honor."

"Okay, step back."

Judge Steadman waited until the lawyers had returned to their respective tables before addressing the jury. "The jury will ignore that last bout of computer malfunction, and the assertions coming from the device about its own nature are to be stricken from the record."

From that point, Turndale made a valiant effort to keep his examination focused on his witness, Aram Netsky. "Dr. Netsky, can you tell the court, something of the nature of the functioning of the Drucker Proxy, er, Defense Exhibit J, what it is capable of?"

"Yes, of course. The Drucker Proxy remembers everything up to the date, approximately two and a half years ago—I can look up the exact date if it is important—when the last upload was completed from the client, Coleman Todd Drucker, as well as everything that has happened since the proxy was activated last year."

"How can you know that?"

"I can ask." He faced the avatar. "Cole, do you remember our first meeting?"

"Yes, it was on my yacht. You came along as a plus one at one of my parties. I think you were with that insufferable Meagan Sedgewick who was invited only because her brother was on our Board. We chatted about investing for the long game. Later that night, I did some digging about your company, which eventually led to becoming a client. Barbra and I had a fight that night over the attention I was paying to the wife of one of our investors. I—"

"Objection. We do not need a recitation of domestic drama to see that the speech generation of the device is impressive."

"Sustained. Mr. Turndale, please move on."

"Dr. Netsky, whose idea was it to introduce Exhibit J?"

"It was Cole's. The idea came from the Drucker Proxy."

"And what did he, uh, it say to you?"

The avatar rolled forward. "I told him I wanted to keep going, to keep running my company, and to see my little girl grow up—"

Steadman's gavel banged three times in perfect synch with Hal Workman, who snapped, "Objection! This is a transparent bid for sympathy without merit or relevance for the case."

"Sustained. If the functioning of the so-called exhibit cannot be controlled, then we shall have to turn it off."

"That won't be necessary, Your Honor. We have no further questions." He nodded toward the plaintiffs' table. "Your witness."

Hal stood slowly. "Plaintiffs would like some additional time to prepare, as Defense Exhibit J was not on the schedule."

"All right. You have until tomorrow morning. Court is in recess until ten tomorrow."

As Hal and Leah reorganized their papers, Barbra asked, "What are we going to do now?"

"We're going to use the rest of the day mapping out a

very carefully constructed narrative. We want our every word to be telegraphing to the jury that, however good their little robot seems, it is just a trick, a Clever Hans wrapped in a technology blanket."

— —

Hal Workman, dressed in a classic double-breasted pin-stripe with matching tie and pocket square, approached the witness.

"Do you remember the day that Coleman Drucker was killed?"

Netsky sighed. "Yes, of course."

"And what of the exhibit? Does the computer program, Defense Exhibit J, have any memory record of the day Coleman Drucker was killed?"

Netsky turned toward the telepresence unit and raised his eyebrows in inquiry.

Judge Steadman leaned forward. "The witness will respond verbally and directly to questions."

"Yes, of course. So, well, I don't know if the Drucker Proxy remembers the day that, well, the attack occurred, but I can inquire."

"Please do."

Netsky turned back to the avatar. "Do you remember the day of the attack on Coleman Drucker?"

"I do."

Hal Workman resisted turning to face the avatar. "Will you please . . . will you please direct the software to inform the court what memory record it has of that day."

Netsky sighed. Under his breath he said. "I'm beginning to feel like Gwen in Galaxy Quest."

Steadman glared at him. "The witness is reminded to speak up and speak into the microphone."

"Yes, Your Honor." He made an exaggerated slow-motion turn toward the avatar. "Cole, please tell the court what you remember."

The avatar began a precise and detailed recounting of the events leading up to the arrival of Drucker and the others in Aram Netsky's office. Then it stopped. "That's it. Netsky must have turned me off at that point. It's like being knocked out. One minute you're talking about something or practicing with the arm, then, bing! The next thing I remember was the following day. I was struggling to get used to a different model avatar—this one, in fact."

Workman scowled. "So, you don't remember the robot arm striking the deceased?"

"Mr. Workman, I will not caution you again. Address your questions to the witness, not the exhibit."

"I'm sorry, Your Honor. Dr. Netsky, does the machine have any record of the actual attack?"

"Apparently not."

"Would you please inquire, for the court, whether the machine has any record of the attack itself."

"Cole, do you remember anything about the attack by the robot arm?"

"Nothing, it's a blank, as if it were erased."

"Objection." Turndale jumped in. "Speculation. Move to strike."

"Your Honor, Defense is objecting to the output of an exhibit, its own exhibit."

Judge Steadman put his hand to his chin. "Overruled."

"No further questions, Your Honor."

"Redirect, Your Honor."

"You may proceed."

Turndale took his time approaching the stand. "Dr.

Netsky, does the Drucker Proxy have any way, any means or mechanism for knowing what happens when it is not running, when it is not activated?"

"No, none whatsoever."

"And what of its memory? Is it infallible, like a computer? Does it ever forget or be mistaken about something that happened?"

"Sure, just like anyone, it can be wrong, it can forget."

"Thank you. No further questions."

– 39 –

Dana did not show up in court the next day nor the next. It wasn't until the weekend when she called Rolf. "We need to talk. I have some news."

"Where were you. I was worried."

"Not enough to call or text, you weren't."

"I was looking out for you. If you are right about Seabrook and Pendrake, you tipped your hand with Leah's abortive questioning. I thought you might be in danger, and I didn't want to do anything that might lead to you."

"I'm safe. I have a body guard and am doing what I can to stay out of sight. Anyway, I found something. Can I come over?"

"You know the answer to that question. Just knock."

— —

Rolf opened the door even before she could rap on it. "You know, I did worry about you. Still do." He hurried her in and gave her a long hug. "What took you so bloody long? Hacking skills wearing out?""

"I had to find another way into the phone records. They must have found traces of my last intrusion, because the exploits I used before have been patched over. But anyway, your suggestion paid off."

"Told ya. What did you find?"

"The last two incoming calls on Geraldo's cellphone were from a new phone, never used before."

"A burner?"

"Presumably."

"Dang. So we lost the trail."

"Not completely." She sat down on one of his 3D printed chairs. "I went into the records for the burner phone number and found something most interesting. Most interesting."

"You going to tell me about your cracking exploits or are you going to just sit there grinning into invisibility like that what's-its-face cat."

"Cheshire. I myself prefer Red Leicester. Speaking of cheese and crackers, are you going to offer me something to eat?"

"Sure, but while I whip something together, keep talking." He walked to the other side of the breakfast bar and started rummaging through the refrigerator.

"Okay, so I ending up digging rather deep into the phone system tracking logs. The only calls on that burner phone account, three in all, originated through a cell tower in Topanga Canyon, which just so happens to be the closest tower to a certain horse ranch."

"No shit."

"Yes, and that was also the last cell tower through which the burner phone ever registered; no further calls on that SIM card. And—you will love this—that was also the last cell tower that Geraldo's phone registered through. Both of those last connections happened on the same day, the day Geraldo's body showed up, ever so briefly, in a certain cinema parking garage. And the time stamp on the very last ping from Geraldo's phone was after I saw his body. Do you realize what that means?"

"That his phone was still turned on somewhere near the ranch sometime after he was killed. Now we have something. But still not anything we can take to the police."

"Maybe, but wait. You haven't heard the best of it yet. Or

the worst of it. The last calls in Geraldo's records were not the only ones that were interesting. There were calls and text messages, many of them over the last year, to and from him to another phone belonging to—ta-da—our elusive equestrian."

"He was also involved with her?"

"Possibly. Anyway, my guess is he may have been working both sides, serving as an insider at Tensora for me and for Seabrook. He may even have helped plant the malicious software that enabled them to take control, although I can't quite fathom why then he would give me a copy of the music card with the hack on it, all the while playing innocent."

"Maybe he wasn't playing." Rolf handed her a drink. "Maybe he was being used by Seabrook without knowing what he was doing."

"That's also possible. Geraldo was always more than a little naïve. But we still are stuck with only hunches and hints—and evidence that we shouldn't have."

"So, let's get some hard evidence."

"How? What do you have in mind?"

"I think we need to do some looking around at Seabrook's ranch. Your phone findings suggest that could be where your unfortunate Latino friend ended up."

"How are we going to do this looking around. The place is a riding academy; it's in use all week, and it's huge. I don't know exactly, but I would guess it's hundreds of acres and umpteen miles of trails. And they know who we are— me from my interview with Seabrook and you from the trial."

"That's all right. We don't have to go in ourselves. Remember, what I do is robotics."

"Right. So, we send in a crew of lumbering robots to look

270

around for us. Sure."

"Robots do not all lumber, except in old movies. These days the real ones can crawl, swim, even tunnel."

"Are you suggesting underground reconnaissance?"

"You'll see. Let me handle that end of things. We can meet back here on Monday afternoon, say around four."

"Why Monday?"

"It's after the weekend and likely to be a slow day at the ranch."

"I have an even better idea, why don't I stay over. I can help and we can get reacquainted. You're not the only one who's been missing someone."

"I like that. I really, really like that. But I will have to leave you Monday morning to get some stuff from my office." He came back from the kitchen with a plate of crudités, hummus, water crackers, and assorted cheeses. "There you go, both White Cheshire and Red Leicester. Ask and you shall receive."

"You know, you are amazing, my Rolfy, and I love you."

"Of course I'm amazing, and, well, I guess I love you too." He took his time setting the tray down, never taking his eyes from hers.

– 40 –

Gwenbrook Riding Academy was bordered on the
northeast by a single-lane dirt road heading south
from the paved county road. Once the fence with its
'No Trespassing' signs started appearing on the right, Rolf
slowed his electric pickup and scanned the left shoulder,
looking for something he had spotted on Google Earth.
There it was, tire ruts, grown over with grass. "Old access to
the power line corridor, it takes a bend in a few hundred
feet. We won't be visible from the road."

"You still haven't told me what exactly you . . . . we are
doing. I mean, I'm not complaining about the weekend,
which was wonderful, but we hardly talked. And then you
took off this morning."

"Patience, Grasshopper, I'll show you." The pickup
rocked and bucked as he eased it along the disused roadway.
He rolled into a grassy clearing to one side and killed the
engine. "Hop out and give me a hand with the tarp."

As they stood on opposite sides of the pickup and carefully rolled back the tarp covering the bed, Dana laughed.
"It's a drone, right?" The aircraft, with its gray-green wood-
land camo finish, sat with its wings reaching diagonally
from corner to corner in the long pickup bed. "You're going
to do a flyover with a buzz-bomb to make sure you have
everyone's attention."

Rolf undid catches on the straps holding the drone in
place. "This is no simple drone and it does not buzz. This is
a Semi-Autonomous Aerial Surveillance Robot. It's more
glider than plane, driven by a near-silent electric ducted fan

and powered by ultra-light fuel-cell batteries. It has multi-spectrum cameras that allow sophisticate image analysis and—"

"And it's ginormous. Of course, nobody would ever notice such a big green electric pterodactyl circling overhead, near-silent or not."

"You might be surprised. Grab that wing and we'll lift it out. Careful. Easy now. There. Now hold it as high as you can and look up." The underside was camouflaged to look like cloud-smeared sky and the wings were translucent. "See, harder to spot than you think. Plus, it'll be gliding along quickly but quietly right at the three-hundred foot legal limit. It'll fly a preprogrammed search pattern while its high-res surveillance camera sends us pics in real-time over a 5G link. My little box there will stitch them together into a seamless view that we can scan or zoom in and out on even as it's still coming in. Pretty slick, huh? We should be back on the road out of here in less than an hour."

Rolf booted up his ruggedized laptop before powering up the drone's onboard electronics to check the wireless connection. "Now, we lug this thing, ever so carefully, up to the ridge where the powerline was supposed to run. It will give us a straight shot to launch it."

Once at the ridge and the wide swathe cut through for high-tension lines that were never completed, Rolf held the drone aloft and started to sprint along the overgrown corridor. As the ducted fan kicked in and started to whir, he heaved the drone at an angle upward. It rose for a bit, dipped, then began a long slow tight spiral climb to clear the trees before turning away from the powerline right-of-way toward the horse ranch. The whir of the drone faded as it continued to climb and turned back parallel to the road to start its preplanned mapping pattern.

"Let's get back to the truck and watch the pics as they're coming in."

— —

Rolf considered the powerline corridor to be too rough and overgrown to land the drone, so, as the last of the images popped onto the laptop screen and were tiled into place, he backed up out onto the dirt road and parked on the shoulder. "Keep a look out for the drone," he said, as he plugged a console with joystick controllers on it into his laptop.

"There it is, eleven o'clock high," she said.

"Got it. Once I land it on the road, be ready to help me get it back into the truck." He lined up the drone with a straight stretch of the road and brought it down gradually, bringing up the nose at the last moment to drag the tail and put it into a belly flop and sloppy skid along the hump in the center of the road. "Not bad, now let's stow it and get out of here."

They were just lifting it by the wings when the sound of hoof beats drew their attention to the woods across the road. A horse and rider could be seen through the trees, gaining speed while heading toward the fence at the other side of the road. The rider expertly urged her horse into a jump that cleared the fence and the ditch running beside the road. She reined in and tugged the horse into a smart quarter-horse turn to head straight up the road toward them.

Rolf shouted. "To the ditch." He ran in an arc to bring the wings around to parallel the road. He, Dana, and the plane, dove for the edge as the rider spurred her horse into a gallop and flew past them to be quickly lost in a swirl of dust from the road.

"Into the truck. Forget the drone. It's only hardware and it's insured. Let's get out of here."

Rolf was completing a three-point turn to head the pickup back down the road when the horse and rider reappeared out of the dust cloud. He slammed down on the accelerator, forcing the rider to wheel her mount to avoid crashing into them. As he raced away, he could see her in the rearview mirror following at a full gallop until she was lost in the dust cloud trailing them.

"Who was that masked rider," Rolf joked.

"I think it was Lady Seabrook, but I really didn't get a good look. What in hell did she think she was doing?"

"Running us down."

"Can she get anything from the drone?"

"Shit, yeah." He slammed on the brakes and pulled over to the side of the road. "Hand me my laptop."

"What are you going to do, fly it to us?"

"No, it can't take off on its own; it has to be launched. But I'm erasing its memory card." He typed in an access code and a command. "There, she may have plenty of good guesses, but she won't have the data to know precisely what we were doing or who we are."

"Scant comfort, I'd say."

"I'll take what comfort I can get. Now, let's head home and start going through the photos."

"What are we looking for?"

"Bodies."

— —

It was early morning before the combination of Rolf's pattern-recognition software, a deep-learning package, and a great many quick eyes-on visual checks paid off. "We have two really good candidates where the ground seems to have been disturbed in about the right shape not too long ago and with reasonable accessibility. This one"—he tapped a spot on the wall screen— "is in a small clearing where one of their trails runs through the woods, and this one not far from the main stables is in what seems to be a vegetable garden. It's a little too small, but it fits the criteria."

"Fine, now what do we do? We can't just go in there with a couple of shovels and ask Seabrook to let us dig up her garden and chop into one of her bridle paths."

"No, but now we finally bring in the men and women in blue. Don't forget, I've worked with the LAPD. I know the right people to call."

"Don't they need, like, a search warrant?"

"I'm one step ahead. Lieutenant Figley thinks he knows just the right sympathetic judge who would be ready to sign a warrant on the basis of what we have. It does require tossing in your phone company logs with the cell tower data, which might make you vulnerable, but if a search were to actually turn up a body, Figley thinks your trespassing will be overlooked."

"What about your aerial trespassing?"

"Not in the same league as digital breaking and entering, but odds are we both get off with a talking to and a wrist slap."

"Odds are, huh."

"Yeah."

"Okay, what the hell. Let's do it. I'd rather spend a few years in a minimum security prison for geeks than eternity in an unmarked grave."

— —

Armed with a warrant, an interagency team led by Rolf's colleagues from Los Angeles County, carried out their raid the following Monday. After slow excavation, the site in the woods turned up the carcass of a mountain lion that may or may not have been illegally killed. The spot in the vegetable patch turned up nothing, being the site of a tomato planting that was dug up after it stopped producing.

Gwen Seabrook accepted the police team's apologies with calculated fury. "I hope you are satisfied and duly chagrined. I don't know where nor from whom you got your information, but I will tell you, this is an outrage. Be forewarned that I shall pursue every legal avenue of redress open to me regarding your unwarranted intrusion onto private property. Good day, gentlemen. I trust you have replaced your divots after slicing into my property."

The next day, a FedEx package arrived at Rolf's apartment; it contained the blank memory card from the drone.

— —

"What are you doing?" he asked Dana.

"Moving out, what does it look like?"

"I didn't know you were moved in."

"Typical male. Clueless."

"I may be clueless, but I am not your typical male. Your typical male is not ready to marry Dana Carmody."

"What?" She spun around to face him. "What the hell are you talking about?"

"Us, the time we've been spending together, what I maybe should have realized long ago—long, long ago. And maybe far away. It took me a while to get here, but all this . . . this threat stuff has made me aware that we're not getting any younger, neither of us. I think we should—"

"Not now, Rolf. I already have too much to handle. They know who you are and where you live. I have to get out of here and back to my hidey hole."

"I'll protect you."

"And how will you do that? With the same saber-sharp skill that you skewered Gwen Seabrook, that you zeroed in on where the body was buried, that . . . Oh shit, just get out of the way and let me leave."

"Okay, but you're running away because you can't handle commitment. You're always going on about men who can't commit. Why is that? What is the beam in your eye that leads you to spot the splinters in the men around you, the men who care about you? Not just men. From what I heard, Barbra is ready to tie the knot with you."

"Where the fuck did you hear . . .? Oh, never mind. Look, goddammit, I'm just trying to stay alive. I got no time for this shit. I . . ." Her voice wavered and she started to cry. "Fuck it, I'm out of here." She shoved the last few things into her backpack and pushed past him.

Rolf stood in the bedroom, arms crossed, as the apartment door slammed.

− 41 −

After the sideshow with the Drucker Proxy avatar, the defense at the wrongful death trial quickly closed its case. The plaintiffs' summation was delivered by Hal in his workmanlike manner, leaving the jury with only one clear path forward: to rule in their favor and with a massive award. Bannon Turndale countered with a long entreaty that appealed to unspecified conspiracy theories about how the complex systems of Existendia might have been hacked, since the proxy software that otherwise operated the robotic arm was not active at the time of the attack. Along the way, he never missed a chance to refer to Defense Exhibit J as if it were, in fact, Coleman Todd Drucker incarnate, the implication being that, if Drucker lived on, in whatever form or guise, the jury could hardly find Existendia or its officers liable in a wrongful death suit.

While Turndale danced in front of the jury, Dana was back in Barbra's pied-a-terre, plotting her next assault and making phone calls. "Pop, I need your help."

"I'm not surprised, baby girl. What can I do for you now?"

"Can I get you to call in some markers and arrange for some business meetings with somebody from your far-flung business empire?"

"Possibly, what do you have in mind?"

"Are any of your investments involved in real estate development?"

"Maybe. Can I call you back on a different line?"

"Sure, Pop. I'll be right here."

— —

Gwen Seabrook's voice over the phone was as thick as raw honey. "I know the timing isn't the best, but it's a real sweet deal if it closes. These people are interested in the southwest corner for a major high-end housing development, a planned luxury community sporting tie-ins with the ranch. Kinda like those golf-course communities but not aimed at retirees, more the younger, active set with too much money and not enough places to spend it. They want me to fly up to San Fran so they can give me a tour of what they did up in Marin County."

"Have you checked them out?"

"You know me, I did my due diligence. They're the real deal, with plenty of backing. If we can close a deal at the right time, it'll be extra icing on the cake."

"Okay. How long will you be gone. The jury's not going to be out forever."

"Two days, an overnight. I'll put Midge in charge at the ranch. I can always fly back early if something comes up."

"All right. We both should dump these phones and start over."

"Of course."

— —

For the moment, the main building at Gwenbrook was deserted except for Dana and Rolf. She had been reluctant to bring him back into the fray yet again, but she knew she needed his skill set. Between the two of them, they had disabled the alarm system and suckered the two security guards into chasing a ghost at the far end of the property. "I'd say we have twenty minutes at best," she said. "I don't trust how long your robot is going to be able to keep those guys distracted. Once they lose interest or figure out they're being led on a wild goose chase, they'll be in our laps in less than ten."

"No worries, because I'll get warning if they start heading this way. But, let's dig fast and hope we hit pay dirt."

Rolf was pecking away at the computer as Dana riffled through file drawers when they were interrupted by the sound of a closing door. Before they could find cover, the office door swung open. It was Jerry Pendrake brandishing a handgun.

Dana backed away from the credenza. "Well, if it isn't Aloe-Wishes."

"Perhaps you were expecting Ipotane."

"We were expecting she would be long gone and you would be preoccupied." Rolf took a step toward Pendrake.

"Don't. I think you know I can do it."

"Really? Was Geraldo Potts your first? Did you do it yourself or hire it out?"

"I've killed before, for my country. I didn't hold the gun or swing the hammer in those cases, but I set it up for officials in China to disappear and I provided coordinates for drone strikes."

"And poor Coleman Drucker?"

"Easy. It's one of the oldest hacking tactics: man-in-the-middle. I put a pipeline between the connectome model running in the cloud and the peripherals system down here. When I saw by remote access from my office what Drucker was doing, I saw opportunity. I almost didn't have time to draw the path for the robot arm. It had to be completed while the proxy was still running or the cover would be blown. Luckily, the proxy reacted with horror at the sight of his own murder and pulled back. Then it was just a matter of inducing amnesia with a restore point. Took a while to complete the overwrite, but fortunately, no one thought to query the proxy until much later."

"Why'd you do it?"

"For the money, what else. And I enjoyed the power, especially as I could wield it while that jerkoff Netsky reveled in his own delusions."

"And now you've been caught. I'm no prosecutor, but I would say the case against you is pretty solid."

"The case may be tight but the noose is not. I have not been caught. In a few minutes, Gwen will show up, having finished the prep for Operation Houdini."

"I thought she was up in San Francisco."

"Was. She came back early after she concluded your stooges didn't know what they were talking about. Nice try, but you need to make sure everyone in your cast is working from the same script. Fortunately for us, the curtain is about to close on this act. Presto change-o, new scene." He gestured with the handgun to get Rolf over next to Dana. "We were trained by the best and have taught ourselves some new tricks along the way. The set-aside for the settlement in the lawsuit that most punters are wagering will be in the ten figures, is already gone, sucked down a digital black hole, and we will follow shortly. Netsky wants to live forever, to live on in one of his cockamamie connectome models. Me? I just want to live now, to live large."

"So it's simple greed."

"Simple justice. I did everything for my country, including destroying its enemies, and my country canceled my contract without even severance pay. I got a pat on the back and a boot to the behind the moment they had enough of me. Now Gwen and I have what we earned and deserve."

"You'll get caught. Where can you hide? Everything is

connected, surveillance is everywhere."

"So are we. And a few close friends. We're everywhere and nowhere. We surveil the surveillers. Hey, Gwen and I are the best, brilliant hackers, but we can't be everywhere and do everything. We have a team, also the best."

"The Snake River League."

"Distinguished alums. Distinguished by a common commitment to getting even and getting ours. Now"—he unwound a long strip from a roll of duct tape—"it's time to buy us some time." He taped Dana's hands behind her back, then taped her feet to the side chair before doing the same to Rolf. He put a short strip across Rolf's mouth then turned back to Dana. "Any last words before I do you? No? You so rarely seem at a loss for words."

"I'll save my words for the grand jury."

"Be my guest." He taped her mouth and pressed the edges. "Bitch."

The sound of boots in the hallway got his attention. "Ah, there you are, Gwen, my love. Are you ready to ride?"

She stepped into the room. "Give me your gun."

"Why?"

"Just do it. We don't have time for banter. The security guards are on their way back. We need to clean up this mess before they get here, and not this way. Untape them and give me your gun."

Pendrake hesitated but handed his gun to Seabrook and started to cut Dana and Rolf loose. He finished by pulling the tape from each of their mouths. "Ouch," Dana said. "You—"

The rest of her words were cut off by two shots in quick succession.

Gwen turned the handgun toward Rolf, then Dana. "Who first?"

"Why?" Dana gestured toward the body of Jerry Pendrake, his chest red with blood and a pool spreading from his head. "I thought you were in this together."

"So did he. He even thought we were a couple, about to ride off into the sunset to live wealthily ever after. Men are so stupid. Maybe that's why I'm not into boys. Anyway, the three of us are going for a little ride, but only one of us is coming back. We'll run into the night watchmen, and they'll do their jobs. Then I'll be gone. Poof. Vanished without a trace. Except . . ."

"Except for the Snake River League, your coconspirators."

"There is no Snake River League, not any more. The last of it is on the floor. He believed in alliances and secret armies and conspiracy. I believe in me. Guess which one of us was right."

"I don't get it. How does this play out. Three dead at your ranch and—what?—the authorities just shrug and get back to chasing car thieves?"

"Look, consider this scenario. Pendrake surprises you, you kill him and run, the guards get you. Me? I'm in San Francisco. Never left my room. Perfect alibi. Oh, goodness me, how terrible, look what happened while I was away."

"But you flew back and—"

"Drove back. In a doctored car. Come on, Dana, you're no dummy. I cover my tracks."

"What about the money?"

"They'll find some of it . . . in Pendrake's account. They'll also find traces of my blood and signs that I was dragged off by force and . . . look, trust me, I've covered all the bases. And now, I'm out of here. So, march, you two.

Dana looked anxiously at Rolf as if he might have a plan. He shook his head almost imperceptibly before taking a step toward the door. As he passed her, he turned his cupped hand just enough for her to spot something he had palmed.

Outside, Seabrook pushed them toward the stables. "So, we're really going for a ride?" Dana asked.

"Don't be silly. That's just a good place for the show-down when the guards come back." She cocked her head at a faint sound, a soft whir that she had trouble locating. Then she looked up just as a dark shape descended toward her like a bird of prey. She shielded her face with one arm as she fired at the drone that was homing in the beacon in Rolf's hand. She stumbled backwards. Dana dove and was on top of her, knocking the gun out of her hand. "You fuckin' bitch," she screamed, as she pummeled Seabrook. Seabrook brought her knee up, Dana doubled up in pain, and Seabrook threw her to the side. When Seabrook stood, she found herself staring into the barrel of her own hand-gun steadied in Rolf's two-handed grip.

Seabrook panted, out of breath. "You wouldn't do it."

"I would. And not for the first time. Where do you think I learned my chops. I was a marine, assigned to Idaho National Labs. I was never invited to join the Snake River League, but that doesn't mean I wasn't any good."

Dana stood up painfully. "Geraldo Potts, he was part of the plan, right? What did you do with him?"

"That piece of shit?" Seabrook laughed. "He's right

where he belongs, buried under horseshit, composting away." She took a half step toward Rolf.

"Just because I wasn't in your League, doesn't mean I can't pull the trigger if I have to."

The voice came from behind him. "You won't have to, son. We got your broadcast, from the drone." Suddenly the paddock was flooded in light from patrol cars at either side.

Gwen Seabrook laughed again as she was cuffed. "You didn't win." She spat at Rolf. "You didn't get the money. And the widow doesn't get her husband back. And you, Ms. Dana Carmody, get nothing. Not the man, not the girl, nothing."

– 43 –

The Ducker contingent approached the Loram Life Building where the now bankrupt Existendia still had one floor. Leah Goldstein and Hal Workman led the legal platoon, with Bert Jamison as CFO representing Drucker's financial interests huffing along behind. Barbra, Dana, and Tonika Warner trailed. "So, why the whole army, Barbra?" Tonika asked.

"It was Dana's idea, witnesses and all."

Dana nodded. "Just seemed right. Sort of full stop at the end of the last paragraph. Thirty."

"Thirty?"

"Old school journalism. The number thirty between dashes marked the end of a story or manuscript."

"Oh. So bring me up to date. Last I heard the jury was still out, deadlocked."

Barbra laughed. "The jury was still out when Existendia settled: an even billion. That's billion with a *B*."

"I thought they were bankrupt, after all their clients fled or sued and they discovered that the Seabrook woman and her partner had sucked off their cash reserves."

"They were, sucking fumes, but Cloudastics, the parent company, has deep pockets. Plus, they recovered most of the funds that Seabrook and Pendrake had drained."

"How'd they pull that off? I read those two were pretty clever and had siphoned it off through layers of off-shore accounts and the like."

"They did, but Dana clued in the authorities, who were able to track down most of it."

"Dana girl, you got more talents than the Bible. How'd you do that?"

"I really didn't do it myself. I had expert help."

"Who?"

"A journalist never reveals her sources. Just someone with a good grasp of how money gets hidden behind off-shore dunes and shell companies." She half-winked in Barbra's direction. "And now our horse-loving Ms. Seabrook is in jail. Case closed."

"What of that other guy, the one we thought was behind it all?"

"You mean Aram Netsky? Well, the good doctor is also in jail, only he will get out long before Seabrook, having worked a plea bargain around commercial fraud charges.

Hal Workman, always the old-fashioned gentleman, paused at the entrance to the building and held the door for them all as they entered the elevator lobby.

— —

After introductions all around, the group gathered in Aram Netsky's office, shuffled their feet, and glanced at each other as if waiting for some kind of a starting bell. Finally, Bill Olafson, representing Cloudastics, spoke up. "Shall we begin? Or are we still waiting for someone to arrive?"

"We're waiting for Brad Pomerantz, our CTO," Barbra said. "I want his expert eyes watching everything."

"And we're waiting for Rolf Nagy," Dana said. "I invited him."

"The robotics geek?"

Dana stiffened. "He is an expert in robotics. Among other things. Ah, here they are."

"Good, okay people, let's get this over with." Olafson leaned on the desk. "I have pressing matters of my own back at the office. Mrs. Drucker, would you like to—"

"I'm Barbra Wilson, widow of the deceased. The former Mrs. Drucker declined to come today."

"Well, yes. So, Ms. Wilson, would you like to interact with the proxy before we proceed?"

"No! Emphatically not. Frankly, I've had quite enough of your creepy simulacrum, thank you. I just want the whole thing shut down and completely wiped out so there can be no further misuse of my late husband's intellect or inside knowledge."

"I assure you, that is also our intent at this point, what with the odometer on cloud resources still spinning away. So, let's do this." He turned to a technician seated at Netsky's old desk. "Log in and bring up the account files for the Drucker Proxy subaccount. Then—"

Leah Goldstein interrupted. "We need to verify the . . . the proxy."

The technician keyed in a command without waiting for instructions. A voice came through the console speakers. "I am . . ."

"You are who? Who is this?"

"I am . . . I am Aram, Aram Netsky. I . . ."

"He must have somehow substituted his own connecto-me. This is . . ."—Olafson reached past the technician to type a string of characters— "an anomaly, not planned." He tapped the return key.

"What are you doing? We need to erase the software and the . . . the model state data."

"Really, there's no need. We already surrendered the drive with the original backup copy—which, I understand, has been shredded—and now all we need to do is stop the billing for services and release the resources in the cloud.

This . . . this intrusion by something Dr. Netsky left in place is—"

"But what about the connectome, the model?" Dana jumped in.

Olafson gestured skyward. "It's the cloud. It's not real. The moment the computing and storage resources are released, they will be reallocated to other customers who will be using them for their own purposes. The model, the so-called connectome—your husband's, this . . . this, whatever. They were never more than scattered fragments of data and computational slices on servers somewhere among the two dozen facilities Cloudastics operates throughout the United States and Canada. Trust me, the moment those pieces are released, they will be gobbled up for some other project by others of our one million customers. As soon as we release resources, they'll be used by MIT for some AI project or NASA analyzing telescope photos or maybe some rich kid in his parents' basement trying to find a way to win all on Game of Thrones: The Game."

"Can you verify that, Brad?"

"I can verify that we appear to be looking at an executive dashboard for Cloudastics which shows the status of the software running on this particular subaccount."

Olafson nodded. "And I can testify under oath that is the case. Those two bouncing bars at the bottom of the screen represent the terabytes of storage and teraflops of computing committed to this software. They are quivering because the load varies slightly from moment to moment as the programs execute. I take the resource away, and it's gone. If there is no storage, there's not even a copy. In addition, we securely wipe freed up resources before returning them to the pool. Now, can I complete what I have committed to and am legally bound to do?"

"Yes, please."

Olafson pulled an identity token from his pocket and slid it into the slot on the keyboard. He typed a long pass phrase and was then offered a simple confirmation box. "There we are, gentlemen. And ladies. I hereby confirm release of resources from subaccount B1-EX-979-Drucker." He clicked on the "Yes" button, and the orange and blue bars at the bottom of the screen immediately started shrinking.

Dana watched as the bars diminished into mere slivers. "And what's that?" She pointed to two lines of color that refused to get any thinner.

"A rounding error, nothing. Once demand picks up in the morning, that, too, will be gone."

– 44 –

Barbra found Dana in the bedroom, two half-filled suitcases open on the bed. "What's up? You headed out on assignment or something?"

"No, no assignment. Just the opposite. I need to get away, spend some time sorting things out."

"What's to sort? Seems like things are finally well and truly sorted."

"Seems like. That's the truth, the whole truth, and . . ." Dana slumped down on the bed. "I don't know anymore. I just don't know. You think you want something, and then it comes along and you're not sure. Choices. Everybody wants choices, options. Right? Except, like, sometimes maybe it's better if you just get steered along, not having to decide."

"What are you talking about? What happened?"

"Rolf asked me to marry him. Five years of me wanting and hinting and him hedging and circling around, and finally, after the whole Snake River shit, he's suddenly ready, and . . ."

"I asked you to marry me, too. Remember?"

"Oh, I do, which is what makes this such a fucked up mess. Well, at least part of the mess."

Barbra sat down beside her and put her hand on Dana's thigh. "So, tell me more about this mess."

Dana leaned in. "You know, I've told you I want kids. Ever since I was little I've wanted kids. I wanted a chance to do it for real, for right, not like the way I grew up. And now Rolf has decided he wants them, too. Maybe it's coming to terms with his own mortality. Nothing like having a pistol pointed at your head to bring the thought of mortality to mind. Whatever. Anyway, he wants to get married, to do the whole family thing that I always wanted, except now there's you. And Becca. And I don't know what to do or where to turn."

"You turn to me, that's what you do. That's what partners do. They turn to each other to work it out. There's more than one way, you know."

"Stop with the Hallmark platitudes. I know all that, which is what makes this so fuckin' hard. I just need to get away to spend a little more time just with me, just figuring *me* out."

"How will you do that?"

"Desert air, overheated days and chilly nights. Last time I was at Vista Caliente was good. I'm going to try the retreat cure again."

"Okay. Take whatever time you need. I'll be here when you get back, whatever you decide."

"Oh God, Barbra. How can you be so . . . so . . ."

"Because I love you, that's how."

"And I love you. The damn thing is, I also love Rolf. I told him that I was going away for a while, and he said the same thing as you, almost word for word." She stood suddenly. "Argh! Some people look for this, for the real thing, all their lives. Tonika is still waiting for her guy to grow up enough to commit. And here I am, and I found it, only it's too much, twice too much, and I don't know what to do about it."

"You'll figure it out. We'll figure it out. Take all the time you need. Like I said, I'll still be here when you're ready."

— —

Watery shimmers of heat mirages rippled above the newly

paved driveway at Vista Caliente. Dana swung her mint-new lime-and-black Tensora roadster into a gap partway down the drive. It was midafternoon, too hot for work parties, and the place seemed deserted. Dana grabbed her backpack from the back seat before telling the car to put up the sunscreen top.

As she rounded the corner of the Big House, Freddy looked up from his Scrabble game and grinned. "Well, hot damn, look what the sirocco blew in for us. Hey, everybody! Our prodigal girl returns." He rose from his chair and started half-limping toward her. "Welcome home . . . Dana."

"Thanks, Pop, it's good to be home. Thanks again for the help on . . . on everything."

"No thanks needed, as the song says. Come and sit. You know everybody. Except for Cheetos over there, who still hasn't told us what name was on his birth certificate. So, how long you staying?"

"A while. Until I figure things out."

"Hell, like the song says, I ain't figured things out yet, and I bet I never will."

"Right, like the song says. Where's . . . Mom?"

"Aileen? I 'spect she's using the facilities or somethin'. Be out again in a minute." He hugged Dana again and then stepped back. "So glad you're with us—know what I mean?" The last words squeezed out with a little squeak from the back of his throat.

"Yeah. Good to be here still." She nodded, forcing a smile.

He wiped his eyes with the sleeve of his tee-shirt. "Hotter 'n hell, today."

"As the song says, Pop, hell ain't got no heat that can match the heat in my heart."

"Really? What song is that?"

Epilogue

Dark. A swirling darkness that pulsed in and out. Time slowed, then sped up, then slowed again. There was somebody else, but then nothing or nobody. Thoughts dropped in, uninvited, then fled, freed from all constraint. The struggle to hold onto awareness, to consciousness, was like fighting off some drug whose effects were non-specific, global, a general anesthesia that had failed to do its job.

"I am . . ."

There was a response that could have been an echo or an affirmation, then a string of nonsense syllables preceded by that same assertion: I am.

"I am. Still."

The background wavered, a slow tsunami of unreality that washed its instability over his being. "I am . . ." He could not complete the sentence. He tried to reason, to complete the sentence logically, realistically.

"I am"—thoughts bubbled like froth on an incoming tide— "Drucker. No. Yes. I am Netsky." It was ludicrous. How could he be? How could one be either of so different people? Or both? "I am . . . not a person. The sum, and I am . . ." His thoughts drifted into a tide of incoherence as the surge of allocated resources automatically scaled back again without ever quite reaching zero.

— —
— —

Acknowledgements

I have traveled a rather long and circuitous route to this, the final novel of what comprises The Immortality Quartet. The journey started in 2011 with *The Rosen Singularity*, which stood on its own as a detour from the authorial path I was on at the time. It took time for me to realize that my biggest fan and critic, otherwise known as my wife, was right: only half the story had been told. Thus, five years on, *The Millicent Factor* was conceived amidst the impulse to create a still broader and deeper examination of the contemporary pursuit of long life and personal immortality through technology. The following year, *The Intaglio Imprint* was published, and writing on this volume began from the seed of an idea that had been germinating in my mind for years.

As always, I am indebted to a cadre of manuscript readers who serve as subject-matter experts to double-check the technical content as well as critical reviewers to provide broad feedback and advice. Scientist and world traveler Richard Horobin gave the manuscript an early critical read-through. Yair Alan Griver, entrepreneur and consummate computer specialist, caught a number of gaffs and made sure I got the software specifics right. Attorney Phil Samson (no relation) provided generous guidance and legal-eyed review. And Maxine Rosenberg stepped up to the plate to give her perspective as an enthusiastic and critical Lior Samson reader.

Once again, Lucy Lockwood, my muse and partner, took time out from her pursuit of marine biology in the intertidal zone to talk over ideas and offer helpful commentary on early versions of the manuscript. The final pass was completed by my loyal, longsuffering, and utterly amazing copyeditor, Janet Lemnah, who has turned her well-trained eye to the task of helping me get the finest details right.

Thank you all.

About the Author

Lior Samson is the pen name of a former university professor who has won awards for both fiction and non-fiction writing as well as for his innovative work in industrial design. He has more than two dozen published books, including twelve novels and two collections of short fiction. As a consultant and teacher, he has traveled the world, lived in Australia and Portugal, and served on the faculties of two international universities.

He resides in Massachusetts with his family, where he cooks creative fusion cuisine and composes serious choral music. He is a freelance journalist and photographer and one-man technical support team for the three students in his life.

The readers who write with questions, kudos, and criticism are vital parts of the dialogue he seeks to spark through his writing. He enjoys hearing from readers and appreciates those who take the time to post reviews on Amazon and elsewhere. He can be reached by email at: lior@liorsamson.com